BEST LAID PLANS

D0465707

Also by Gwen Florio

The Lola Wicks series

MONTANA
DAKOTA
DISGRACED
RESERVATUINS
UNDER THE SHADOWS

Novels

SILENT HEARTS

BEST LAID PLANS

Gwen Florio

SEVERN
HOUSE

First world edition published 2020
in Great Britain and the USA by
SEVERN HOUSE PUBLISHERS LTD of
Eardley House, 4 Uxbridge Street, London W8 7SY.
Trade paperback edition first published
in Great Britain and the USA 2021 by
Severn House, an imprint of Canongate Books Ltd,
14 High Street, Edinburgh EH1 1TE.

British Library Cataloguing in Publication Data
A CIP catalogue record for this title is available from the British Library.

ISBN-13: 978-0-7278-9024-5 (cased)
ISBN-13: 978-1-78029-715-6 (trade paper)
ISBN-13: 978-1-4483-0436-3 (e-book)

All Severn House titles are printed on acid-free paper.

Severn House Publishers support the Forest Stewardship Council™ [FSC™],
the leading international forest certification organisation.
All our titles that are printed on FSC certified paper carry the FSC logo.

Typeset by Palimpsest Book Production Ltd.,
Falkirk, Stirlingshire, Scotland.
Printed and bound in Great Britain by
TJ Books Limited, Padstow, Cornwall.

To my mother
whose wanderlust was hereditary

ONE

Nora Best blew up her life when she turned fifty – said take it and shove it to the day job, goodbye to the friends who turned out not to be, along with the home touted with neither irony nor exaggeration by the realtor as a dream house. Ditched the husband; went on the run for real, not some Eat-Pray-Love lark; saw herself arrested, finger-printed and mugshot, the whole nine yards. But those last came later.

First, the party to end all parties.

That's how she and Joe billed it on the invitations. 'Our house is empty but our hearts are full. Help us celebrate.' Nora's wording. She was the detail queen, the one who'd done the necessary financial tap-dance that made it possible for them to leave their careers, sell the house, and sink the proceeds from the sale and a book contract into a tricked-out Airstream in which they'd cruise the country for the next two years. At the end of which time, they aimed to have a bestseller from the book deal Nora had wangled.

'Every overworked, stressed-out cubicle jockey's dream! With sex! A whole new travel genre!' her agent chirruped in an email, another in a series so relentlessly exclamation-pointed that her actual speaking voice – all ball-busting gravel – never ceased to startle. She'd been hounding Nora for a follow-up to her first book, *Do It Daily*, a treatise on the benefits of sex – lots and lots of it, six days a week minimum (because even God rested) – with one's spouse. Despite its provocative premise, book sales had proved disappointing. Apparently nobody, not even the evangelical crowd, was interested in having that much sex with his or her spouse. Her agent blamed polyamory. 'It's all the rage now. Maybe we should have said spouses, plural,' she groused, hinting at a sequel, bait Nora refused to take.

Escape, though. What about that? 'It's the new fantasy,' her agent had agreed with reawakened enthusiasm. 'People would rather run away than fuck. But be sure you put some of that in the book, too.'

Now it was time. The Airstream crouched in the driveway, hitched to a chrome-laden, black, double-cab pickup that farted testosterone whenever Joe stomped the gas. The truck, its side panels flared to accommodate dual fuel tanks, had been Joe's one contribution to the entire enterprise.

She'd stood aghast when he tossed her the keys. 'I thought we agreed on a Land Cruiser?'

'I went for the cowboy Cadillac.' He slapped its flank as though he'd just dismounted after a long day on a dusty trail. Standing there in his boat shoes and khakis, collar turned up on his polo shirt, for God's sake. She pinched the keys between thumb and forefinger, held them away from her. A Chevy. No one she knew drove an American vehicle.

But Joe could have his truck. The Airstream was her baby. The sounds of the backyard party faded as she slipped around the front of the house. Before her, the trailer gleamed like a promise, catching the day's last light. Her own reflection, a wavering funhouse distortion, smiled back at her as she approached and ran her fingers just above its famously riveted surface, afraid of smudging the aluminum.

'It's beautiful.' Another reflection bent and swayed behind her, wafting scents of perfume and bourbon, cut by the faint tang of sweat. Charlotte, wife of Joe's best friend and law partner. Their reflections merged as Charlotte pulled her into a hug. 'We're going to miss you guys so much.'

Nora sank into softness. Charlotte had, in Nora's mother's dismissive phrase, 'let herself go', all breasts and stomach and hips, the perfect shape to cradle a grandchild, not so much for the neon-yellow summer sheath with its cruel color and unforgiving outlines. Had the woman never heard of Spanx?

Nora waited for Charlotte to let go. Finally pulled away. Refocused on the Airstream. 'I named her Electra.' Forestalled the question. 'For Amelia Earhart's airplane. See?' She'd paid someone to paint a decal of Earhart's Lockheed Electra, its lovely rounded contours, wheels just leaving the ground, nose angled skyward, on the trailer's front flank.

'Are you fucking nuts?' That had been Joe's reaction. 'The thing went down in flames.'

'It disappeared. There's a difference.'

But Charlotte nodded immediate understanding, greying curls bouncing around the long face that gave her an unfortunate resemblance to a sheep. 'Because it's an adventure. God, Nora. I'd kill for some adventure.'

Of course she would. The adventure didn't exist that could pry Charlotte's husband's hands off the next rung of the career ladder. Artie had tried to stage something of an intervention when Joe and Nora announced their plans, oblivious to his own wife's yearning expression, her eye-rolls at his exhortations of common sense. Recently, though, Artie seemed to have succumbed to the inevitability of the venture, even urging them to move their departure date up. 'Once you've made the decision, why wait?'

Nora thought Artie's new attitude might have cheered Charlotte, but maybe it had yet to take hold.

'If it's adventure you're after, we'd better get back to the party. I hear Joe and Artie talked the caterers into mixing up some kind of killer rum punch.' Nora stepped back, willing Charlotte to lead the way.

But she couldn't keep herself from looking back over her shoulder at Electra, still shimmering in the dying light, poised for morning take-off.

Strings of twinkling lights framed the back yard. Nora would take them down at party's end, pack them away in a flat box, slide it into one of the Airstream's clever compartments. At each stop, they'd festoon the Airstream and their campsite with the lights, making for the Instagrammable ambience they'd flaunt throughout the trip, building their future book's audience along the way. The assortment of baguettes, boules and ciabatti in another box were fake; the wines that would appear beside them real, waiting in cases padded against potholes and other insults of the road. She'd even packed a red-checked tablecloth.

An arm slid around her waist. 'You done good, babe,' Joe said. 'Just look at all this.'

The house sat atop a hill east of downtown, with a sweeping view of Denver's ever-more-vertical skyline, the corporate headquarters' striving grandeur made petty by the peaks beyond, purpling in the twilight. Alpenglow backlit the holy trinity of Pikes Peak, Mount Evans and Longs Peak, along with the lesser ridges between. The lawn sloped gently downward toward the food tables and bar. The catering team had cleared away the platters of salumi and cheeses and moved among the crowd with trays of mini-desserts and champagne flutes filled to the brim. In one corner of the yard, a large screen flashed a rotation of photos. Nora and Joe twenty years earlier, part of the first wave of right- and left-coasters to invade Colorado: Joe still sporting the techie jeans-and-hoodie uniform he'd had yet to abandon for button-down law-school duds, his hair sweeping his collar; Nora's own hair boy-cut then, less blonde than it would become in gradual stages over so many years it now seemed natural.

Joe and Nora on the slopes, Steamboat and Mary Jane in the early years, Aspen and Beaver Creek later. Joe and Nora running the Colorado, raft tilted precariously, rapids boiling up white against the redrock canyon walls. Joe and Nora atop one fourteener or another, gym-toned calves anchored by clunky hiking boots, the whitecapped sea of the Rockies stretching infinitely away at their feet. No kids; whether they'd never been part of the plan or things just worked out that way, Joe and Nora were vague even in their own minds on the topic. At some point, a decision had been made by default, leaving them plenty of time and money for all that adventuring.

But – the inevitable *but* of modern, mortgage-laden life – each exploit was grabbed in weeklong chunks of vacation, the weight of work pressing ever more claustrophobic over the years, phones vibrating in their pockets, watches flashing alerts on their wrists. Emails flagged urgent. Actual phone calls: 'I know you're on vacation, but . . .' 'It'll only take a second . . .' 'Sorry. This can't wait.'

Done with all that now, belongings boxed away in a storage unit, house stripped bare and echoey, keys waiting on the counter for the new owners' arrival the next morning.

For this last hurrah, Nora had specified finger foods,

simultaneously lavish and stripped down. Yet somehow Artie had procured a spoon, probably from the caterers, and tapped it against his glass – *tink, tink, tink* – calling for a toast.

'To Joe and Nora . . .'

It ran around the lawn in murmurs rising to a shout, subsuming Artie's carefully crafted farewell. Joe and Nora! Whistling, stomps. Joe and Nora! A glass shattered against the patio's bricks. How much rum had the guys mixed into whatever preceded the champagne? Charlotte stood to one side, her slow sheep eyes blinking away tears. Nora eased away from Joe, slipped beside her, stroked her plump forearm. 'Oh, sweetie. It'll be fine. I'll text you every day.'

'It won't be the same.' Almost a pout.

Of course not; their weekly, wine-soaked brunches while the guys golfed the only exciting thing in Charlotte's empty-nest life. Nora wouldn't miss those brunches nearly as much as Charlotte, the familiar recitation of Artie's faults long gone stale. And other than the truck, a topic quickly exhausted, what was she supposed to offer in return about Joe, a man known among her friends as the Perfect-Ass Husband, double-entendre intended. Joe in his jeans was a sight to behold.

No wonder they'd had all that sex, her friends' envious glances said, as clearly as they'd spoken the words aloud. Those same friends now kept an eye on their own husbands when Nora was around. Because a wife who actually wanted it, who wasn't coming up with one excuse, or another, or another still – who wouldn't want a little piece of that action? No, Nora wouldn't miss the eggshell-walk her life had become ever since she'd written that damn book.

More toasts. Another glass sacrificed to the patio bricks, the caterers collecting things, broad hints written on their tight-lipped faces. *Time to go.* Yet people lingered. Nora slid her phone from the pocket of her sundress and snapped a few photos, something for the blog that would precede the book, building both audience and anticipation. Someone brought out tequila, a saltshaker, limes. A knife. Who in God's name had come so prepared? No shot glasses, though, and the caterers had rounded up all the champagne flutes. The bottle passed mouth to mouth. Now they'd never leave. But if you can't beat 'em . . .

Nora joined them, muscle memory from the carefree young woman in those long-ago photos kicking in. Touched her tongue to the meat of her thumb. Shook salt. Tipped up the bottle. Holy hell, it was the good stuff. Teeth into lime. *Damn.*

Nora! Nora! Chanting now. Where had Joe gone? Who cared?

She reached for the bottle again, glugged, coughed. Laughed and shook out her hair. Nora!

The bottle made the rounds. The landscape tilted. Nora kicked off her shoes, planted her feet in the grass, everything still aslant. She headed for the house, step by careful step, vowing to double the caterers' tip if they'd cleaned up all that broken glass. Dark inside, floor cool and smooth and safe against her feet, just a few silent steps now to the bathroom, where she'd splash cold water onto her face, the back of her neck, and maybe jam a quick finger down her throat to hasten the inevitable.

She stopped. From the bathroom, a light. Motion. Sound – a male groan. What was it with men and their bathroom noises? And this idiot, maybe thinking himself alone in the house, not even shutting the door behind him. Nora slid a step back, started to turn away, registered all the wrongness of it one wrong thing at a time. He stood, not in front of the toilet, but before the long marble counter between the double sinks, hands braced against its edge, body a blur of motion.

What was he doing? What were *they* doing? Oh, Jesus.

Another step back. Too late. She'd already seen the khakis down around ankles. Yellow sheath pushed above hips – not only sans Spanx, but total commando. Perfect ass bobbing between jiggling thighs.

No. Fucking. Way.

Her hand went to the phone in her pocket. She looked again. Way.

Later – many, many years later – she'd make a joke of it. You want to go from drunk to sober in two seconds flat? Get a gander of your husband helping himself to his best friend's wife.

And maybe she *was* sober as she made her way across the lawn, phone clenched in hand, toward the laptop powering the photo montage. Soberer still as she clicked at the phone and then the computer, a quick download, a few more clicks to stop the running carousel, to freeze a single photo on the screen. She reached for the extension cord running from the house, found the plug to the lights. Yanked it.

The lawn plunged into darkness, alpenglow long gone, the only light supplied by the screen with its image of Joe fucking Charlotte.

Nora's voice shattered the silence more thoroughly than any fling of crystal against patio brick.

'Party's over.'

TWO

She bolted back through the house, scooping up her keys and purse, past Joe and Charlotte emerging from the bathroom.

'Your fly's open,' she called. 'And there's a big wet spot on your dress.'

Was there? It didn't matter. Worth it, almost, to see the way they leapt apart, launching into stuttering explanations that she didn't have time to hear, intent as she was upon getting the hell out of there, only to confront an issue that nearly foiled her escape before it was begun.

Joe hadn't just selected the truck. He was going to drive the truck.

Not that Nora had any qualms about driving the truck itself, although it would be the biggest vehicle she'd ever operated, larger by several factors than the Prius she'd traded in. But towing twenty-four feet and three-and-a-half tons of Airstream – that was a whole different matter. They'd agreed that Joe would get them out of Denver, through the first couple of weeks of the trip, over to California, up the coast, catching the ferry to the islands off Seattle for some magical days kayaking among seals and orcas. She'd wait to drive until they hit the big empty stretches of eastern Washington, Idaho, Montana, taking the wheel when the roads were straight and empty, nobody around to honk their horns in annoyance at the woman of a certain age, hands clutched at ten and two, creeping along like a first-time driver with a parent grinding a foot against an imaginary brake.

All of which she made a split decision not to think about as she slammed the front door behind her, sprinting to Electra, pain registering in her bare toes as she kicked the chocks from beneath the trailer's tires, tossed them atop the suitcases in the truck's roomy rear seat, muttering *go-go-go* as the engine caught and she disengaged the emergency brake. Light flashed in the rear-view mirror, the house ablaze with it, front door flung open, people streaming out, Charlotte standing frozen as Joe stumbled toward the truck. 'Nora, Nora!'

A great gathering beneath her. The truck rumbled, surged, yanked, Electra resisting. Then not.

Take-off.

The last thing about Joe she'd ever be thankful for: he'd done the guy thing, backed the truck and trailer into the driveway. The first few feet of her escape were a breeze, a straight shot onto the street.

Which at this hour, like the rest of their neighborhood – save the unfolding disaster at their house – lay locked up and buttoned down, houses dark, cars in garages instead of presenting terrifying obstacles on the streets. She took the corners wide and slow. So far so good. Onto the blissfully broad boulevard leading to the interstate, the few cars out and about swerving around her with condescending bursts of speed. She negotiated the on-ramp at fifteen miles per hour, took a breath and hit the gas onto the highway, hugging the right lane, praying as she hadn't since she was a child approaching the confessional with her child's sweaty handful of sins.

'BlessmefatherforIhavesinned . . . I hit my brother five times. I didn't do my homework two times. I wished hurt on Sister Pancratius seven times.' Praying so hard she mostly forgot about Joe and Charlotte, might have even promised God she'd forgive them if only He'd (She'd?) let her make it alive through the Mousetrap where I-70 hit I-25 in a spaghetti bowl of overpasses and restricted lanes. An obliging God bestowed a miracle. Nora was through, shooting onto I-25 north toward Wyoming, Electra flying straight and true behind her as she drove the reverse of the route she'd planned so painstakingly with the asshole who'd turned out to be just like every other husband after all.

Her wedding ring with its engraved infinity sign – because of course theirs was to be the rare lasting marriage – sailed out the window near the big limestone bluffs at Chugwater in Wyoming. The engagement ring very nearly followed it until

Nora remembered she was mostly sober and that someone with a functioning brain didn't toss away a two-carat, emerald-cut, platinum-set ring that could very well provide some much-needed cash in the future.

Her thoughts slithered around, treacherous and unreliable, from hysteria to practicality and back again.

She'd need money. Not only was the planned book dead in the water, but the publisher was going to want the advance back – money already put toward the Airstream. The goal had been to spend the next year touting the benefits of living lean, conveniently ignoring the fact that the combined cost of truck and trailer amounted to that of a small starter home. Or, considering Denver's punitive housing market, maybe a condo in one of the more undesirable suburbs. She'd lined up free-lance assignments throughout their trip, all of them with editors counting on rhapsodic accounts of a life free of fetters, a lot of scenery, some adorable mishaps, wrapped in the romance of middle-aged love on the road. Apparently, she and Joe represented a demographic.

Had represented. A safe guess that newly single, toweringly pissed-off women on the cusp of their sixth decade were nobody's idea of a desirable demographic. So, scratch the freelance gigs.

And scratch money as something to think about, at least for the moment. She had another, more urgent worry. All that tequila and champagne and rum punch, while thankfully fleeing her brain, apparently had taken up temporary residence in her bladder and now begged, nay, demanded escape. But she was in Wyoming, the most sparsely populated state in the union, and lack of people apparently meant a corresponding lack of facilities. There'd been a rest-stop sign in Chugwater, too many miles back now to contemplate a return, and besides, while she was getting the feel of hauling the trailer on these deserted straightaways, the prospect of turning the thing around was too terrifying to contemplate.

The trailer.

'Remember the wet baths in those smaller models I just showed you?' The salesman at the RV dealership, all anticipatory glee, led them down the line of Airstreams, so many silver bullets at the far end of a lot full of lesser vehicles. Knew people with money in their pockets when he saw them coming. The wet baths were cunning toilet-shower combos – close the toilet seat, turn on the shower, try to scrub down without bruising your elbows in the squeeze-box space, wipe it all down when you finished.

He led them to a larger trailer, up the stairs, into the galley. A couple of steps down the 'hall'. Pulled open a door. 'Voila!' A full bath, little round sink, vanity cabinet beneath, and a separate, enclosed shower. The salesman actually giggled as he showed them the retractable clothesline within.

Wyoming may have been short on rest areas, but the base of each long, rolling hill featured a chain-up area off to one side for semis, testament to the prevalence of winter's hazards. But it was summer, and the pull-outs were free of parked trucks that would populate them in just a few months, their drivers crouched low against screaming blizzards, cursing the wind and snow as they fought to fasten chains to tires.

Nora tried to recall the *Towing A Trailer* manual she'd skimmed too many weeks ago. She tapped the brakes far in advance of the pullout, tentatively at first and then with a surer tread. Exulted in coasting in for a smooth landing. Then stomped the emergency brake, flung open the door, and sprinted back to christen the trailer.

She'd be forever grateful for portable creature comforts of Electra's bathroom. But she could have done without the mirror, not to mention the vaunted brightness of the lights.

Was that her actual face? The one she'd present to the world as a single woman? Because, as she'd spent the last hundred and more miles reminding herself, that's what she was now, her whole reality changing in a split second. That's how these things happened, wasn't it? The truck bomb, the tornado, even the pink slip. You cruised along on automatic pilot, and then *boom*. You turned around and everything that had come before was obliterated.

Including her bathroom at home, with its muted lighting, its cabinet full of concealers and creams and foundations that she patted on each morning without thinking, a routine grown familiar as the face in the mirror, the one she seemingly had not taken a really good, long look at in far too many years, secure in the knowledge that, compared to a lot of her friends, she looked pretty damn good – oh, how the words came back to her now – *for her age.*

She stared at the stranger confronting her, the smeared mascara, the incipient grooves from mouth to chin, the triplicate lines across the forehead. The deltas of crow's feet spreading away from her eyes, the bags beneath them dark and puffy as plums, and let's not even get started on the neck. She tucked in her chin. Combed her hair across her forehead with her fingers. Thought a minute. Pushed the button that kept the vanity drawer from sliding in and out while Electra was in motion and sorted through the stuff she'd stocked there – her comb and brush, hair dryer, emery boards, tweezers, and there, right where she'd placed them, a pair of nail scissors. She ran her fingers through her hair again, pulling a hank forward, down over her face. Eyed it through the strands, lifted the scissors, and cut. Another hank, another cut. A third time. She shook her head, scattering cut hairs across the little countertop. There. Not much she could do about her neck, but now a fringe hid the offending forehead lines.

She tore off a piece of toilet paper, moistened it, wiped up the hair and flushed – flushed! No roadside Port-a-Potty, her Electra. Washed her face, working at the delicate skin beneath her eyes until she was satisfied that the mascara was gone and the remaining smudges were attributable solely to exhaustion. What was it, three in the morning? Time to get back on the road.

THREE

The sky lightened an hour later, not dawn, nowhere close, but blackness fading to grey, stars that had hung low and startling now winking out, abashed before the emergence of a deep, thrilling blue. Landscape appeared as outline, low undulating lines, nothing manmade. Casper was long past, a sprinkling of light and then a full flare of shopping centers and motels; the reassuring signs of habitation too quickly in the rear-view mirror, nothing ahead but the unending roll of prairie.

How had she lived a full two decades in Denver, a mere hundred miles from the Wyoming border, and never been through this state? Highway signs pointed to side roads, beckoning travelers to Yellowstone to the west, Devil's Tower to the east. Routes requiring two-lane roads. No thank you.

On the other hand.

Her exhaustion grew apace with the fast-fading stars. She had to pee again. She was hungry. She needed to get off the road and eat and sleep, and a highway pull-out wasn't going to cut it.

Time to grow a pair – oh, wait. That cliché wasn't hers. Pull up the big-girl panties. Something like that. She was punchy. She turned on the radio and scanned through the static. Joe had wanted to spring for satellite radio, but she'd demurred, pointing out that listening to local stations would lend authentic detail to their narrative. She could tweet country music lyrics, amusing quotes from hog futures or some such. She finally found a newscast, with a breathless account of the search for the killer of a long-haul driver, found with his throat slit at a truck stop outside Blackbird, the next town of any size she'd encounter. According to the sound bite from the local sheriff, authorities were seeking a 'lot lizard' seen leaving the truck – necessitating a quick, embarrassed-sounding explanation from the reporter that lot lizard was slang for truck-stop prostitute. He went on to note a string of break-ins in the same town that night, but Nora had stopped paying attention.

She reached for her phone to record a quick note – lot lizard was exactly the sort of telling detail she'd work into an anecdote for the book – before remembering that there would be no book. Besides, once she'd gotten enough confidence to take a single hand off the wheel, she'd silenced her phone, until then buzzing and jumping around on the passenger seat with unceasing texts and calls. She could just imagine. She wondered who'd left more texts and voicemails – Joe? Charlotte? Or their friends?

God, what if someone had already told her widowed mother? Her alone in Nora's childhood home on Maryland's Eastern Shore, nothing to do but stare at the waters of the Chesapeake Bay where sloops from weekending Washingtonians had long ago displaced the oystermen in their paint-peeling skipjacks of days past. She passed her days writing long, fretful emails to her daughter about the changes fast forcing the taxes on her enviable waterfront property beyond her ability to pay. In others she fretted about the racial unrest spurred by police abuses in Baltimore, fearing a resurgence of the race riots that swept the Eastern Shore in the sixties, filling Nora's inbox with links to stories about violence a hundred miles away.

Nora had often entertained impossible daydreams about cutting off her mother's subscription to the local newspaper, somehow jamming her radio frequencies and internet access, anything to keep her from obtaining ever-more fodder for the disaster scenarios she spun in their weekly phone calls. She'd have a field day with this one.

A green exit sign rose ahead, some nowhere place to pull off, Blackbird – scene of the truck-stop murder – still a few miles up the road. The sign sported a gas pump symbol by the exit. No knife-and-fork indicating restaurants (no need for those, anyway; as with the bathroom, she'd stocked Electra's galley); but – hallelujah, amen – the little triangular tent that meant a campground. She'd have to negotiate a two-lane road, but it couldn't be far. She could do this.

* * *

She conquered the gas station, grateful that the place was closed, the pumps operating on credit-card swipes, no one to see her easing the truck and trailer up beside the pumps inch by tentative inch.

The truck's dual tanks took forever to fill and registered a shocking dollar amount on the pump. Money, again. She'd have to figure it out. Right after she'd found the damn campground. Eaten. Slept. The Problem of Joe slipping ever farther down her list of immediacies.

Forty-five minutes out of the gas station, with no campground in sight, she deemed herself the Trailer-Hauling Queen of the Two-Lane Highway. The things you learn when you don't have a choice. Beyond the gas-station-and-nothing-else spot in the universe, the road snaked up and away, emphasis on *up* in an increasingly tight series of switchbacks that kept her gaze flicking constantly to the side mirrors, checking to see that Electra wasn't swaying across the center line, nor too close to the edge of – oh, for the love of God, hadn't they ever heard of guardrails in this place? A canyon yawned wide, displaying fanged rocky outcroppings. On the far side of the road, bare foothills gave way to pine-forested slopes. She supposed people considered it beautiful. You want beautiful? How about vast gentle valleys, or those Utah salt flats that were on their original itinerary? Or even a Walmart parking lot, its outer reaches nothing but lovely level stretches of macadam.

People liked to talk about white-knuckle driving, but if she'd been foolish enough to take her eyes off the road for the split second she'd need to glance at her own knuckles, she was sure they'd have gone beyond white to some bloodless no-color stage, fingers already beginning to necrotize. They'd pull away from her hands, fingers staying stuck like a leper's to the wheel as soon as she tried to release herself. If she didn't die first. With such macabre thoughts Nora kept herself awake and ghoulishly entertained until she realized with a single last jolt of adrenaline she'd gotten the trick of it; that Electra was staying safe in her lane, sedate as a stolid mule plodding behind the fairy coach pulled by a fancy four-in-hand.

The road began to unkink, turns long and lazy now, farther between each one until finally achieving something akin to straightness along a high-elevation plateau. And there, like a woodsy species of mirage, a sign pointed off to her right: National Forest campground.

Nora took the turn at a crawl, pulled up to the entry booth, and burst into tears.

'Ma'am? Ma'am? Are you all right?' A young woman in a dark-green Forest Service ball cap leaned from the booth, her blonde ponytail swinging forward. 'Can I help you? Are you in some kind of trouble?'

Tears morphed into climbing yelps of laughter. Was she in trouble? Oh, honey. Where to begin?

The woman left the booth and approached warily, cellphone in hand. Probably had her finger poised over the emergency button. Nora rolled her window all the way down and took calming gulps of cool mountain air.

'I'm sorry. I've been driving all night. It's my first time driving a trailer. I'm tired and hungry and I just want to get this damn thing parked somewhere so that I can eat and sleep but I have no clue how to park it and . . .' Crap. Again with the waterworks.

The woman shoved her cellphone into her pocket. She was so tall her face was nearly even with Nora's, perched as she was in the truck's high seat.

'It's OK. You're fine now. You don't have to worry about any complicated parking situation. There's a campsite right next to ours with a horseshoe driveway. All you have to do is pull in and turn off the engine. You can follow me there. I'm Miranda.'

She waited.

Nora wondered if she should give her real name. Why not? She hadn't done anything wrong. It wasn't as though she'd cracked Joe over the head with a golf club like Tiger Woods' wife. Now there was a woman who knew how to handle things. *Christ, Nora. Focus.*

'I'm Nora. Lead the way.'

Miranda finally left her after breaking off a long recitation about bear-proofing her site, and the location of the restroom.

'Although,' she said, sweeping the Airstream with an openly envious gaze, 'I guess you're not going to need it.'

Nora had glimpsed the campground hosts' site as she'd pulled into her own, their battered camper a fraction the size of Electra, enough years on it to raise concern, not so many to qualify as retro cool. And she'd noted Miranda's newly questioning glance when she stepped from the truck, barefoot and shivering in the mountains' morning chill, the short sundress she'd donned for the party wrinkled and worse from the wear, as she herself was from the long night in the truck. She could just imagine Miranda's thoughts: what was this woman who probably looked like a haggard, aging version of the lot lizard described on the radio news doing with a $100K trailer?

Miranda broke off. 'You're tired. You should be able to sleep like a baby here. You won't believe how quiet it is. We're off the main tourist path. Not like some of those campgrounds around Yellowstone – real zoos, a party every night.' Again, Nora thought she detected envy. She nodded along with Miranda's recitation, the words hypnotic . . . her head jerked.

'Oh, shoot. There I go again, running off at the mouth when I'd just told you to get some sleep. Now I'm telling you for real. Come by and say hey when you wake up. We've got beer.'

Nora closed the door on Miranda without even saying goodbye. A quick pit stop in the bathroom that, despite the lights, was quickly becoming her favorite feature in the Airstream. Until she fell face down onto the bed and then it all came back to her – not the business of Joe and Charlotte; that would have to wait – but the salesman's words: 'Goose down duvet. Top-of-the-line memory foam mattress. You'll be asleep before your head touches the pillow.'

Oh, yes, she was.

Consciousness came slowly, memory slower still.

She slid a leg across the sheet, feeling for Joe. Nothing. He must have already gotten up. She groped for her phone, usually charging on her nightstand, but her hand dangled into space. She opened one eye and lifted her head. Pain slammed it back down. She lifted her wrist to check her watch, which returned a blank black stare even after she shook her arm and tapped the watch face, its charge long gone.

She lay motionless, breathing slowly, cautiously, and worked on getting the other eye open. Above her, a curved aluminum ceiling. Right. She was in the Airstream. They'd started their trip.

No. Not *they*.

Hello, memory.

The party, the tequila – she put a hand to her throbbing head – Joe and Charlotte, all the dominoes toppling in the wake of her discovery. Marriage gone to hell. Book contract – poof, vanished. House sold, no place to go back to. She was stuck here in . . . where, again? Some campground in the mountains of Wyoming, with a truck-and-trailer combo she was still learning how to drive, whatever cash was in her wallet, along with credit cards that she supposed she could max out, and a couple of cases of really good wine. The infernal banging in her head intensified. Only one way to stop it.

She sat up by degrees, claiming victory in not falling right back down again. Made her way the few steps to the galley and freed a bottle of wine from the three-bottle rack under the counter. Damn straight she'd packed a corkscrew. She held the bottle up, toasting herself. 'Hair of the dog.' Chugging straight from it had the unfortunate effect of reinforcing the memory of the previous night's tequila, but the immediate effect – not a cessation of pain, but some notable subjugation – was worth it. Head tamed, her stomach asserted itself: food. *Now.*

She opened the fridge. Eggs nestled in a foam-lined container. A pepper, red and waxy. A wedge of Manchego. An omelet would be great, but her stomach said no. Too much prep time. She pulled a knife from a drawer, slapped the cheese onto the removable cutting board atop the sink, and whacked off a chunk, gnawing on it between sips of wine. She belatedly studied the label. A Rioja, perfect with the cheese. 'Breakfast,' she congratulated herself, 'is the most important meal of the day.'

A few sips – oh, who was she kidding? She guzzled it – of

the wine muffled the worst of the clanging in her head. At some point, sanity prevailed and she switched to coffee, its comforting aroma nudging her into automatic pilot. She carried her mug to the dinette and turned on her tablet, a daily routine from a life abandoned.

A weak cell signal barely powered it. She'd rig up the gizmo they'd bought to provide Wi-Fi on the road later. Still, the screen showed the blog they'd designed to keep people apprised of their progress, its introductory post written and shared with the world, now awaiting its first update from the road.

Best Laid Plans, they'd called it, same as the book's title.

Nora had argued against it. 'Don't you remember the rest of the line?' she'd said to her agent and Joe, her words bumping up against their identical frowning, arms-folded poses.

'"The best laid schemes of mice an' men gang aft a-gley",' she quoted anyway from the Robert Burns poem, in the Scots, the way she'd been taught in high school, taking some pleasure in ignoring the usual 'go oft awry' translation that would have kept Joe's brow from furrowing in confusion.

'Please,' Lilith growled. 'First of all, it references the fact that you're tossing aside the best laid plans, the kind everyone makes, the safe ones. And then, *laid*, a nice little wink and nod to your previous book. Maybe that'll give us a bump in sales.'

Nora typed, fingers stumbling over the keyboard, backspacing to fix the typos.

> Maybe we – I – should have called this *God Laughs*. As in, 'Man plans and God laughs'. Woman plans, in this case. We were supposed to be bobbing in the hot pools at Glenwood Springs right now, an easy trip our first day, just three hours out of Denver. A soak in the spa, dinner in some cute cafe, and then breakfast the next morning in the Airstream. Eggs and peppered bacon, sliced avocado and fresh-ground coffee. I should've packed a damn ruffled apron.
>
> Instead, I've washed up in the mountains of Wyoming, a place apparently populated by hungry grizzlies and murderous lot lizards, a phrase I only just now learned.

I imagine someone teetering around on high heels, Daisy
Dukes riding up her butt, carving knife in hand, and I
have to say, given the discovery of my soon-to-be-ex-
husband's recent escapades, I feel a certain kinship. Not
with the Daisy Dukes and definitely not the heels. But
that knife – thank God I only had a phone in my hand
when I caught him in sweaty flagrante.

She stopped typing, an incipient laugh at her own turn of
phrase dying as the memory sank in. She went full Scarlett
O'Hara: 'I'll think about that tomorrow'. She couldn't spend
her whole day in hysterics over her situation. She needed a
day to recover. Then there'd be time for a strategy.

She clicked 'save as draft'. She'd never send it, of course.
But there was some satisfaction in getting it down. She stared
off into space, all the evasive *tomorrows* catching up with her.
She'd always known exactly what she'd wanted, switching her
college major from journalism – so many gray areas, the
necessity of always seeking out other viewpoints, and weren't
those endless? – to communications and the surety of pushing
a single point of view.

And those trips she and Joe had taken over the years, each
one so goal-oriented: climb that mountain; run that river;
through-hikes only, no end-up-where-you-started loops. Even
the first book, written fifteen years into their marriage when,
let's face it, things had been stale for a good long while and
one after another of her friends had come to her sobbing out
some tale of infidelity, either their husband's or their own
guilt-soaked straying. Hence, all that sex, so much damn sex,
making sure Joe would be too exhausted to wander, even if
she herself was resorting to Meg Ryan-esque moaning and
oh-yes-yes-yes-ing through gritted teeth by the time they were
only three months in.

This new book project another variation on the same theme,
just the two of them on the road, always on the move, not
enough time in any one place for dangerous distractions – for
either of them. Because truth to tell, she'd had her share of
chances. The surprise of a colleague's lingering kiss in the
Xerox room, never repeated, resulting in weeks of abashed

mutual avoidance, but so searingly erotic that the memory turned some of all that yes-yes-ing into the real thing. Drinks with an old boyfriend, in town for a conference, memories of his never-since-experienced combination of wizardly skill and thoughtfulness – 'Is this what you like? Here? Better here?' – intertwining with the knowledge of his hotel room just a few floors above them, his knees brushing hers under the table . . . She'd panicked, looking at her phone and pleading an urgent work text, rushing from the bar. And regretted it ever since.

What did she want her *tomorrow* to be now?

She wanted things to be the way they were. The same thing everyone who'd been the focus of God's laughter wanted. The only goal impossible to achieve. She'd always looked aghast at friends who'd shrugged off affairs, citing their children, their comfortable lives, their *understandings*. But this was no discreet affair, no unspoken understanding, no anonymous encounter on the road. As tortuous as imagining one's spouse with another person must be, at least the friends who'd confided in her had been granted the mercy of never having seen the act in the flesh, as it were, and practically in public, too. Anyone could have walked in on them. And if anyone else had, would that person have told Nora?

No going back, not in time, not to Joe.

Her best laid plans had gang agley. Time for a new plan.

But for a plan, she'd need to know what she wanted.

And she had no freaking clue.

FOUR

Baby steps.

Nora had always hated the term, the mantra offered people in tough situations, its cheerful condescension, its 'you can do this' reassurance somehow an admission of defeat, a looking away from the ultimate prize to something small, attainable, and as a result near-worthless.

Baby steps were for, well, babies, inches of progress achieved on unsteady legs prone to veering off in the wrong direction. Nora had always preferred long, galloping strides, her own mantra learned during early years riding horseback, the necessity of keeping one's eyes on the next jump even as your horse rose over the one before it. Because to look down at the immediate barrier was to risk doubt, hesitation, a sensation that would somehow transmit itself to the thousand-pound animal ostensibly in her control, causing it in turn to doubt itself, swerve, sit back on its haunches, dip its head, sending her cartwheeling off its back and often into the very obstacle they'd meant to surmount.

Now, though, the concept of incremental progress appealed; her immediate goals a shower and clean clothes, warm ones. She'd flipped on the Airstream's heater, gratified that it warmed exactly as quickly as the salesman had promised, but the sundress was at the end of its usefulness. Luckily her packed suitcases were in the truck. She retrieved one, then headed back into the bathroom, ignoring the harpy in the mirror, and was delighted to discover that the shower delivered as advertised, too.

Twenty minutes later, hair wet and combed and her new bangs evened out with a few more snips of the nail scissors, clad in jeans and a fleece, feet jammed into the hard-soled slippers meant for nights around a campfire, Nora stepped out of the Airstream and into her new reality.

*   *   *

'Hey, girl.'

The ponytailed blonde in the next campsite waved a beer her way. A signpost at her side proclaimed: 'The campground hosts are IN'.

'We were afraid you'd gone and died in there. You slept the whole day.'

The surrounding pines striped the campsite with long shadows. Eight or nine in the evening, maybe? Summer darkness came late this far north. Nora, disoriented, reminded herself to retrieve her phone from the truck and charge it later, along with her watch. She waved back, a hesitant flap.

'C'mon over.' The young woman sat at a picnic table next to a smoking grill tended by quite possibly the best-looking man Nora had ever seen. Full head of wavy dark hair, check. Toothy Kennedy smile, check. Double dimples, check and check. And while the girl – Nora fished for her name. Miranda – looked as cute as could be in her green Forest Service duds, this guy gave a whole new cachet to the man-in-uniform mystique.

He flashed that smile again and Nora considered that maybe she'd had a little too much of the hair of the dog that morning, the way she nearly stumbled. 'Trick knee,' she muttered.

He raised his own beer by way of greeting. 'Name's Brad.'

Of course it was.

'Come join us,' Miranda urged again. 'When I told Brad we had company, he got some elk steaks out of the cooler.'

Nora had never eaten elk. But while the Manchego had staved off the worst of the pangs, her stomach grumbled low and forceful reminding her that it still needed some serious attention, so no more of that foraging around in the fridge nonsense.

'Just a minute.' Nora popped back into the trailer, ducked into the bathroom, and scrabbled around in the drawer. She rubbed moisturizer into her face, and patted foundation atop it with a wedge of sponge guaranteeing a smooth application. She slipped the lid off her eyeliner pencil, then held her breath so its motion wouldn't result in a jagged line as she drew the pencil above and beneath her eyes. She daubed on shadow – just a touch – combed her new fringe across the offending wrinkles and called it good.

She retrieved a new bottle of wine, opened the trailer door, and stopped.

A woman walked between her own campsite and Miranda's, her back angled beneath the weight of a pack that seemed far too large for her frame. A red bandana fluttered from one of its straps, and a six-inch knife in a tooled leather scabbard gone dark with age hung from her belt. The woman had the stringy, near-emaciated look of the Continental Divide Trail through-hikers Nora had occasionally seen in Colorado. Nora's nostrils flared. The light breeze carried the woman's scent, a robust waft of dirt and the tang of exertion, cut with hints of fresh air and pine needles, not entirely unpleasant.

The woman performed a skittering sidestep when she saw Nora, the unwieldy pack nearly turning it into a stagger, then recovered her balance and raked Nora with an assessing gaze. Nora stood within it, uncomfortably conscious of her freshly scrubbed skin, her clothes smelling of detergent and softener, her hair soft and brushed. This woman had woven her oily strands into two shoulder-grazing braids that, when clean, were probably blonde. Her gaze, no less judgmental, shifted to the Airstream.

'Huh,' she said with a snort, and trekked off toward a campsite farther within the campground, probably to sleep on the ground and gnaw on something like beef jerky for her dinner.

Nora accepted the woman's implicit judgment as fair. When she and Joe had moved to Colorado they'd embraced the state's outdoors ethos – to an extent. They climbed fourteeners near hot springs resorts, the better to soak sore muscles while sipping chilled Chardonnay at the end of their hikes. Their trips into the backcountry had been on horseback, gear hauled on an outfitter's mules. And while she'd slept under the stars every night during their Grand Canyon trip, she'd awoken to a bacon-and-eggs-and-espresso breakfast prepared by the tour group's minions. Send her into the woods alone, like this woman, even with a pack loaded with every gadget cheerfully and expensively supplied by REI, and she'd last about five minutes.

Brad and Miranda watched the wordless exchange, grinning.

They stood beside one another like paired images of health and beauty, blonde Miranda nearly as tall as her dark-haired husband, sun to his shadow, the two of them provoking the sort of automatic envy Nora had once supposed the province of herself and Joe. Now she wondered: was Brad and Miranda's marriage, too, a façade?

Even as she squelched the thought, Brad slipped an arm around Miranda's waist and pulled her to him, the sort of unforced gesture of affection Nora wondered if she'd ever experience again.

'Glad that's not your style, sweetheart,' he said after the woman had rounded a corner. 'I don't get it. Hauling all that stuff on your back, walking up and down mountains all day – where's the fun in it?'

'And all alone, too,' Miranda said. 'She showed up a few days back, claimed a campsite, then took off right away. Why would anyone want to do that?'

Maybe because she had a cheating husband? Nora pushed that thought, too, down deep where it belonged (*tomorrow, tomorrow*), some sort of internal version of a computer's trashcan. Not everybody set out on their own because of some cataclysm in their life. Some people actually chose it. What would that be like?

She slid onto the picnic bench. A third place had already been set with a metal plate, and a folded paper towel for a napkin. She thought about her checked tablecloth, her plastic-bread props, the twinkle lights – *Get a grip, Nora. Think about that tomorrow, too.*

She held out the wine. 'I know you've got beer. But I thought maybe with the elk.'

'Uh, sure. Thanks.' Miranda eyed the wine as though it might bite.

'Or, you could save it for later.'

Miranda's second 'sure' came with far more enthusiasm.

'Ever had elk before?' Brad again. 'It's a whole new experience,' he said when Nora shook her head. 'It'll blow your mind.'

When had she heard those words before – not so much the words, especially accompanied by that tone? In bed, probably.

A long time ago. A very long time. Nora was pretty sure that during their year of daily sex, she and Joe had exhausted every new experience under the sun. She'd have termed her mind incapable of being blown. Now she wondered.

'Caleb brought them.'

Nora gave thanks for Miranda's interruption. 'Who? What?'

'Caleb. He's the forest ranger. You'll meet him if you're here any amount of time. He brought us the steaks.'

Smoke drifted across the table and Nora's stomach knotted with impatience. If the elk tasted half as good as it smelled, it would put to shame any piece of meat Nora had eaten in her life, ever.

She spoke more to cover the rumbling within than from actual curiosity. 'What is this place? And how does someone end up as a campground host?'

Brad turned from the grill with a lancing glance. Nora's knees did that quick dance again. Thank God she was sitting down this time.

'You're in the middle of the Bighorn Mountains. They call this area the Cloud Peaks and you can see why.'

She could. Through a break in the trees, she saw mountaintops wrapped in diaphanous shawls of mist.

'As to ending up here, all you've got to do is wake up one morning and find yourself out of a job. Two jobs. We made the mistake of each working at the same company. You know how it is these days. Layoffs everywhere.'

Nora knew. She and Joe had dodged round after round at their respective jobs – his at a big law firm getting smaller every year, hers in the communications department of a university staring down a dwindling endowment – with the irrevocable knowledge their turn would come. Hence, salvation in the form of the road trip/book project, except . . . *Tomorrow, Nora. Tomorrow.*

'We thought we could hang on until we got new jobs.' Miranda's voice was small. 'But nothing worked out.' She shook her head, ponytail lashing the air, visibly rallying, her own version of *tomorrow*. 'And then I found out about being campground hosts. We can stay here free all summer while we get back on our feet. Head into Blackbird every few days for supplies.' Hope and heartbreak warred across Miranda's pert features. She'd clearly opted for Making the Best of Things. Nora's own heart broke a little. Is that how she'd look, once she fully faced her own situation?

'Yeah.' Brad sprinkled the elk steaks with salt and pepper from plastic shakers. 'Miranda saved our butts.' He threw his wife a grateful look. Miranda turned her head aside and touched the back of her hand to her eyes. 'We're in it together, sweetie,' she said, her voice thick.

Something that, not twenty-four hours earlier, Nora had thought about herself and Joe. She tried to change the subject. 'Blackbird's the nearest town, right? Wasn't someone just killed there?' Murder and mayhem, a sure-fire distraction.

And it worked, providing long minutes on the kind of speculation as to the type of woman who would do such a thing – Miranda, wide-eyed and whispering: 'They say she cut his throat!' – until Brad deposited a steak, redolent and running with red juices, on her plate and Nora forgot about everything but wielding knife and fork in the interest of getting as much of that meat to her stomach as fast as possible, so intent that she very nearly choked on Brad's question.

'So when do we meet Mr Nora?'

Nora coughed and spat a piece of elk into her paper towel.

Brad swung a leg over the bench and settled himself across from her, next to Miranda, who enthused in italics about the meal. '*Sweetheart*. These are *delicious*.'

Nora mumbled affirmation, hoping to distract him. But Brad nodded toward the truck, its twinned kayaks bungee-corded atop it, the two mountain bikes on the tailgate rack.

'Is he joining you later? I mean, I assume it's a he. You never know these days.'

Nora slid her left hand under her thigh. She'd tossed her wedding ring but the engagement ring still flashed a telltale attachment.

'Honey.' Miranda elbowed her husband. 'You're being nosy. Nora doesn't need all of your questions. She's probably still tired from her long trip. All that way from Colorado.'

How had she known . . . of course. The license plates.

'We get a lot of greenies in Wyoming.' Brad, too, referenced the plates, their distinctive kelly-green color with the raggedy white outline of the Front Range. 'But mostly they're headed for Yellowstone. You're kind of far afield, aren't you?'

'*Brad.*'

'It's OK.' Even though it wasn't. 'I like to wander.' Since when? But at least they were off the subject of a traveling companion.

'Are you going to stay for a few days?' Miranda, nakedly hopeful. 'We don't get much company up here.'

Nora could see it. The one-two punch of the double job loss. The weeks stretching into months, running through the savings, then the retirement accounts. Kiss the house – they were young, though, so maybe just an apartment – goodbye, along with friends, family. Days spent with Miranda staring off into space from the campground's check-in booth, Brad making the rounds of the campground, picking up litter, scrubbing out the restroom. Both of them repeating that bear safety lecture ad nauseum.

'Except the bears.'

Nora jumped. It was as though he'd read her thoughts.

'There's been a yearling coming around, a grizzly. Caleb – you know, the ranger – says we get them once in a while. They get used to people food, and then he has to put them down. That's probably what'll happen to this one.'

Nora sniffed the air, still scented with elk steak, and looked into the trees, standing black in the twilight. Was the bear in there, likewise lifting its snout, inhaling? What would happen if it lumbered into camp and found the elk steaks gone? Would it look for something – maybe someone – else to eat? Now she was more thankful than ever for Electra's little bathroom. No need to make her way in the middle of the night to the camp restroom, with maybe a hungry bear lurking beside the path.

'What about mountain lions?' They were forever showing up in Denver's suburbs, slinking out of the foothills and into backyards, in one case even squeezing through a dog door and helping itself to the cowering pooch's dinner.

'Oh, they're here, too. You just don't see them, the way you do bears. They're pure carnivores, and mostly stay in the woods. But bears, man, they'll scarf up anything. A campground, all these coolers and backpacks full of food, is an all-you-can-eat special as far as they're concerned.'

'Brad, enough. You're going to scare her off.'

She play-slapped him. He caught at her hands and they tussled, laughing, a few seconds before falling into a quick hug and then breaking apart.

Brad turned to Nora with a broad smile that activated both dimples. 'I've got something that'll keep you here.'

Oh, yes, he did. But Miranda was sitting right there. He wasn't possibly suggesting a threesome, was he? Had she stumbled into some sort of backwoods sex ring? Or was this part of the polyamory thing her agent insisted was a lasting trend?

But he pulled a flask out of a side pocket and held it across the table. Nora was pretty sure she was relieved.

'Miranda said you had a rough trip up here. This should help take the edge off.'

To refuse would have been rude. Just one taste. As long as it wasn't tequila.

It wasn't. Nora took a thankful swallow of bourbon, sweet and smooth, promising a far gentler night ahead than the previous one.

'Go ahead. Have some more.'

Tomorrow was still a long way away. So she did.

Another morning, another jackhammer at work inside her skull.

The bourbon? But, mindful of the tequila disaster, she'd only sipped it. Still, the night had closed in fast, her vision going cottony around the edges, Brad and Miranda's voices coming from far away. The slow rise from the table, an apology.

'I think I'm still getting over that drive. Off to bed with me.' Trying to sound jaunty. Knowing she'd failed.

'Same here. Except I don't have the excuse of the drive. Just a tough day hanging around in the check-in booth.' An exaggerated yawn and stretch from Miranda, faking her own tiredness so Nora wouldn't feel bad. Sweet kid, Nora thought as she returned to the Airstream on legs strangely wobbly, even though Brad's dimples no longer flashed before her.

The banging went on. *Slam. Slam. Slam.* She opened an eye and beheld the tabletop. She'd never even made it to the bed just a few feet away. She remembered typing some nonsense, a blog post that wouldn't see the light of day. She lifted her head a couple of inches and touched a hand to her flattened, numb cheek. Registered the stiffness in her spine.

Maybe because she'd mixed beer with bourbon? But she'd only had a single beer, and truly, hardly any of the bourbon all.

'Nora? Nora! Are you in there? Nora, help me, oh, God, somebody please help me!'

The voice, Miranda's; the pounding, her fists against the trailer door.

Nora flung open the door, catching Miranda as she fell into the trailer, gasping, quivering.

'Miranda?'

She held Miranda away from her, gave her a shake, a role reversal from their previous morning's encounter, when Nora was the hysterical one.

'Miranda, what's wrong? What happened?'

Miranda fastened her hands around Nora's forearms and pulled her outside, only her grip saving Nora from falling down the steps.

'You've got to come, you've got to come,' Miranda babbled. 'It's Brad. He got up in the middle of the night. Said he heard something outside. I thought it was that stupid bear again. Oh, Nora, I guess I was a little drunk. I fell right back asleep. And when I got up this morning, he was . . . he was . . .'

Dear God. Not—?

'He was gone.' Nora relaxed a millimeter. Too soon.

'He was gone, and Nora, look there. I think he's . . .'

She pointed to the dark spreading stain on the packed earth near the picnic table, gone brown and crusty where the sun hit it, still red and wet in the shade, and voiced the word Nora's mind had rejected.

'Dead.'

FIVE

The sheriff looked to be half cop, half cowboy, what with his khaki uniform shirt and usual accoutrements – radio, duty belt, and an overly large handgun riding his hip – but also a broad-brimmed hat, jeans and boots.

So much for an anonymous hideout, Nora thought, as he took down her name, birthdate and address. Then reminded herself that it wasn't as though he was going to broadcast it to the world.

'The purpose of your visit here?'

To ditch my cheating bastard of a husband? She wondered how that would read in his report.

'Camping.'

He quirked an eyebrow at the gleaming trailer across the way. 'Roughing it, huh?'

Let me tell you, she wanted to say, about the nights in the desert during that years-ago Colorado River trip, sleeping bags atop sand, not even a tent between herself and the curtain of stars that nearly brushed the ground. She could rough it. She just didn't want to anymore. Silence seemed the best option.

'Your eventual destination?'

What did that have to do with anything? She thought of the signs she'd seen at seemingly every exit. 'Yellowstone.'

He did that thing with his eyebrow again. 'You're taking a pretty roundabout route from Denver. You should've hung a left about a hundred-fifty miles back.'

'I wanted to take the scenic route.'

'Because I-25 is so scenic?'

Parry and thrust. He did have a point. He also seemed satisfied to have had the last word on that particular subject. 'How well do you know the Gardners?'

'I didn't even know that was their last name. We just met. They asked me over for dinner last night.' She glanced toward their campsite, where two deputies sat at the picnic table on either side of a weeping Miranda.

Another deputy organized a fast-growing search party, each sporting a holstered canister of bear spray, and several people carrying rifles.

'How did they seem? Any sign of tension between them?'

He was one of those men who spreads out and fades as they age – sandy hair going gray, jowls sliding into a slack neck that lapped the collar of his shirt, belly on its way to outmatching his barrel chest – instantly forgettable but for the haphazard uniform. A bland tone to match his bland appearance.

She succumbed to an unfortunate urge. 'They're married. Isn't there always tension?'

Now both eyebrows got in on the dance. 'Not in my personal experience. Luckily.'

You don't know your wife very well, then. She was fast tiring of Sheriff – she checked his nametag – Duncan and his inane queries. 'I thought the bear attacked him.' She pointed to the splotch of blood, now surrounded by small plastic yellow triangles with numbers on them. Yet another deputy stooped beside it, taking photos.

'We have to check all possibilities. But that certainly seems likely. We've called in the ranger.'

Right on cue, a green pickup pulled up.

'There he is.' Duncan waved over to the lanky man who swung down from its cab. The man hesitated, looking toward the group at Miranda's campsite. 'They're busy over there,' Duncan said. 'But this lady here might be able to help you. Might.'

His voice tightened on that last word and Nora considered the fact that maybe Sheriff Duncan wasn't quite the dimwit he appeared.

'Caleb Dexter.' He held out his hand. Nora took it warily. Caleb had the lithe self-confidence of someone who spent much of his life in physical pursuits. She saw the type frequently in Denver and even more so in Boulder, with its contingent of skiers and climbers and ultrarunners, people whose leisure time involved pushing themselves to the limit.

Some ranchers and farmers had it, too, at least in their younger
years, before too many seasons of bucking bales and fixing
fences in all kinds of weather took their toll on backs and
knees. Too often, in her experience, those men had an unfortunate tendency toward the kind of handshake that turned bone
to jelly, as if to bring home the point that, compared to them,
you were some lesser specimen. Nora put Caleb Dexter in his
forties, about ten years younger than the sheriff and twenty
times more fit.

He enfolded her hand in a grip that was just right, warm
and firm and reassuring. 'Pleasure,' he said automatically. She
watched him register the inappropriateness of the word. He
coughed and hit some sort of mental reset button. 'Right.
What's your name? What have we got here?'

His face looked as though it had been assembled from
disparate parts, mouth too wide below thin cheeks, nose veering
off to one side, jug ears below a fright of brushy bright-red
hair. In her experience, ugly people turned out one of two
ways – snake-mean, coiled and ready to strike at a world
looking askance at their appearance, or almost overly kind,
taking care never to inflict the kind of pain they endured daily.
Caleb appeared to be the latter, though without the wounded
aspect that sometimes accompanied those people, his brown-
eyed gaze direct, curious and entirely lacking in judgment.

'I'm Nora Best. And I don't know much of anything. Just
that both Miranda and Brad told me about a bear that's been
coming around. Miranda said he heard a noise in the middle
of the night and went to check. She just assumed he was going
to scare the bear off, and she went back to sleep. But when
she woke up, he was gone and there was . . . that.' She pointed
to the bloodstain. 'Does this happen often? That they attack
people? Am I safe here?'

It hit her even as she posed the question: she didn't want
to leave the campground. She wanted to stay a few days, linger
in the pine-scented air and clear starry nights until clarity
returned and tomorrow was no longer the guiding principle of
her life.

Caleb started to laugh, then glanced toward Miranda and
cut it off. 'I probably get that question twenty times a day in

the summer when all the tourists show up. We've only had a handful of people killed by grizzlies in Wyoming in the last hundred years, and those were either in Yellowstone, or when someone got between a mother and cubs, or in the fall, when a hunter startled one in the brush. From what you say, this one sounds like a trash bear, poking around the campground, looking for easy pickings from slob campers. It's a shame. Even before this, given that it sounds like he's become food-habituated, I'd probably have to take him out.'

'Take him out – you mean, tranquilize him and move him?'

All traces of the smile fled. 'I wish. But grizzlies are way too smart for that. I could tranq that bear and drop him two states away, and I guarantee you he'd be back at this campground in a few weeks, parked at one of the picnic tables, chowing down on Pop-Tarts or whatever other goodies he managed to find. Bears like that get way too familiar with people. You put eight hundred pounds and five-inch claws up against some pathetic human specimen, and it doesn't go well. Unfortunately, as a species we're not fond of Darwinism. The bear always loses in that equation.'

He ran a hand through that hair, adding a few different directions to its general disorder, and shook his head as though to bring himself back to the matter at hand. 'I've run on far too long about bears. Duncan, you know where Costa is these days?'

At Nora's questioning look, he added, 'Corey Costa runs dogs. We'll do a couple of things. Bait a live trap and see if we can catch a likely culprit. If that doesn't work, Costa's dogs can help us track it down. In the meantime' – he looked at the line of pickups parking along the campground's winding gravel road, the group of men disappearing into the forest, and turned to the sheriff – 'looks like you've already got a sizeable search party out trying to find our victim.'

The air above them pulsed with sound. He stopped talking and cocked his head. 'The helicopter, too. If he's lying all tore up someplace, we want to find him fast. How much longer do you think your guys will need with . . .'

'Miranda,' Nora supplied.

'Thanks. I want to talk to her, find out just where in the campground the bear's been seen, whether it comes in from the same direction every day – aw, *hell*.'

Another pickup pulled up. Nora glanced around and realized there was not a sedan in sight. For a brief second, she was grateful for Joe's testosterone-fueled purchase, although her own truck was considerably newer and shinier than the battered specimens increasingly crowding the campground, including the most recent arrival.

'Hey, Sheriff. Hey, Caleb. Want to fill me in?'

The young woman advancing upon them looked to be college-age, but the narrow notebook in her hand and a mix of curiosity and excitement on her face proclaimed her a full-fledged reporter.

Caleb shot the sheriff a grin and stepped aside. 'I believe this is your bailiwick.'

The sheriff had shown flashes of skepticism with Nora; now, outright annoyance took over. 'Chrissakes, Bethany. You sleep with a scanner or something?'

She held up the hand, showing the phone beneath the notebook. 'I've got an app. Plus, I think half the county called me. Turns out a grizzly attack trumps a truck-stop murder. So what's going on? Just so you know, the AP's already picked up on this. You're going to have national press breathing down your neck any minute now. So you might as well practice your spiel on me.'

She turned to Nora. 'Are you a camper here? Did you see anything? Hear anything?'

Like the sheriff and his deputies, Bethany wore jeans with sharp and centered creases. Unlike theirs, her jeans sported a fleur-de-lis design in sparkly decals on the butt, oddly festive, given the matter at hand. They caught the light and, as Bethany turned toward Nora, Duncan's eye.

'No, no, nothing,' Nora stammered. She felt a hand on her arm, tugging her away.

'I just need to finish up a conversation with this lady while you talk with the sheriff,' Caleb told Bethany.

He lowered his voice so only Nora could hear. 'If you're checking out, this would be a good time. This place is going to be crawling with reporters by the end of the day. Looky-loos, too. Doesn't matter whether you saw anything or not.'

'I wasn't planning on leaving right away. I don't really have a plan at all.' Maybe she could just keep going the way she'd started, following her and Joe's planned route in reverse, head north into Montana, where – to the best of her knowledge – no one had been killed in a truck stop or eaten by a bear recently.

He looked at her quizzically, but refrained from questions, a bit of good manners for which she was grateful, given that she couldn't have explained why in the world she'd stay put, given the situation.

'You at least might want to move to a different campsite. Something a little farther from the scene of the . . .' He stopped himself from saying 'crime'. 'From whatever this is.'

Yes, she would. But . . . 'I can't.' She'd glanced around at the other campsites within her line of sight and realized that hers had a feature that those lacked.

Caleb naturally misunderstood. 'There's plenty of empty sites. It's early in the season. There's a really good one back by the creek. I can show you. Can't imagine a lot of people are going to want to stay here if this really turns out to have been a bear attack, but you might as well claim it now just in case.'

Nora looked at Electra, so beautiful and so unwieldy and still hitched to the pickup. 'I just . . . can't.'

He opened his mouth and closed it, politeness winning yet again. 'OK. Good luck, then. Nice to meet you. Sorry about the circumstances.' Another quick handshake, the gentle pressure conveying competence.

She fought an urge to cling, and succeeded, almost. 'I don't know how to drive with the trailer,' she blurted as he dropped her hand.

Curiosity finally triumphed over courtesy. 'Then how'd you get here? Are you here with someone?' He looked at Electra's door as though he expected a mysterious driver to materialize.

'No. Just me.'

He didn't even bother to ask. Just waited.

'I drove it here. But I only made it into this site because I could pull it in. Look at those.' She gestured toward the other sites. 'I'd have to back it up. Turn it. I'd take out some trees, completely wreck the trailer.' She felt herself grow smaller with every word, becoming the sort of woman she always despised. Helpless. Making excuses. 'I can just stay here. I'll be fine.' Even though, clearly, she wouldn't. The old Nora would have Handled It. The only thing that saved her from complete humiliation was that Forest Ranger Caleb Dexter had never met the old Nora. And, also, that once this new Nora got her mojo back, she'd be gone from this place and wouldn't ever have to see him again, or Miranda or any of these people who'd seen her at her most diminished.

The thought brought the lacerating realization that she'd just writhed around in self-pity over her inability to drive a truck and trailer, the kind of rig piloted by flotillas of senior citizens across Colorado's twisting mountain highways every summer – as only a few feet away a woman wept over her husband's likely demise in the most horrifying fashion possible.

'Never mind,' she said. 'I'll figure it out.'

'Get in the truck,' he said.

'Excuse me?'

'In. Now.' He moved toward it. Maybe he was going to drive it over to the new campsite for her? She hurried around to the passenger's side, pride be damned. This was an offer too good to pass up. His voice halted her.

'No. You're driving. You've got a pretty sweet ride here and an even nicer trailer. Stupid to have it and not be able to use it. Let's get it figured out.'

'Yes,' she said faintly, as she climbed up into the truck and took the wheel. 'Let's.'

It was probably the shortest distance Nora had driven in her life – barely half a mile – and definitely the most nerve-racking. When Caleb finally waved goodbye and strode off into the midmorning sunshine shafting through the trees at the far edge of the campground, Nora slumped in the driver's seat, pried her cramped fingers one by one from the wheel, and flicked sweat from her forehead and the pool in the hollow of her throat.

Caleb's slow patient cadences, spoken barely above a whisper, lingered in her mind: 'OK, now you want to cut it a little to the right. Your side mirrors are your friends. Remember, if you want the trailer to go right, you turn the wheel left – the opposite from where you want things to be. Kind of like my ex.'

Oh, so there was an ex. For a moment, Nora forgot she was handling seventy-three-hundred pounds of recalcitrant metal. Well, she was about to have an ex, too. A club she'd never wanted to join.

'Better, better. See how much easier it is when you relax?' Words, of course, that snapped her back to attention, muscles tensed anew, nerves twanging. And it wasn't enough to just get the trailer in place. There was a quick tutorial on unhitching it, and once that was accomplished – wiring and chains detached, tongue unlatched, safety keeper (a label Nora especially appreciated) lifted – it was back into the truck to pull it forward a few feet, leaving a firmly grounded Electra behind.

Caleb hopped out and came around to the driver's side. 'Now you can do it all by yourself. You can drive into Blackbird without hauling the trailer, stock up on groceries, maybe grab dinner and a beer at the Buckhorn. You'll find me there most nights. I'm not much for cooking.'

With that he was gone, leaving Nora puzzling over something she could only interpret as an invitation.

SIX

'**B**est campsite in the whole place,' Caleb had said when she'd finally maneuvered the trailer into place.

She'd been too wrung out to notice. Her first instinct, upon his departure, had been to flee into Electra's creature comforts, plug in her very dead phone, boil up an espresso in the stovetop Italian-style pot (so much more charming than a modern electric version), and add a jolt of Sambuca for a *corretto* to smooth her ragged nerves, falling back on the old day-drinking excuse that the sun was over the yardarm somewhere.

She took the coffee, along with her tablet, out to the campsite's picnic table and, out of habit, crouched to snap a photo, golden sunlight spilling like syrup across the tiny blue-and-white demitasse cup sharp in the foreground against the blurred green backdrop of lodgepole pines. She settled herself at the table and shifted to avoid a sticky spot smelling faintly of bacon, cursing the site's previous occupants, and reminding herself to wash it later. She didn't want that bear joining her at mealtime, and she especially didn't want to become the meal. She turned on the tablet, clicked to her unpublished blog, and tapped idly at the keys.

Desperate Woman Drinks Alone in the Woods.
Today, glass half empty version:
Husband, ditched. Man missing, presumed dead.
Murderous grizzly on the loose in the woods. Murderous lot lizard on the loose in town.
Today, glass half full version:
Learned how to park the trailer. And unhitch it. Espresso + sambuca.
Toto, we're not in Denver anymore. Nor is there a 'we' anymore.
And it's not even noon.

She uploaded the photo and barked a laugh at the entry. If Lilith saw that, she'd kill her. Of course, Lilith was going to kill her anyway – right after she'd somehow reclaimed the advance she'd negotiated for the book.

'Tomorrow, tomorrow,' Nora reminded herself, and took a good long look around the campsite by way of distraction. Then looked some more, forgetting all about tomorrow and returning to the present with a long *oohhhhh* of appreciation. Even without having seen the other sites, she was willing to accept Caleb's superlative about this one.

It sat within a horseshoe bend of a creek, water on three sides, tucked out of view of the neighboring sites. The trailer and picnic table occupied the sunny side of a clearing framed by a fringe of lodgepoles. A lone Ponderosa pine towered among them, its spreading branches shading half the site. Thick strands of whippy willows and aspen lined the creek banks. A breeze lifted and stirred their leaves, their rustling barely audible over the creek's urgent hubbub as it rushed over rocks rounded and smoothed by its constant caress.

Nora covered the cup with her hand to preserve the coffee's warmth, lifted her face to the sun and inhaled the mixed scent of pine and damp earth and thought that if she could just sit like this long enough, easing into her first moments of peace since walking into that bathroom some forty-eight hours earlier, either the answers would come or – more likely – it wouldn't matter so much if they didn't.

'Thank you,' she breathed. She wasn't sure she believed in a god, but whatever power had created this spot deserved some gratitude. She'd stay here a few days, soaking up sun and seclusion. Formulate a plan. Get back to being Old Nora.

No. She'd become New Nora, a woman who could . . .

A sound pierced her reverie, tinny and, truth to tell, a little whiney.

'Baby I'm Yours'. The Arctic Monkeys version, the ringtone she shared with only one person.

Joe.

*　　*　　*

'Nora. Finally. Where are you? Everyone's been trying to reach you. What were you thinking, running off like that? Are you all right?'

Had she imagined that pause before his last question?

'None of your damn business.' An all-purpose answer to each of his questions. Even as she spoke, it occurred to her that if Joe really wanted to know where she was, the phone in her hand could probably lead him directly to her. They, like nearly everyone else they knew, each misplaced their cellphones so routinely that they'd installed tracking apps. He wouldn't come after her, would he? Because her barely baked plan did not involve figuring out her next move with Joe in her face.

'Wherever you are, we need to talk. Work through this. You've got to come home.'

She laughed, if you could call that dry, rasping sound a laugh. 'We don't have a home anymore, Joe. Have you forgotten?'

His reply, when it finally came, pointed out the thing *she'd* forgotten.

'Oh, yes, we do. And you're in it.'

The campsite, so serene just moments before, transformed to mirror the menace she read into Joe's response, the sun's gentle warmth now a furious glare, the pines looming close, the creek clamoring a frantic warning.

New Nora would have seen this coming, would have formulated the perfect response, words of lethal – and legal – precision. But New Nora was still the barest concept, as inky and muddled as the dregs of coffee fast cooling in its china cup.

The best this Nora could manage was a reversion to some twelve-year-old self, as if the preteen Nora would ever have gotten away with such language. Her mother's voice rang in her head – 'We don't speak that way in this house' – even as the words left her mouth.

'Go fuck yourself, Joe.' She clicked off.

The phone very nearly went into the trees, her arm already cocked when the same belated impulse that saved her engagement ring kicked in. She placed the phone with exaggerated care on the picnic table and instead shoved her way through the willows to the creek and spent a satisfying few moments hurling surprisingly weighty rocks into it, where they cracked like gunshots against their streambed-bound compatriots before sinking beneath the glacial-green waters. She wished she could rid herself as easily of the fears stirred by Joe's words.

Would he come after her? Demand to share space in Electra? But Electra was *hers*.

She'd researched trailers for months, ultimately paying double what any of the others cost, unable to resist Electra's sleek, seductive lines, her clever shipshape interior flooded with light from her curved, expansive windows. She'd chosen the color scheme, all cool grey and beige, warmed with burgundy throw pillows and bedding and a tiny table lamp with a fanciful fringed and beaded red shade that had prompted a sarcastic comment from Joe: 'You're turning this thing into a Gypsy caravan.'

'That's the whole idea, isn't it?' She'd grinned, undeterred, as she papered a section of wall with a map of North America, upon which she planned to trace their route with red magic marker, their progress to be featured, of course, on her blog.

'Gypsies are thieves,' he muttered.

'I believe the term is Romani. And it's not like you to be so prejudiced.'

Wasn't it? Now she wondered. Joe had protested the cost of the Airstream but he'd also turned up his nose at the cheaper models. 'Tin cans on wheels.' And he'd chosen the ridiculous truck, even as he'd proclaimed himself a 'real redneck now'.

'Wonder if I should get some shitkickers to complete the look?' he'd said.

Which is what she supposed he'd call the boots worn by Caleb and everyone else she'd seen in the campground that morning; people whose boots no doubt had crusts of real cowshit on their soles.

'Shhhh, shhhhh,' the wind whispered, tracing feathery fingers across her forehead, a mother's soothing touch. The sun shifted in the sky, no longer hammering directly from above. The trees' shadows stretched, tossing a protective skein across the large flat rock on which she stood. The creek chortled along.

The campsite worked its magic.

Nora, beguiled, returned to the picnic table, where she stretched out along the bench, took a few deep breaths of the pine-scented air, and slept.

SEVEN

S he awoke oddly at peace.

She sat up cautiously, unkinking muscles whose protests reminded her that Electra had a perfectly good bed with a mattress far more forgiving than the narrow slab of concrete from which she'd somehow managed not to tumble to the ground. Her stomach asserted itself next, a low warning mutter threatening to quickly become a full-throated growl. When had she last eaten? With Brad and Miranda, sharing the elk steaks that had sent a well-fed Brad, no doubt smelling irresistibly of meat, off to his death?

And before that, the impromptu snatches of wine and cheese from Electra, and before that still, the hors d'oeuvres at the party. She hadn't had a real meal – protein, starch, veggies – at a proper table in days. Even the most rudimentary cook could prepare exactly such a meal in Electra's compact kitchen that was a miniature version (Moen faucets! Quartz countertop! A microwave and Instant Pot!) of the one in the house that was now somebody else's dream abode. But the idea had been to buy groceries on the road, so Electra's fridge and cupboards were stocked mostly with boxes of pasta, along with fruit and snacks. She contemplated another spread of cheese slices, maybe some fruit and granola in yoghurt. Don't even think about it, her stomach groused, its objection becoming a rumbling chant: feedmefeedmefeedme.

What had Caleb said about Blackbird? With the truck unhitched, she could drive into town, buy provisions and maybe fool herself into thinking she wasn't going to get dinner at that place he'd mentioned solely on the chance that he'd be there.

Town was a good thirty miles away, back down the mountain switchbacks, taking the sharp turns with one eye on the yawning abyss that was not nearly as frightening without the threat of a fishtailing trailer dragging her over the edge.

The pickup, so big and brawny, felt comfortably manageable without the trailer attached and she settled into it, familiarizing herself with its fingertip-responsive steering, the surge of power when she touched toe to accelerator. She glanced around when she hit the flat, assuring herself of an empty road, and pressed down hard, the speedometer leaping joyfully to eighty-five, ninety, beyond, just brushing triple digits before she eased off, laughing at her own foolishness. What was she, a teenage boy?

Her laugh ended in brief, bitter resentment, memories of the doom-laden drumbeat of *be careful*s aimed at teenage girls, and the implicit unspoken coda accompanying each. Be careful, don't drive so fast, you'll crash and die – and break our hearts. Be careful, don't eat so much, you'll get fat – and we'll be embarrassed to be seen with you. For God's sake, be careful and don't have sex, you'll get pregnant – and ruin us all. Every action guided by the reminder of the effect it would have for someone else.

What would it have been like to be a boy, living only for oneself? Indulging in delicious, thrilling speed, tires whining across blacktop, wind rushing through open windows, no worry about how it might mess one's hair? To chow down with gusto and then see a second serving pressed upon him by a grateful cook? And the pursuit of sex – sweaty, fumbling, each new variation more mind-blowing than the one before – taking one's pleasure as a right?

Nora had grabbed an apple on her way to the truck. She retrieved it from the console's cupholder and took a savage bite. The truck topped a rise that presented a view into a wide valley, its center strung with streets and buildings and cars and restaurants offering real food, not a measly piece of fruit. She lowered the window and flung the core into the evening.

She'd just driven like a teenage boy and now she was going to eat like one, too.

She cruised Blackbird's ruler-straight main drag, past a travel plaza proclaiming 'Little Town, Big Truck Stop', and wondered if that was where the unfortunate driver had met his demise. She searched storefront signs, trying to remember the name of the place Caleb had mentioned, but saw only touristy-type shops selling T-shirts and tchotchkes, along with a ranch store whose wares looked interesting enough that she considered exploring it. But first, food. The rest of her body had joined her stomach in its increasingly urgent demand, hands shaky with hunger, brain fogging.

Where the hell was that place? She passed a Mexican restaurant. That wasn't it. A brewpub – she might as well never have left Denver, which was lousy with them. Posters advertised a rodeo. And there, like a visual echo of the posters, a red neon sign, the twisting outline of a cowboy atop a bucking horse, hat held high in one hand, brandished against a fast-darkening sky. The Buckhorn.

Inside, she made a beeline for the first empty booth she spotted and pulled a plastic-coated menu from between the ketchup bottle and mustard pot. It featured photos of steaks, chicken smothered in dumplings, bowls of cheese-topped chili in danger of overflowing. Salads were listed, but not pictured. She'd come to the right place.

She contemplated a steak – the chicken, no matter how heartily prepared, seemed pale and wan, too close to how she herself felt. She needed a culinary kick in the ass. But the steak queasily reminded her of the elk steaks she'd eaten with Brad and Miranda. The inch-thick slab in the photo had been cooked rare, juices running red, a little too referential to how Brad had likely met his end.

The server arrived just as her eyes fell on the perfect solution.

'That.' She pointed, so hungry now that anything beyond the single word seemed impossible.

'Chicken-fried steak?' The girl confirmed Nora's choice of the dish that had nothing to do with chicken, despite its name. She looked barely old enough to be working, at that age where she hadn't become accustomed to the power of her own prettiness, no make-up to enhance the clear skin or outline the wide blue eyes, brown hair naturally tousled and a little flyaway, not disciplined into artful disarray by tedious application of product. 'You good with mashed and gravy?'

'Oh, yes,' she managed, speaking past the saliva pooling in

her mouth. She swallowed. 'And can you please bring me a roll – no! A basket of rolls – while I'm waiting?'

Her hands stopped quivering after the last bite of the second roll, butter laid on thick. When five extra pounds had ever so slightly rounded her hips in her forties, Joe had patted his still-flat belly in solidarity and banned butter, along with full-fat milk, ice cream, white bread, bacon, cookies, an endless list of all the things that made life worth living. They piled vegetables atop mushy, whole-wheat pastas, limited red meat to once a week, became adept at various preparations of fish. They hit the gym with the fervency of religious converts and if ever Nora was tempted to skip a session with the trainer she referred to as the Cruella of Cardio, she thought of her friend Charlotte with the flapping skin beneath her upper arms, her wobbly thighs – the same thighs she'd wrapped around Joe's famously firm ass. So what had all that sweat and deprivation been for, anyway?

Nora ran her finger through a smear of butter on her bread plate and popped it into her mouth and, with the worst of her hunger pangs held at bay, took stock of her surroundings, belatedly grateful, given the way she'd tucked into those rolls, that Caleb was nowhere in sight.

Wood defined the Buckhorn – its walls, its booths, its wide floorboards – not the polished mahogany variety of the bars, all high gloss and brass accents, she and Joe frequented in Denver for the once-a-week cocktails they permitted themselves. This was pine, its raw yellow gone golden with age, varnish worn bare in spots, floorboards warped and mildly treacherous. The clientele looked to be mostly local – more pressed jeans and scuffed boots, either the pointy-toed cowboy variety or heavy work boots – along with a few people who were clearly tourists, bodies bared in tank tops and shorts, exposed flesh sunburnt and peeling, feet grimy in flipflops or sandals.

Sepia-toned photos of mountains and cowboys populated the walls, along with big game mounts gone dusty and moth-eaten – a moose with red-and-gold Christmas ornaments dangling forgotten from its antlers, several glassy-eyed deer and the obligatory jackalope – along with corny sayings burnt

into varnished boards: 'Don't Squat With Yer Spurs On.'
'Always Drink Upstream From The Herd.' And an image of
a cowgirl bent low over the neck of a galloping horse with
the saying, 'When They Say You Can't, You Have To.'

She raised her water glass in a sort of toast just as the server
returned with a dinner that broke every taboo of the last several
years of her life. Almost. Something was missing. She called
the server back and pointed to a pie case at the corner of the
counter. 'What kind of pies do you have?'

'Blueberry, blueberry-peach, cherry, Boston cream, lemon
meringue, coconut cream, pecan' – *pee*-can, she said it – 'apple,
apple crunch, strawberry rhubarb. I think that's it today. We're
getting low on some, though.'

Nora deposited a pat of butter – more butter! – atop the
mashed potatoes and watched with deep reverence as
the puddle of gold spread across the lake of gravy. 'Would
you please save me a piece of blueberry-peach?'

Because, sometimes Handling It meant pie.

She'd never had chicken-fried steak before. She would, she
vowed after the first bite – savoring the peppery gravy that
preceded the crunch of breading, the protein surge of steak
– have it again.

She lifted her phone and snapped a photo of her plate before
she inhaled any more of its contents, then put the phone away
and proceeded to make like a Hoover.

'Nice to see a woman enjoying her food.'

Nora nearly spit out a mouthful of steak, saving it just in
time. She choked it down and turned to face Caleb Dexter
with what little of her dignity was left intact. She'd been so
intent on getting food into her stomach she'd forgotten she
might see him.

He slid into the booth across from her. The server appeared
with a PBR tallboy and a frosted glass. 'Your usual?'

'Abby, have I ever changed it up on you?'

The beautiful blue eyes rolled so hard they practically
spun. 'Gee. Where to begin? Maybe when you and Mom
split?'

Nora, who'd returned her attention to her meal during the

exchange, nearly choked again. Would she never get to enjoy this new concoction?

'Cheeseburger and fries, same as always. And don't even think you're getting a tip.'

'Same as always,' she retorted, although with a hint of a smile.

Caleb popped the top on his beer, tilted his glass and held the can over it, beer sliding down the side until it was within a half-inch of the top. He straightened the glass and let the head foam reach just above the rim before setting the can aside.

He took a long pull at the glass and licked a line of foam from his lip. 'Been waiting for that all day long.'

Abby returned with his burger and fries. When Nora raised her eyebrows at the speed of its arrival, she said, 'We started it when he walked in the door. Word of warning. He's nothing if not predictable.'

She might not have delved into the mysteries of hair and make-up but she'd perfected the smartass sashay, Nora thought as the girl sauntered away.

'Her mother and I split when she was eight,' Caleb said. 'Amicable, I guess they call it. Wife got the Buckhorn and I got to stop being a constant disappointment. Win-win and all that. Except for not seeing Abby every day. That part's hard. I try to eat dinner here on the days she's with her mom.'

Nora chewed and nodded encouragement, hoping he'd keep talking so she could keep eating. He obliged.

'I thought I'd lose my mind before the split, cooped up in that kitchen all day. Look out there. Those mountains.' He turned toward the picture window, which framed a sunset just a few flame-colored brushstrokes from being a masterpiece. Nora swiped a couple of his fries.

'Soon as we divorced, I went back to college and double-majored in forestry and wildlife biology. I've worked in the woods ever since.' He returned his attention to his plate, and Nora posed a quick question, hoping to distract him from the reduced heap of fries.

'What about your daughter? Does she live in the woods when she's with you? And isn't that . . . hard?'

He threw back his head and laughed. Another couple of fries disappeared from his plate. 'Well, sure,' he drawled. 'All that chopping wood for the fire, hauling water in buckets from a creek' – he said it *crick* – 'it wears a young girl down. To say nothing of how many squirrels you've got to shoot and skin to make a decent dinner. It's easier during hunting season, when we can get a deer. You ought to see Abby here at work with a buck knife. Girl's got a future behind the meat counter at Safeway,' he said purposefully loud enough so that Abby, who had returned, could hear.

'Daddy, stop being a jerk. We live in a house in town. Running water, electricity and everything. Look.' She held up a Nike-clad foot, the first non-booted one Nora had seen. 'I even wear shoes.'

She glanced at Nora's gleaming plate, wiped clean with a roll. Yes, Nora nodded, appreciating that the girl hadn't simply whisked it away, she was done.

'You want your pie now? Or want to wait 'til he's done? Gee, Dad, you sure made short work of those fries.'

'I'll wait,' Nora said faintly. The girl winked and bore her plate away in full sashay.

Caleb stared at his plate in puzzlement, shrugged as though accepting the fact that he'd unwittingly consumed all of his fries, and tackled the remainder of his burger.

Nora's eyes strayed to the pie case. 'You drive all the way back to town every night?' She told herself the question was more an attempt to distract herself from the pending pie than actual inquisitiveness.

'Not every night, just the ones Abby is with me. I've got a cabin up there I can use. It's not too far removed from that whole wood-chopping, water-hauling scenario, but it's tight as a tick and warms up fast in the winter. You'd be surprised. Summers, though, I usually just pitch a tent in the campground. That's how I know about that site I showed you.'

Abby appeared with pie, holding it high as though bearing a sacrament. 'I warmed it. And added a scoop of ice cream. You didn't ask, but I figured.'

'Hey. How come I don't get that kind of treatment?' Caleb handed her his empty dinner plate.

'You didn't ask. You want pie?'

Nora held her breath. You could tell a lot about a person by their attitude toward pie. Did they prefer cake? Or, if they leaned toward pie, was it the gooey, creamy kind, all sugar and fluff, the crust – the most important part – almost an afterthought?

'You got triple berry?'

Nora perked up. Abby hadn't mentioned triple berry in her run-through.

'Only one piece left. I saved it for you. Sorry' – she shrugged toward Nora – 'it's his favorite. Blueberry-blackberry-raspberry. I'd be grounded for a week if I let it go to someone else.'

'Nice kid,' she managed before she dove into the pie.

'Mostly. Even though these teenage years are exhausting. Apparently, I don't know anything about anything.'

Nora barely heard him. Whoever made the Buckhorn's pies deserved some sort of prize, well beyond a purple ribbon at the county fair. Nobel, maybe. Pies for Peace, something like that. It could work.

Caleb stopped talking and watched. 'Good, huh?'

'More than.'

When Abby came back with his own slice, he put it in the middle of the table. 'Go ahead. I'll share. Save you the trouble of stealing again.'

Damn. She'd thought he hadn't noticed. The triple berry combo was, if possible, even better than the piece she'd just eaten.

'It's the crust, right? Diane makes it with lard.' He picked up the menu, scanned it, and put it back down. 'Pretty sure that's noted somewhere in very fine print. Don't want to lose the vegetarian tourist business.'

'Diane?'

He cut his eyes toward a redhead with her back to them. She wore denim shorts and a black T-shirt with: 'Everything's better at the Buckhorn' printed across the back, the telltale strings of an apron tied at her neck. She chatted briefly with a customer and then ducked back into the kitchen.

'If your ex is still single, I'll marry her for this pie.' Nora forced herself to push the plate back toward him with half the slice left. A different kind of man might have urged her to finish it, but Caleb was not that kind of pushover.

'Too late. Somebody else snapped her up before the ink was dry on the divorce papers. Maybe before.' He grimaced.

'How long ago was that?'

He passed his hand over his face. 'Seven years. A little more. Prehistory.'

He'd described their parting as amicable. Yet it seemed there'd been an affair, and nearly ten years later, it still stung. Would the body blow Joe had dealt her still burn a decade hence?

'Anyway,' said Caleb, 'looks like you've got somebody lined up.'

'Excuse me?'

'That rock on your hand. When's the big day?'

Oh. She'd meant to put the ring away after those early queries from Brad about a 'Mr Nora' but had forgotten.

'That. Well. We broke up.'

Broke up. It's what high school kids did; at least, they did when she was in high school. Back then boys and girls went steady, a venue for pushing sexual boundaries to the limit – hands over clothes or under? Above the waist or below? How long did you have to go steady to do *it*? You only got one chance, with one boy, for *it*, so that steady relationship had better be rock-solid. Because no matter how he swore he wouldn't, he'd tell his friends, just as you'd tell yours, so everyone would know you'd done it, and that was fine – until you broke up, at which point other boys would swarm, full of presumption. No more weeks of working up to it, delicious slow kisses, hands tentative, shaking. Once you wore the label of willing, they dived right in, tongue down your throat, hands everywhere, dick out of their pants the second you'd achieved anything remotely achieving privacy. 'C'mon, just with your hand.' Said even as they pushed your head downward. 'I won't tell.'

Bullshit.

Would Caleb ask her back to his tent or cabin or whatever rustic accommodation he preferred – maybe under the stars – tonight? Invite himself into the Airstream and promise not to tell? And how would she respond if he did?

She decided to come at the subject obliquely. 'Where will you stay if I've got your favorite site?'

'I don't know if you've noticed, but there aren't a lot of people rushing to check into a campground where a bear might have attacked someone. There's plenty of empty sites.'

For a little while, wonderful things – the meal, the pie, the company – had pushed the bear from her consciousness. 'Do I need to worry about the bear? Should I move to a different campground?' She'd have to leave the site that felt so sheltering, hitch up the trailer and maneuver it away with her newly acquired knowledge. She could do it. She just didn't want to. She'd posed a version of the same question earlier that day and was glad to discover his answer hadn't changed.

'Even if it was a bear' – she took note of the doubt he cast, and filed the thought away for future examination – 'I don't think you should give it a second thought. The woods are full of people looking for that guy. The helicopter flew grids for hours today. There's all sorts of unusual commotion. Every bear in fifty miles, along with the elk and the bighorn sheep and the mountain lions and all the other creatures, has probably headed for Montana. A shame.'

She didn't think the absence of bears – not to mention mountain lions – was a shame at all and said as much. 'I'll sleep better at night.'

'You will, but they won't,' he retorted. 'This whole area is part of a natural wildlife corridor between the Beartooths' – he caught her look – 'that's a mountain range just to the north, in Montana, and the Winds to the southwest of here.'

Another look, another explanation. 'The Wind River Range. The Eastern Shoshone and Northern Arapaho tribes have a reservation there. And the Crow Reservation in Montana borders this area to the north.'

'What about here? Aren't there any reservations?'

'There should be. But the tribes got driven out of here a long time ago. Same thing's happening to the animals, in a way. I know this probably looks wild and woolly to you, but there's more people moving into this area all the time. Everybody wants a log mansion in the mountains, it seems. If it were up to me, they'd shut down this campground tomorrow. It's on national forest land, so it can't be developed. Closing it would give the animals that much more breathing room.'

'But then I wouldn't have my pretty campsite.' She tried to make a joke of it. 'And you wouldn't get it back when I leave.'

'I'd give it up tomorrow if it gave the bears more of a break,' he said. 'In the meantime, there's no need for you to rush off. Abby's with me the rest of the week, so I won't be staying up there, anyway.'

He hadn't been about to ask anything of her. Was she disappointed? She couldn't tell. Nora didn't know enough about her new self yet to trust any of her emotions.

'Time Abby goes back to her mom's house, you'll be out of here. Speak of the devil.'

She stood beside their table, check in hand. Nora dug in her pocket for the neat packet of rubber-band-wrapped credit cards, driver's license and cash, the way she'd learned to keep them after she'd lost her purse in a brazen midday mugging in Denver's LoDo neighborhood. Caleb waved her away. 'Put it on my tab. Sort of a Welcome to Wyoming treat.'

You'll be out of here. Would she?

EIGHT

He walked her to the truck, a quaint gesture that left her wondering yet again. How would they part?

The night had felt oddly date-like, to the extent that she remembered her decades-ago dating life. He'd mentioned dinner, and the restaurant. Then he'd showed up and bought her meal. Would they shake hands now? Kiss – in this pea-gravel parking lot, in full view of the Buckhorn's rough-hewn clientele? She laughed aloud at her own foolishness.

'What?'

She was saved from having to concoct an explanation when a burly man hailed Caleb from the detached cab of a semi-trailer.

Caleb raised a hand. 'Hey, Bobby. What brings you here?'

Bobby climbed down from the cab in a series of cautious moves that betrayed the toll too many hours of sitting took on one's back. Blood veined his eyes. He drew a grease-blackened hand across a stubbled chin.

'Food's better here than at the truck stop. You guys found that bear yet?' Something in the way he posed the question made it sound like a threat. Nora took a step back, but Caleb's reply was easy, relaxed, albeit tinged with regret.

'Not yet. But we will. They're creatures of habit. *If* a bear did it' – again, he stressed the if – 'he'll come sniffing around the campground again.'

'Well, get on it.' Bobby's lower lip pooched out in telltale fashion. He turned his head and spat a brown stream of tobacco juice that landed an inch from Caleb's left boot. Nora took another step back.

'The sheriff's up there chasing that bear when he needs to be down here, finding that lot lizard who killed Dale. People are going broke, waiting. We're none of us sleeping in our trucks now. Pretty much everybody's taken a room in the motel, and the ones that haven't are carrying – well, everybody carries. But they're sleeping with the safety off. Somebody's going to get shot before this is over, and it probably won't be the right somebody.' Another streak of tobacco juice arced through the air and splattered at their feet.

'Jesus, Bobby. I don't like the sound of that. I'm sure they'll get her. Although, my guess is that she's moved on. Way I understand it, to the extent that I do, those women don't stay in one place very long. Can't imagine she'd hang around here after what she did.'

Bobby harrumphed and headed off into the cafe, one hand to the small of his aching back.

Caleb shook his head. 'Truckers running around with guns. And now, because of this bear thing, people in the campgrounds will be doing the same. What could go wrong? There's a reason I'd rather deal with bears than people.'

Nora dug a toe into the gravel, trying to anchor herself in reality. She was only a couple hundred miles from Denver, but felt as though she'd landed on a new planet. None of her friends in Denver so much as owned a gun, let alone carried one, at least, not as far as she knew. She said as much, followed by a question that would have been unimaginable a few days earlier.

'Should I have one?' And if she should, where would she get one? Was there a registration process, as with a car? And how would she learn to shoot it?

A flock of sparrows, cruising in for a landing on a tree beside the cafe, swerved hard in midflight at Caleb's laugh, a full-throated bellow. 'Please don't. We've got enough going on around here without amateurs in the mix.'

Still chuckling, he sauntered away without so much as a glance back.

Evening came later at this new latitude, the sun still high in the sky at nine p.m. as Nora drove back to the campground. She lowered the visor against its glare, and took the curves fast, eager to return to Electra's shelter.

Despite Caleb's assurance, she'd feel better once she was behind its locked door. But when she drove into the camp-ground, she saw Miranda alone at the picnic table in front of her camper, finally deserted by deputies and reporters and curious campers.

She lifted her foot from the accelerator and let the truck glide to a stop, trying to buy herself a few seconds' time, searching for the right words. Whatever did one say in these circumstances? Maybe Miranda wouldn't want company.

But Miranda leapt from the table at the sight of the truck and ran toward her, enveloping her in a fierce hug as soon as her feet touched the ground.

'Nora! I'm so glad to see you. I thought you'd gone.'

Nora, never a hugger, held herself stiff within the embrace. She forced up a hand and patted Miranda's back once, twice, before easing herself from an unexpectedly sweet-smelling grip. She sniffed. Had Miranda shed the hovering men and made her way to the campground's bathhouse, changing into fresh clothes fragrant with some sort of scented fabric softener?

She chided herself for the sort of questions she'd always hated when applied to victims. Because Miranda was very nearly as much a victim as her husband, presumably widowed in shocking fashion at such a young age. Who was Nora to judge how Miranda should behave?

'Come, sit with me.' Miranda pulled her toward the picnic table. 'I've done nothing but talk to the sheriff and EMTs and search parties and reporters all day long. The last of them just went away. It's getting too dark to search. I'm just as glad. I haven't had a minute to myself to process this.'

Nora got it. Wasn't that why she herself was lingering in the campground, seeking time to process what had happened with Joe? Then chided herself anew for comparing her own situation in any way with Miranda's. Still: if Joe were possibly lying somewhere grievously wounded, perhaps dying, wouldn't she want the search parties to work through the night, eating on the fly, not stopping for so much as five minutes?

'What do they think? Are they sure it's a bear?'

Even in the fast-dimming light, Nora could see the reddened skin around Miranda's eyes, despite the attempts at concealment. Maybe the layer of make-up and the clean clothes were a kind of armor, the thinnest defense between herself and a world turned hostile; maybe Miranda had stood beneath the

campground's shower, furiously working shampoo into her
scalp, trying to wash reality away, much as she herself had
upon arrival. Maybe.

'What else would it be? It's not like Brad would up and
leave me. He's not that kind of man.'

A blow, unmeant, that nonetheless landed so perfectly Nora
doubled over, fighting for breath. Joe hadn't been that kind of
man, either. Until he was. Probably not the sort of thing to
tell Miranda, not under the circumstances.

'Are you all right?' A woman's reaction; no matter how
shattering her own circumstances, turning to meet the needs
of others.

'Fine,' Nora managed. 'I just . . .' She spread her hands.
She didn't know what to say. What could possibly be the
matter with her, given the enormity of Miranda's situation?

Miranda decided for her. 'You're still exhausted. That long
drive, and now all of this. It's no wonder. When does your
fiancé get here?'

That damned ring. She trotted out the break-up line that
she'd foisted upon Caleb, feeling even more foolish. 'It just
happened. I hadn't even thought to take this off. No time like
the present.'

Miranda's covetous gaze followed the ring's progress from
finger to pocket. 'I'd wear it, too. That's a beautiful ring. What
are those, amethysts?'

'Sapphires. They're so dark that sometimes they look almost
purple.' Nora succumbed to the unspoken request, pulling the
ring back out and laying it on the table between them. The
blue stones framing the diamond caught the color of the sky
and held it. 'It can be somebody else's beautiful ring, especially
if I want to eat until I find a new job.' Reminding herself of
her own harsh realities, applying logic. Isn't that how it went?
First, define the problem.

'Oh, Nora. You're unemployed, too? I'm so sorry. Isn't it
awful?'

It wasn't supposed to be. But she couldn't imagine telling
Miranda that her own joblessness had come by choice, cush-
ioned by a fat book contract. She just nodded. Because now
it was, in fact, awful.

Miranda lifted the ring, held it to the light and then slipped it onto her middle finger, turning her hand this way and that, admiring it.

Nora stiffened. She'd just proclaimed herself ready to get rid of the ring, but she wasn't prepared to see it on someone else's hand. It hung loose on Miranda's slender finger, sliding easily to the table when Miranda lowered her hand.

Nora snatched it back, probably too quickly, and this time tucked it more deeply into her pocket.

'Was it a bad break-up?'

'The worst.'

'I'm so sorry,' Miranda said again. 'I don't know what I'd do without . . .' She clapped her hand over her mouth and burst into tears. Mascara traced wet, black lines down her cheeks.

Nora patted her hand silently, fighting envy. She wished she could cry over Joe. Or did she? Would she really rather have Joe dead than faithless?

She ignored the small, emphatic voice within saying *yes.*

NINE

Nora left Miranda, and the hard questions she'd raised, with a sense of escape. As she drove up to her campground idyll, the Airstream glowed in the headlights in the seconds before she switched off the truck's engine. The patch of sky above the campsite was fast shading indigo, stars teasing with their uncertain light.

She stood in the center of the site, letting its deep peace settle around her, the sound of the creek smoothing her roughened nerves, working on them the way it wore away the jagged edges of the river rocks. Electra's comforts beckoned, but she wasn't ready to go in, not yet. She quickly retrieved her tablet and sat at the picnic table and uploaded the photo of her meal into another draft post that would never see publication. Still, the routine soothed, a touchstone to the life she was supposed to have been living.

Goodbye health, hello happiness.
I'd heard of chicken-fried steak, of course. But I'd never eaten it. Why would I? Why would anyone do that to their body?
Well, now I know why. Maybe it's the lure of the forbidden, red meat and white flour and the mortal sin implicit in the word fried. But as the song goes, I'd rather laugh with the sinners than cry with the saints, and if I hadn't been so intent upon scarfing it up, I'd have laughed through my whole meal. Because, my God, what a revelation. Eve sold out, settling for an apple. She should have sent Satan's ass straight back to hell and told him not to come calling again without a plate of chicken-fried steak in hand.
Where did my own downfall occur? The Buckhorn Cafe in Blackbird, Wyoming, a town just off the interstate and well worth the detour.

Oh, and get the pie. Because if the steak is worth a dance with Satan, the pie is an express train to heaven. Photo? Sorry. My slice (think warmed, and a la mode, duh) disappeared too fast. You'll just have to see it for yourself.

She sat back and smiled at the tiny screen. Exactly the sort of thing Lilith had imagined. 'Keep up with the posts and half the book will be written by the time you're done. And don't slack off, or else I'll be chewing on your ass.'

A memory that only served to remind her of the epic ass-chewing that awaited once Lilith found out how profoundly she'd detonated The Plan. The darkness descended, sudden, complete, and with it a swift chill.

She retreated to the Airstream, flipping switches for light, heat. She leaned against the counter, positioning herself in front of the heater, enjoying its quick comfort. Maybe she'd take off in the morning, head for someplace warmer. Something knuckled her thigh; the ring, so carelessly relegated to her pocket. She dug it out and made a quick circuit of Electra, latching and unlatching drawers and cupboards. Finally she overturned one of the banquette cushions, unzipped the cover, and dropped the ring within. Out of sight, out of mind and out of the highly unlikely possibility of thieving campground denizens.

The next morning found her perched on a high stool in the campground's claustrophobic checkout booth, tugging at one of Miranda's beige uniform shirts, the sleeves too long, the front too baggy. Where had Miranda found a shirt to fit a torso so simultaneously slender and curvy?

The knock at her door had come early, rousing her from the deep sleep the campground induced, the Airstream's screened windows opened to the bracing night air, the tang of pine, the soothing shush of the creek. For a moment, she'd frozen, remembering that first knock that had brought the news of Brad's disappearance. Her breath caught at the sight of Miranda. Nora braced herself for news of Brad, perhaps even worse than the previous morning's shock. But even as she tried to ready an appropriate response, Miranda thrust a forest-green uniform shirt at her.

'I'm supposed to work today. But I can't, Nora, I just can't. I left the booth unattended all day yesterday, and the sheriff and everyone will be back today. The searchers went out at dawn. Could you possibly sub for me?'

The shirt fluttered in her shaking hands. Nora realized she was meant to wear it.

Miranda babbled on, her voice as unsteady as her hands. 'I can't lose this job, Nora. Brad and I need the money so badly. And it's as easy as could be. When campers come in, you just fill out the forms with their names and license plates and give them the map that shows the tent sites and the trailer sites. Then take their money – the fee scale is posted – and have them check back in within a half-hour with the number of whatever campsite they pick. They've got to clip the form to the sign with the campsite number.'

A mandatory task Nora had neglected. The sign at her site was partially obscured by a huge, ragged tree stump, its blackened splinters telling of the lightning strike that had felled the tree. The entrance into the site curved sharply past the stump, leaving the site's interior shielded from the gravel track that formed one of the campground's three main loops.

Now that she was leaving, it didn't matter, she'd told herself the previous night, when she'd thought vaguely of moving on – a plan abandoned upon her response to Miranda. She allowed herself a few seconds' regret, then stepped down from Electra and took the shirt.

'Of course.' Because what else could she say?

Miranda sagged so abruptly Nora feared she'd fall. 'You don't know what this means to me. To us.' A determined insistence upon Brad's survival that made Nora ashamed of her momentary reluctance. She looked away, giving Miranda time to collect herself and was relieved when the conversation turned to practicalities.

'Be sure and mark off the campsite on the whiteboard when they check back in, so we can hang out the "Full" sign if that happens,' Miranda said. 'But I can't imagine there'll be much business, under the circumstances.'

Nora made mental notes, reminding herself she could just as easily figure out her future during the empty hours in the booth as she could in the Airstream. Still, she cast a reluctant glance backward at her new haven as she followed Miranda to the booth.

The gravel track into the campground took travelers well off the main road. Within the booth's confines, Nora couldn't even hear cars or trucks passing, if indeed any had. Miranda's campsite (how quickly she'd left Brad out of the equation!) was nearby, but behind her, out of sight. The trees pressed close, casting the booth in shade even on a bright morning, leaving her grateful for the shirt's long sleeves, even though the cuffs fell uncomfortably over her fingers. She peered into the woods, wishing she'd thought to ask Miranda exactly where the bear had been spotted on its campground perambulations. For some reason, she'd never given it much thought in her campsite. Something about its open clearing, the sun streaming in, banished thoughts of furtive carnivores.

But here, with the trees crowding so near, the underbrush so thick, the possibility seemed imminent. She saw something. Jumped. Over there – was that a swatch of gingery fur? She reached for her phone, wishing it were bear spray. She didn't see any in the booth, despite warnings on the campground's bulletin board that all hikers should carry it.

But she wasn't a hiker. She was a sitting duck in a flimsy wooden booth with a door that didn't even lock and windows that a chipmunk could probably punch through with a single tap of its furry little paw. The wind stirred the trees. The branches swayed and parted, revealing a shrub that had been hit by some sort of disease, its leaves brown and brittle. Not a bear. Just a bush.

The first truck pulled up just as Nora was wiping tears of slightly hysterical laughter from her eyes.

The fact that the truck was unencumbered by trailer or camper shell should have tipped her off.

Still, its occupants could have been tent campers. There were a few in the campground, their neon-hued shelters looking impossibly flimsy in this land of prowling predators. 'Sack lunches,' Brad had dismissively referred to the tents and their occupants before he himself became something's lunch. (Maybe, Nora reminded herself. Given that the searchers were back at it, there was still hope.)

But as the truck approached, Nora saw one of the few people in this part of the world whose face she recognized, a woman whose own puzzled expression cleared as she braked beside Nora's window.

'Hi! I'm Bethany James. I met you yesterday, I think. You were in the campsite next to Brad Gardner's, right? I didn't realize you worked here. What's new today?'

Of course. The reporter, that damned notebook already at the ready in her hand.

Nora lifted her shoulders higher than necessary, trying to convey with the exaggerated motion that she was useless for Bethany's purposes. But Bethany just waited, with a bright, expectant expression. A technique Nora had sometimes used herself, back during the interminable rounds of meetings in her office at the university. Keep quiet long enough and eventually someone else will fill in the unbearable silence. An old trick, and one she fell for anyway.

'I don't really work here. I'm just filling in for Miranda. She needs to be available for the sheriff and the search parties.'

'Oh, the searchers are out again today?' Bethany made a note on her pad. 'They definitely think it was a bear then?'

'What else would it be?'

Bethany shot her a world-weary look at odds with her age. 'People leave their spouses all the time. Or so I hear. I wouldn't know.'

I would. But . . . 'There was all that blood.' Although, there hadn't been that much. Still, why was she even having this conversation? 'Miranda's in her campsite. You'd better talk with her.'

Bethany snapped her notebook shut, a sound as lovely to Nora's ears as the soughing breeze.

'That's the last thing she needs. I'll probably just hang around awhile, wait for the sheriff or some of the searchers to show up, talk to them. But just in case, do you mind if I get your name and phone number? I might need to check on some small detail, and like I said, the last thing I want to do is bug Miranda. Can't imagine what she's going through.'

Nora hesitated, but eventually spelled her name and recited the number, mentally kicking herself as Bethany punched it into her phone. Still, if it made Bethany go away, it was worth it.

TEN

Two mornings later found her back in the booth, considerably better prepared.

She wore a fleece against the early chill and laid out her provisions – a Thermos of coffee goosed with a couple of shots of espresso, a bottle of water, a sandwich in a Tupperware container, and an apple – on a narrow ledge inside the booth. Finally, she sat a canister of bear spray within easy reach, its safety tab already pushed aside. 'Locked and loaded,' she said aloud. Things got lonely in the booth, and cell service had a habit of fading in and out, making it impossible to scan her phone's lengthening list of texts, most of them from Joe, her mother and her agent.

She'd set up an 'out of office' type of notification for all the ways in which people might try to contact her, and in an act of self-preservation permitted herself only a single text each day, to her mother. 'I'm fine. Taking a little break. Talk soon.' Some variation on that theme, never the same wording each day so as not to provoke the type of panic that might spur her eighty-year-old mother to book a plane ticket and march to the rescue with the aid of the cane she'd recently come to use.

She'd bought the bear spray the previous day, a purchase that necessitated a trip to Blackbird, and – naturally; after all, she had to eat – another visit to the Buckhorn. This time, she forced herself to forego the chicken-fried steak in favor of the chicken and dumplings she'd rejected on her previous visit. But she reasoned the chicken would be slightly more healthy than the steak, and to her delight it proved no less delectable, dumplings slick with pan gravy, the chicken so fresh and tender she suspected it had been plucked from some local farmer's backyard coop only a few hours before. Pie was nonnegotiable. She'd eat salads for the rest of her life before she passed up a piece of the Buckhorn's pie.

'I'll try the triple berry this time,' she told Abby, waiting with pencil poised above pad.

'You're in luck. Dad's already been in tonight. Otherwise I'd have to steer you to something else.'

The pie more than vanquished the thump of disappointment she was embarrassed to feel at the news. She was chasing the last crumbs around the plate before the agitated conversation at the next table worked its way into her consciousness.

'*Another* one?' A group of burly men bent over a newspaper. One ran a stubby finger across the page, announcing its contents to the rest.

'Looks like it. This one was in Texas, couple of months back. They're backtracking, trying to put together a pattern. Same deal – looks like he picked up a lot lizard, same as what happened here. She got out of the cab, he never did.' The man lifted his finger from the newspaper and drew it across his throat. Soft curses ran around the table.

'What's this make now? Three?'

'Near as I can tell. This Texas deal, El Paso it says. Then one in, hold on a second.' The men, along with Nora, held their collective breath, as his finger returned to the page, searching the paragraphs. 'New Mexico. Wait. There's four. There was one in Colorado just last month.'

'Looks like she headed straight up I-25.'

'And now I-90.'

Nora, no longer even making a pretense of not listening, remembered how I-25 had veered into I-90 not long before she'd pulled off for gas and ended up in the campground.

'Way she's been doing, she'll hit Montana next. Anybody headed that way? Billings, Bozeman? Or peeling off in Billings to North Dakota? Maybe headed to the oil patch. Plenty of truckers up there. For sure, she'd find plenty of business there. Isn't that where you're going, Wayne?'

Another silence. 'Not anymore,' one man finally said. 'I don't need money that bad.'

Nora counted out bills from the dwindling stash in her pocket. She'd gone to the ATM the previous night to raid their diminished account. They'd stashed most of whatever had been left over after the purchase of Electra and the truck in retirement

accounts, partially as a tax strategy and partially to give Nora
incentive for as much freelancing as she could handle. She
paid the check and brushed past the men's table. Part of her
sympathized with them, but on the other hand, it seemed easy
enough to avoid the fate of their four unfortunate compatriots.
Don't patronize truck-stop prostitutes. Problem solved.

If only it were so easy for women. She thought of a lifetime
of precautions, of parking under street lights and never next
to a van, of walking with her keys poking between her fisted
fingers, of varying her route, of locking, locking, locking – car,
house, even her office door at work on nights when she stayed
late in a building gone empty and echoey. Of the low-level
exhaustion of constant awareness, because God forbid you let
your guard down. Like the woman making the trip from
unlocked house to unlocked car to retrieve bag after bag of
groceries, not noticing the man who'd slipped unnoticed
through the open front door while she leaned unaware into
the car. Or the woman who stopped to answer the question
from a man standing beside the van in a busy parking lot, only
to be pulled into it with shocking speed, scream cut short by
a quick, brutal blow. The woman who forgot to keep her drink
covered with one hand on an evening out with friends and
woke the next morning, dazed and sore, with a terrifying blank
spot in her memory. The woman who was the last to leave
her office. The woman who went on her customary morning
– or afternoon, or evening – run. The woman who, the woman
who, the woman who. Every woman spent a lifetime hearing
about *that* woman, the woman who was simply living her life.
About the things she had to do, the thousand restrictions, small
and large, that would keep her from becoming that woman,
the world seemingly intent upon turning her into some scurrying, fearful creature, always looking over her shoulder, tense,
braced, like – let's face it – the prey she was.

So Nora permitted herself a small stab of satisfaction in
hearing the men grapple with the unthinkable notion that the
tables could be turned; that they, too, could be prey. She'd
glanced at the newspaper sitting beside the cash register as
she paid her bill. It showed a police sketch of the woman
suspected in the trucker's death. White, neither pretty nor plain,

light hair pulled into long pigtails that flowed over her shoulders, a face so nondescript that if you put pigtails on half the women in the restaurant, they'd match the drawing.

The crunch of wheels on gravel outside the check-in booth brought her back to the present, and to the job at hand. Such as it was. Miranda had been right about the campground's new wallflower status. Other than the sheriff's deputies, the searchers and repeat visits by Bethany, nosing about for new scraps of news, the campground was a ghost town. Gone were the vague impressions from her first, foggy night in the campground – the clotheslines strung between trees, hung with towels and sweaty hiking clothes hoping to pick up a pleasant overlay of pine; gone, the folding canvas chairs circling the fire rings; gone the childhood-recalling whiffs of woodsmoke.

After collecting cleaning supplies from a distracted and jittery Miranda – if Brad had managed to live through the attack, his odds of survival were dropping by the minute – Nora had spent half her first day on the 'job' canvassing the grounds, collecting the trash from the bearproof containers that were the Fort Knox of garbage cans, wiping down the pit-toilet latrines with a bleach solution and liberally spraying air freshener around the concrete enclosures.

She reached for her check-in pad and pencil as the car approached, but pulled back as the reality of the word *car* sank in. She'd seen precious few sedans in her short time in the campground, or even on the two trips to Blackbird. Pickups predominated, with SUVs a distant second. Probably another searcher, late to the party, she thought. Then reassessed. The late-model car had yet to acquire the patina of dust that filmed most surfaces in these dry mountain reaches, where the rains disappeared in mid-spring and wildfires made their reliable appearance by August.

No, this car's size and gleaming presence likely announced Someone Official, Nora thought. She slid the window back.

'Nora. What the hell are you doing in this godforsaken place?'

Joe.

ELEVEN

'What the hell are *you* doing here?' *And how the hell did you find me?*

She didn't have to ask. Joe brandished his phone.

'I've got a Google alert for your name. I was afraid you'd end up dead in a ditch somewhere, given that you'd never hauled a trailer before.'

Afraid? Or, hoped?

'I didn't. Obviously. But where was my name?'

His phone did its semaphore dance again. 'It came up in a news story. This is the last place I expected to find you.'

He hadn't had to use the phone tracker after all. Goddamn that Bethany. When Nora saw her again, she was going to wring the woman's neck.

'What are you doing out here in the middle of nowhere?'

'Traveling, Joe. Just like we'd planned. Until you decided to fuck your best friend's wife. When were you going to tell me?'

The dumbest question, nonetheless asked by anyone who'd ever been deceived, the answer screamingly obvious: never.

'There wasn't anything to tell. It was just a one-off. A mercy fuck. It didn't mean anything.'

It meant something to me. She trained her gaze ahead, staring so hard down the empty stretch of road behind Joe's rental car that her eyes watered. Damn. Now he'd think she was crying. Which she wasn't. She didn't want to weep. She wanted to shriek. Throw something. A punch, maybe.

Or . . . she allowed herself a quick sideways glance, toward the bear spray. It claimed to be able to stop a charging eight-hundred-pound beast in its tracks. What might it do to a hundred-seventy-five-pound man? Would he fall to the ground, dig at his eyes, cry out in agony, beg for forgiveness?

Which, she noted, Joe had not done.

She slid the window shut.

* * *

She wondered how long they'd have stayed like that, Joe shouting questions and challenges, herself turned stone statue, humming beneath her breath in a child's defense against a lecturing parent, had it not been for the arrival of the sheriff, barreling up the road, chased by gritty cloud of dust.

He gave a single *bloop* of the siren as the white pickup fishtailed to a stop behind Joe's car. Joe stuck his head out the driver's side window. The sheriff did the same. 'I need you to move this vehicle. Now.' For good measure, he blipped the siren again.

'What's going on?' Joe turned the same demanding tone on the sheriff that he'd used with Nora.

The blip turned into a rising wail. Joe started the car and began to pull forward, but the sheriff, face tight with annoyance, was already backing up, jerking at the wheel, steering around the booth and entering the campground via the exit lane.

Joe rolled up his window against the dust. Nora took advantage of his momentary silence and slipped from the booth, not even favoring him with a wave or middle finger goodbye, and sprinted after the sheriff, equal parts relieved for the excuse to run from Joe (again!) and apprehensive as to the sheriff's grim purpose.

She rounded the corner, the fire in her lungs competing with the burning in her side, wishing she'd driven to the booth instead of opting for a morning walk. She'd stopped her daily workouts a few days before her departure from Denver. She really needed to get back into the habit. She slowed to a gasping walk as she neared Miranda's campsite. The sheriff and Miranda stood silhouetted within the dust, the sheriff an unmoving dark presence, Miranda flitting about him like some small, wounded bird.

The veil of dust sifted back to the ground just in time for Nora to see Miranda collapse against the sheriff's chest.

The sheriff looked up, saw Nora. His arms tightened around Miranda for a long moment. Then he jerked his head, the meaning unmistakable: get over here and do that womanly comfort-and-succor thing.

Once again, Nora stepped into her reluctant role as hugger, cradling Miranda's trembling form, twisting to look a question at the sheriff.

'Searchers found something. Not much. Some clothes, a shirt, I think. But at least it lets us know we're on the right path.'

So it *was* a bear. Once again, Nora wondered: given a choice between being abandoned by a husband, or losing him to a carnivore, what would she choose? Abandonment the only correct answer, of course. But, really? In her secret thoughts, wouldn't any wife prefer noble sorrow to public humiliation?

'What kind of shirt?' Miranda's words were muffled, indistinct. She addressed the sheriff but spoke into the top of Nora's head. Damp soaked her hair. She forced herself not to hold Miranda away from her.

'Give me a minute.'

The sheriff moved a few steps away and spoke into a walkie-talkie. It squawked in return, a spew of static, followed by a garble of words. Nora, straining, couldn't make them out and was glad of it. Who knew what the person on the other end might be describing to the sheriff? Maybe a droning hum that seduced them off the trail and deeper into the woods, toward something dark and shiny, pulsating on the forest floor. A cloud of flies rising heavy and reluctant from a bit of fabric crusty with dried blood, enclosing chunks of shredded flesh, splintered bone.

The sheriff's face revealed nothing. Nora revised her initial opinion of him upward yet again. He nodded once, as though whomever was on the other end could see it, then re-holstered the walkie-talkie.

He returned to Miranda. Nora released her, and she stood with hands clasped at her chest, prayerful.

'What was your husband wearing that night?'

'I don't . . . I don't . . .' Nora watched Miranda willing away recall. Because what if that memory matched what the searchers had found? What if her own words confirmed her worst fears?

The sheriff looked to Nora, eyebrows raised. 'You saw him that night, too, didn't you? Do you remember?'

Nora closed her eyes and thought. She remembered Brad's face clearly, an embarrassing realization. It took a little longer to dredge up, from the evening that ended on such a strangely fuzzy note, the impression that both Brad and Miranda had been wearing their green Forest Service shirts. Yes, that was it. She remembered how the buttons strained at Miranda's chest; how the rough material was nipped in at the waist, an effect so pronounced she'd wondered at the time whether Miranda had altered the shirt. Brad's by comparison had hung loosely on his rangy frame. He'd rolled his sleeves partway up, a look she'd always liked.

'He got up in the middle of the night when he heard the bear.'

Oh, so now she was certain it was a bear. Nora opened her eyes.

'We sleep, uh, naked, you know. But he wouldn't have gone outside that way. He would have put on his clothes.' She spoke haltingly, each word pulled from a place of dread. 'Jeans, probably, and an old flannel shirt he keeps for when he gets up in the morning and makes the coffee. Brad always makes me coffee . . .' Her voice broke.

The sheriff waited until the freshet slowed. 'Can you tell me any more about that shirt?'

'It was so old you could hardly tell the color.' Still leaving room for doubt, for a shirt someone else might have worn.

'Plain? Or some kind of pattern?' The sheriff was relentless.

Miranda glared as he forced her toward the unwanted conclusion. 'Plaid,' she whispered.

'Black? Brown? Green?'

She hunched her shoulders. Wrapped her arms around herself. Nora thought of a small, cornered animal, bracing for the pounce. 'Some kind of brown.'

The sound of engines intruded as the sheriff relayed Miranda's information to the search team. Reinforcements, now that something – and maybe even someone – had been found?

But it was only Joe in his rental car, Bethany's pickup so close behind that Nora worried she'd clip him. Bethany was out of the truck almost before it stopped moving, clicking photos with her phone as she headed toward them. Nora moved out of the frame. Too late, she knew.

Seconds later, still another truck pulled up; Caleb's this time. He hurried to join the group, with a quick, curious glance toward Joe.

'I just heard they found something.'

The sheriff, bowing to the inevitable, delivered the same snippet of information to Bethany and Joe and Caleb that he'd just given Nora and Miranda.

'Searchers bringing it in?' Caleb asked.

'Some. The rest are staying out there, looking for the . . . looking for Mr Gardner.'

Bethany tapped something into her phone and turned toward Miranda. 'Mrs Gardner. I know this is a difficult time for you.' Leaving it at that, not bothering with questions, giving Miranda space to speak into the silence. Nifty trick, Nora thought.

Miranda made her hands into fists, rubbed them against her eyes, childlike. Squared her shoulders, lifted her chin, seemingly grateful to be free of the sheriff's grim inquiry. Looked Bethany straight in the eye and spoke in a trembling voice. 'It's a sign that he's out there somewhere. It's just a shirt. There's no . . . no . . .'

Nora watched her search for the right word. How would you say, tactfully, no piece of Brad?

'No sign of my husband. It means he got away. I'll bet the searchers will find him any minute now.'

Forty-eight hours, Nora thought. Brad, if he'd even survived the original attack, would have lain that long without water or food or medical care, leaking blood, wounds necrotizing, probably in shock, temperatures plunging at night. The crisp mountain air so good for sleeping as long as you were snug in a bed or sleeping bag, so likely lethal to a grievously wounded man with only bits of shredded clothing for protection.

'I'm sure they'll find him.'

Everyone turned to Joe. Nora hadn't heard him get out of the car, had missed his approach. He stood at the edge of their little circle, this man so anxiously questioning her just moments before now speaking to Miranda, a stranger, in low, soothing tones, bowing a little at her grateful, tearful smile.

'And you are?' Bethany asked.

He moved to stand beside Nora.

'I'm her husband.'

TWELVE

Caleb's eyebrows crawled up his forehead.

Nora tried to remember what she'd told him about Joe. Nothing beyond the fact that they'd broken up, implying that said split involved a mere engagement. She'd never said anything about a spouse, let alone one who still introduced himself in the present tense. Not the sort of thing she could explain now, not with a sheriff and a reporter hanging on her every word.

Nora's mother had a term for the expression on Bethany's face.

'Lit up like Christmas,' she'd have said.

Indeed, given the gift she'd just been handed, Bethany advanced upon Joe with high-wattage attention, not a smile – that would have been inappropriate under the circumstances – but with the kind of focus most people, especially most men, found impossible to ignore. And Joe, as Nora had recently come to know, was more like most men than she'd ever realized.

Bethany tilted her head. She wrinkled her brow. She looked deep, deep into Joe's eyes. 'Mr . . .' She hesitated.

'Crane.'

Bethany's gaze flicked toward Nora.

'I kept my own name,' she supplied. *And a good thing, too.*

'Mr Crane. I'm Bethany James from the *Mountain Messenger*. What's it like to be working in a place where something like this happened? Aren't you worried?'

'Working here? What do you mean?'

Nora enjoyed Bethany's brief discomfiture.

'Your wife works in the check-in booth, so I just thought that you worked here, too.'

'She does?'

Heads swiveled, gazes ricocheting from Nora to Joe and back again. Caleb's eyebrows were back where they belonged, at least.

'I'm filling in for Miranda. Under the circumstances.'

'Not anymore, she's not.' Joe moved a step closer to Nora, so close she caught the rosemary scent of his metrosexual shaving cream, the one that always made her miss the straightforward quality of her father's Old Spice.

'It's typical of Nora to want to help out. She's such a generous person.' Oh, she knew that tone. It had, in its roundabout way, brought her to this very time and place.

He'd used it when he'd bought the truck, walking her around it, showing off its features, opening the door and taking her hand and running it over its buttery leather seats with both heating and cooling elements, the USB ports, cup holders to the right and left and in the center console, too. 'But if you'd really rather get the Land Rover, we can take it back. Because if you're not happy, it's not worth it.' But *he* was happy. So, of course she was, too.

Same as he'd done with the trip, working on her for more than a year, a wistful comment here, a bold suggestion there. 'Wouldn't it be great if we could just chuck it all? Do all the things we want to do while we're still young?' Of course it would. Everybody felt that way.

'Nora-Nora-bo-bora!' Sweeping her into his arms and dancing around the kitchen to an old, old tune. 'Let's sell the house and hit the road. Just you and me, baby.' Saying that sort of thing often enough that it became a running joke between them, so much that she started saying it, too. Until the day she came home to find Joe deep in conversation with a real estate agent, the two of them standing close together, bent over papers spread out across their kitchen table. The woman turning a beat too late, advancing upon Nora with hand outstretched. 'You must be Nora! What an adventurous spirit you have. Joe's a lucky man. It's so romantic!'

Joe behind her, rolling his shoulders in an exaggerated shrug. 'I just thought we could run some numbers in case we ever decide to take the leap. You always say it yourself: it's best to be prepared.'

Nora understood from the look on the agent's face that she'd thought it was already decided. That woman didn't know Joe.

For all his talk of preparation, that part fell to her. Joe was the ideas man, floating them cloudlike and dreamy. It was up to Nora to pull the trigger. And if things didn't work out, whose fault would it be? Hence, her acquired skill of Handling It. Because even as half of her writhed in exasperation at the unexpected appearance of this woman and her comps and her slick sales pitch – 'Just a few suggestions about staging. Trust me, they'll add another ten-thousand dollars to your asking price. And I'll get it.' – her mind snagged on something else the woman had said.

'So adventurous! So romantic!'

'You need to get 'em in the gut,' Lilith, her agent, had growled in dismissing one book idea after another Nora had pitched her after sales for what Lilith called 'the sex book' had proven disappointing. 'If people don't react on a visceral level, it'll never sell.'

Nora was kind enough – cowed enough, more likely – not to remind her that people had reacted on a visceral level to her first book. Unfortunately, their gut reaction had been something she herself had felt within a few weeks of starting that particular project. She'd tarried in the bathroom every night (except the days she decided to change things up by waking Joe early, or even surprising him by greeting him naked after his weekend golf games), and trying so very hard not to think of the book she'd rather be reading, the bath she'd rather be taking, the brain-candy show she'd rather be streaming. She wet her finger, touched herself, got a predictable reaction. *Leave me alone, already. I'd rather be sleeping.*

But . . . setting out for parts unknown, exploring a whole new geography, physical, emotional and maybe even sexual, after years of sameness. Apparently, *that* was romantic. If this woman thought so, Lilith might, too.

Nora stepped into the handshake. 'Let's see those numbers.'

Now, standing in a dusty clearing in a Wyoming campground, surrounded by near-strangers, he was at it again. What did he want this time? Correction: what was *she* supposed to want?

Bethany stood with phone outstretched, presumably recording the lengthening silence. A new attentiveness layered

the sheriff's deadpan. Caleb's eyebrows crept upward again.
Even Miranda stood open-mouthed.

'Nora was kind enough to take our new rig' – rig? More
of Joe's new cowboy persona? – 'on a test run. We're spending
the next couple of years driving around in our new home.'

Our. Twice, he'd used the word. Had she imagined the slight
emphasis? A way of highlighting the fact that he, too, had
claim to Electra?

Nora had told both Caleb and Miranda that she and the man
she'd never precisely identified as her husband had broken up.
Now here he was, painting a picture of marital bliss. Caleb
caught on quicker, arms crossed, judgment at the ready, once
he figured out where to aim it. Miranda, poor, shell-shocked
Miranda, hung on every word, probably having forgotten that
Nora had told her just the previous evening about the demise
of her relationship.

No one questioned, at least not verbally, the weirdness of
Nora making this so-called test run alone, or Joe's showing
up in a rental car to cut it short. Although, Joe being Joe, he
followed up with a smooth explanation before anyone could
even ask. 'As soon as I read this business about a bear attack,
I got up here as fast as I could. I just didn't trust a phone
conversation. That bear could park at Nora's picnic table and
she'd tell me everything was fine. She's a tough cookie.'

She was?

He bestowed upon her a look full of affectionate concern.
'What a rough couple of days you must have had. I can follow
you back down to the highway, ditch the rental car in Blackbird.
To hell with the one-way expense. Come on, honey. Let's take
our truck and trailer' – there was that word again – 'and get
out of here.'

Honey. A word from The Time Before. So casual,
unthinking, practically meaningless – but only if you thought
a brush of fingertips while passing was meaningless, a shared
glance at a speaker's bon mot was meaningless, one of a
thousand in-jokes acquired over two decades together was
meaningless.

Let's get out of . . . where? This anonymous campground
somewhere in Wyoming's high country? Or this disaster that

had befallen them? And go back to their old life, even though it wouldn't be the same, could never be the same. There'd be the inevitable period of estrangement, of tiptoeing, thin-ice caution around one another, every sentence freighted, acres of space between them in bed. And then? They'd move on, as so many had before, into a new reality, perhaps better, more likely just good enough, but preferable to the goddamn unknown that had yawned vast and terrifying before her these last couple of days.

Let's get out of here. Because really, why not? What was the alternative?

Joe moved closer still and put his hand to the small of her back, a gentleman's move, as though to steer her through a door, his touch light as breath. But he touched her nonetheless. He fucking touched her.

'Get your hands off me, you lying, cheating bastard. And get the hell out of my sight. I never want to see you again.'

That.

That was the alternative.

THIRTEEN

Back in the refuge of her campsite, in the Airstream, in bed, under the covers. Pillow pulled tight around her head, but not tight enough to block out *the now what now what now what* thrumming through it – soon interrupted by a *taptaptap* at the door so nearly in time to the rhythm of her thoughts that she had the crazy notion someone had divined them.

Not just any someone. Fucking Joe. She hurled the pillow across the room, threw back the comforter – no giver of comfort, alas, despite the vaunted thread-count of its coverlet, the loft of the down – and stomped so hard to answer the door the trailer shook.

'Leave me the hell alone,' she shouted as she threw the door open, nearly catching Caleb across the face.

He leapt nimbly from the trailer steps, landing on the balls of his feet. An ax swung in one hand. He flung up the other one. 'Whoa, whoa. Sorry to have bothered you. I'll come back another time. Or maybe not.' He began to back away.

'No, wait.' Her voice angled upward, retaining its knife edge of anger and confusion. What must he think of her, a shrieking harpy, her words echoing around the campsite? She forced the volume lower. Had less success with the shaking. 'I thought you were my—'

'Husband?' He finished the sentence for her. He stopped. He didn't come back. But he didn't leave, either.

'Soon-to-be ex,' she clarified.

'Have you told him that? Because he seems, oh, I don't know, a little out of the loop.' That last, at least, said with a hint of a smile.

'I think he's starting to figure it out.' She couldn't muster a smile in return but managed an offer of coffee.

He nodded warily. 'I'll just wait out here.'

She couldn't blame him. Who knew what the crazy lady might do to anyone foolish enough to step into her lair?

She coarse-ground the beans and filled the lower part of the aluminum espresso pot with water. She spooned the grounds into the basket, screwed on the top of the pot, and set it over a flame, her movements slow and deliberate, imposing calm on her roiling emotions. It didn't work, not completely. But at least her hands no longer shook as she carried the tiny cups to the picnic table and set one before Caleb.

'You call that coffee? Shouldn't you just serve it in a thimble?'

She finally smiled, back on surer footing. 'Try it.'

He snorted. 'Is there even enough for me to get a decent taste?' He took a sip, sat up straight, and peered into his cup as though expecting to see whatever had just delivered such a decisive kick to the synapse. He took another, then held up his cup in a kind of toast.

'Like it?' Fishing now. But she figured she was entitled.

'That would be a hell, yeah. Got any more where this came from?'

She ducked back into the trailer and came out with the pot. 'There's a little left. But when you're still wide awake at three a.m., don't say I didn't warn you.'

They sat and sipped. The campsite spun its spell. The creek chuckled obligingly over the rocks. The breeze sighed past in a slow caress. Sunlight shafted across the table, highlighting a shiny spot.

'I thought I got all of that.' Nora retrieved a bottle of spray cleaner and a sponge from Electra and went to work on the spot, rubbing hard until she was satisfied it was gone. 'Whoever was here last spilled something on this table. The last thing I need is that bear coming around.'

'He's probably way too comfortable around people, exactly because of stuff like that.' He pointed to the spot Nora had just cleaned, now reeking of Clorox.

He, Nora noticed. Not *it*. This bear was personal to Caleb. Maybe all bears were.

He ran a finger around the inside of his cup and popped it in his mouth. If Joe had done something like that, he'd have followed it up with a suggestive smile. Joe did very little without an eye to effect.

But Caleb was still focused on the bear. 'This isn't a popular thing to say, under the circumstances, but I hate the thought that I'm probably going to have to kill him. That was clear even before he killed Brad. If he killed Brad.'

Nora choked on her last swallow of coffee. 'What do you mean, if? I thought whatever they found today made it clear that's what happened.'

Caleb rubbed a hand across his head. Nora hadn't realized hair could stand up in quite so many different directions. 'His wife said she fell back asleep after he went outside. Maybe I'm projecting too much here, but my general experience is that when people think there's a grizzly around, they go on full alert. It's kind of primal.'

Nora didn't know, but she could imagine. The very conversation had dropped the emotional temperature a few degrees. She rubbed her arms, subduing goosebumps as he talked.

'You were in that campsite right across the way that night, right? Did you hear anything?'

She didn't even have to think about it. 'I didn't hear a thing that night. And if Miranda was half as drunk as I was, no wonder she didn't, either.'

She caught his look, no interpretation needed. She imagined him stacking judgment upon judgment: a bitter soon-to-be divorcee, and a drinker, too.

'Sounds like you all were partying pretty hard.'

'Actually,' she thought back, 'we weren't. I only had one beer. And a little whiskey, and not the way people usually mean it when they say a little, when they've really had a lot.' She held thumb and forefinger a quarter inch apart. 'Only about this much. But it hit me hard. I could barely walk back to the campsite. Slept in all my clothes. I think it was because I was still so tired from the drive. And maybe the altitude. Anyhow, I didn't hear anything.'

'I have to think you would have heard this. Unless that bear killed him on the spot – and if that had happened, which is unlikely, there'd have been a lot more blood. But if Brad were still alive when the bear dragged him off, there'd have been . . .' He looked at her, judging again, but in a different way. Trying to see what she could handle.

'Signs of a struggle,' he finished.

Judged, and apparently found wanting. Nothing about the unearthly screams a person might utter, for some reason so much more horrifying for being a man's, when he realized he was being eaten alive.

But Miranda hadn't heard them, either.

'The ground should have been all torn up. At the very least, there'd be drag marks, big ones. I suppose the searchers might have erased them by walking over them, but it's not like they headed out in the nighttime. You think they'd have seen them. Said something.'

'Maybe they did to the sheriff. Did you ask him?'

'I did. He doesn't remember anything to that effect. You know, for him this isn't a crime scene anymore, not if the bear took him. But to me, it still is. I'm the one who's going to have to determine if the bear is guilty, administer the capital punishment. I need all the evidence I can get. But right now, beyond a little blood on the ground, and apparently a piece of a shirt, I've got squat.'

Nora thought both of those things sounded like more than enough. If there was even a chance that a bear had killed Brad, she wanted that bear gone. What if it came back? She said as much – not about wanting the bear gone. From his remarks so far, she guessed that she and Caleb had a difference of opinion on the subject. But she hoped it wouldn't show up in the campground again.

'I doubt it. They're bringing in dogs tomorrow. Now that they've found that piece of shirt or whatever it was, there's a good chance there's a . . . that Brad is somewhere in the vicinity. The dogs will sniff it – him – out.'

Nora wondered if Miranda knew about the dogs, knew that the rescue operation had morphed into a search for a body, or whatever was left of one.

She eyeballed the ax Caleb had brought, now lying on the bench beside him. 'What's that for? Surely that won't help against a bear? Shouldn't you be carrying a gun?'

He threw back his head in that way he had and laughed. 'Against a grizzly? Their skulls are a couple of inches thick. And if you shoot one anywhere else, the bullet's just likely to get lost in all that muscle and fat. All you'll do is make it mad. As bad as they are when they're just hungry, a mad grizzly is one of the most destructive creatures on the face of this earth. A gun!' He laughed some more. 'Bear spray is really the only thing that works. When it does.'

Nora waited until he was done having fun at her expense and tried again. 'So why the ax?'

'Oh. That.' He picked it up. It hung easily in his hand. 'It's for you.'

FOURTEEN

Nora shrank away from the lethal weapon so casually brandished by Caleb.

'What do I want with an ax?'

He went to his pickup and opened the tailgate. Rounds of wood, big ones, filled the bed. He pulled at them, sending them bounding heavily onto the ground.

'Brought you some firewood. You've got the prettiest camp-site in the whole place, and if I'm guessing correctly, as soon as it gets dark you go back inside that trailer, when instead you should be sitting around a campfire. It's one of life's great pleasures. So I'm going to show you how to make one.'

He upended a piece onto a flat-topped stump at the edge of the campsite, hefted the ax and whacked it in two with a single blow. He picked up one of the pieces, returned it to the stump, stood it on end, and handed her the ax. 'Your turn.'

She held it away from her, not needing to say she'd never used one. 'Why do I have to cut them up? Can't I just burn them the way they are?'

To his credit, he didn't laugh; didn't so much as smile, nor take that oh-so-patient tone that let her know just how oh-so-stupid her question had been. 'They're too big. They won't catch. And even if they did, they'd take forever to burn down. We're in wildfire country here. You want to make sure your fire is good and out before you go to bed. You want a bunch of nice small pieces, about the size of your forearm. They'll flare up pretty and burn down fast. You just keep feeding it with more wood until you're about half an hour from bedtime. Then let it burn down and douse it. Don't walk away from it until you can put your hand right into it. Seriously. You don't want to be responsible for a fire.'

That much she knew. Every summer smoke from faraway fires had curtained their neighborhood in the middle of Denver, miles from the Rockies' forested slopes, leaving exposed surfaces grey and greasy, reddening eyes and roughing up throats.

Still. She was wary of that ax, its smooth solid handle nearly as much a weapon as the gleaming blade that caught the sunlight and flashed it back at her like a warning. She tried again.

'Can't I just buy firewood in town?' She'd seen bundles of it in front of the gas station and convenience stores, likely aimed at campers just like her, already chopped up by someone else with an ax. No need for her to use one.

'Why pay for something that you can do yourself?'

Because I can't?

But he'd already taken her hands and folded them around the handle. Nudged her feet shoulder-width apart with the toe of his boot. 'Bend your knees just a little.' Nope, nothing erotic about any of that, she thought crazily even as she hefted the ax.

He showed her how to swing it – 'Make sure to come down straight, unless you want to see your foot and your ankle part ways. OK, now give it a try.'

She positioned her feet. Bent her knees. Eyed a straight path. Swung.

Two pieces of wood obligingly fell at her feet.

Nora gave a little jump. 'I did it!'

Caleb's smile was its own reward. 'Yes, you did. The rest is all yours. You'll want a pile of it. Do you know how to start a fire?'

Her home – her former home – in Denver had two fireplaces, one in the living room and the second, a major selling point, in the bedroom. She started fires in them all the time, by pushing the button that ignited the whoosh of gas rushing through the 'logs'.

Her hesitation provided his answer.

'Never mind. Go bring me some twigs. Tiny ones, smaller even than this.' He hooked his forefinger around her pinky and raised it. Normally, she hated when men touched her unasked, a dominance move that always put her on edge. But this was so natural, so utilitarian, and so quick that the flash of irritation she expected never materialized. 'Dry, not green.

Look down by the creek. Animals are always snapping branches off when they come down to drink. There should be plenty.'

Animals? Like bears? She eased into the willows just a few yards from the campsite, glancing wildly about, wondering why she hadn't thought to consider the possibility the first time she'd visited the creek. But all she saw, snapping beneath her feet, were the twigs Caleb had promised, scattered here and there along the creekbank.

She returned with a handful. He inspected them with a critical eye and she was unaccountably pleased when he pronounced them satisfactory.

'Good. Now find some duff. Dry stuff,' he said, at her questioning glance. 'Bits of moss. Word to the wise, if you ever go camping.' He looked at the trailer. 'Real camping. Dip some cotton balls in Vaseline and take them with you in a baggie. They make a great fire starter. Then you don't have to bother with all of this. But for now, let's pretend you're roughing it.'

He showed her how to make the twigs into a tiny tipi over the duff, to hold a match to it, breathe upon the glowing strands of moss until a flame stood up and bowed to her. 'Most people pile on too-big pieces too fast and wonder why the fire goes out. Something you could apply to a lot of things in life.'

Nora shot him a look, but his gaze, aimed at the little flame now creeping along a sliver of kindling, was guileless.

He stood up and dusted his hands.

'You can thank me when you're sitting next to it tonight. Don't forget to look up once in a while. The stars out here are something to behold.'

Said without irony or, as far as Nora could tell, an eye to effect. Just a simple statement of fact: the stars were beautiful. She'd spent so many years in verbal gamesmanship, every remark freighted, at work, in friendships whose smooth surface concealed depths of envy and resentment and of course within the earthquake zone of marriage, fault lines everywhere, the tiniest crack at any moment liable to open into a yawning abyss.

By the time she remembered to thank him, he was gone.

*   *   *

Caleb's departure left her edgy, restless. She wondered where Joe had gone, if he'd headed back to Colorado or was still lurking somewhere, as much of a threat to her emotional well-being as the bear to her physical survival.

She shucked out of her jeans and T-shirt and pulled on her running gear and laced up her shoes. During her time in the booth, she'd read all the pamphlets handed out to campers, with boldface warnings about not running away from bears or mountain lions, or running at all on backcountry trails, so as not to appear prey. But she figured the dirt road snaking through the campground was probably safe. That way, if she encountered Joe, she could just claim she was going on a run and not sneaking around looking for him.

She went through her stretches – never as many as she should – grabbed a can of bear spray and set out at a walk – not as far as she should – to warm up, and then broke into a trot, shaking out the stiffness, calves berating her for too many days of inactivity. She passed campsite after empty site, some with signs of a hasty departure, a clothesline tied between two trees, the grill for the firepit left propped against a picnic table. She reminded herself to come back later and put things in order. She saw only a single tent and high above it, hanging from a branch as per bear-prevention protocol and swaying gently in the breeze, a backpack with a red bandana dangling from a carabiner. She recognized it as belonging to the hiker she'd seen her first night in the campground.

Her stride lengthened and smoothed. She picked up the pace, staying in the middle of the road, far from any bushes where animals might lurk, although soon she forgot about them, losing herself in the satisfying rhythm and pleasurable exertion. Sweat dampened her forehead, sliding toward her eyes. She lifted an arm and swiped it across her face, lowering it just in time to see Joe's rental car pull away from Miranda's campsite.

Miranda stood at the edge of the site, back to Nora, waving a goodbye. She turned at the sound of Nora's approach. Her arm fell.

Nora slowed to a walk and paced back and forth in front of Miranda, not wanting to stiffen up.

'I guess you all are going through a bit of a rough patch,' Miranda said finally.

Nora blew out a long, cool-down breath. 'You could say that.'

'What a jackass.' The reflexive offer of female solidarity.

'He can be nice.' A wife's reflexive comeback. But in defense of Joe? Or of herself, in having chosen him, having stayed with him for so many years of what she'd assumed was a reasonably happy marriage?

'Of course he can. All men can, when they want something.'

They shared a quick grin, a moment of airy lightness, humor bobbing to the surface of the dark waters in which they both floated.

Miranda sat at the picnic table and nodded to the other bench, inviting Nora to follow suit. 'He came by to ask my help. He said he didn't blame you for being mad at him. That he just wants to work things out. He said he'd do anything to get you back.'

Nora had never understood her friends who'd recounted just such pleas from their straying husbands. 'You fell for that?' she'd always had to stop herself from saying.

But hearing it now, even if indirectly, she felt a surge of . . . what? Power? Vindication? And she let herself wonder: what would it be like to be the one who called the shots? Not the sort of marriage anyone was supposed to want; still, the swift, fierce appeal of it momentarily shocked her into silence. Is that why her friends had stayed with their husbands? She tried to push such thoughts aside and focus on what Miranda was saying.

'He asked if I'd put in a good word for him. I said I would, of course. But I figured you must have left for a reason.' The unspoken question hovering just beneath her words: why *had* Nora left?

Nora sat. 'He . . .' She stopped. She couldn't tell whether it felt more like a betrayal to Joe or to herself to reveal his dalliance with Charlotte. She didn't want people to think of her as the kind of woman someone would cheat on. Heck, she was the sex-every-day goddess! Besides, she had a more immediate concern.

'I think he wants to take the trailer away. And the truck, too, probably.'

The look on Miranda's face was clear: that doesn't seem so bad.

'Right now, it's the only home I've got.' Joe's, too. Although as far as she was concerned, he'd forfeited his right to it.

Miranda's apology was quick and heartfelt. 'Oh, Nora. That's terrible. Tell me how I can help.'

Nora turned her palms up. 'I can't imagine how anyone can help. Technically, it's his, too. We paid for it out of our joint account. But my name is on the papers.' It had something to do with taxes, the way she'd claim the trailer and the truck as work-related expenses in relation to the book.

The crunch of boots on gravel interrupted their conversation. The backpacker, tramping past, eyes averted from their frankly curious stares, braids swinging in rhythm to her steps, gone before it occurred to Nora to look more closely at her face.

'That's funny.'

'What?'

'I saw a newspaper at the Buckhorn. There was a police sketch of the woman they think might have killed that trucker. She had pigtails. Not braids.' Nora shook her head, dismissing her own suspicion. 'Somehow, I don't see this woman dolled up as a hooker.'

Miranda leaned across the table, whispering as though the woman could hear them, even though she'd disappeared from sight. 'She does carry that big knife. And they said that trucker's throat was cut.'

They considered this awhile, content to sit in contemplation of anything other than their own troubles.

'No,' Nora said finally. 'Whoever killed that guy has been killing truckers from Texas all the way up here. What'd she do, walk all the way from Texas?'

A short laugh rewarded her, and she felt unaccountably proud of being able to bring another moment of brightness to the shadows that were probably going to haunt Miranda's life for a long, long time.

Miranda, perhaps holding onto the same emotion, played along. 'Maybe she carries hot pants and fishnet stockings and heels in that big pack.'

'And soap and water.' Nora, always practical.

Who cared if their momentary merriment floated on the periphery of hysteria? They were women, together, their laughter their only defense against their twinned catastrophes.

Miranda, perhaps relieved to focus on troubles other than her own unimaginable burden, turned back to the issue of Joe. 'What are you going to do about him?'

The previous night's instinct returned. 'Leave, I guess. Until he catches up with me again.' Because he would. He'd pursue her as relentlessly as he'd pushed the notion of going on the road in the first place. She told a little of that to Miranda, omitting of course the reason for her abrupt solo departure.

'The trailer was his idea originally. Thing is, I love it.' And she had, from the moment she'd seen it on the lot, gleaming its promise of the fresh start she hadn't known she'd needed.

'What about the truck?'

'Hah. That was all Joe, too. And I'd be happy to let him keep the damn thing. But I need it to pull the trailer to wherever I go next.'

Miranda caught at her hand. 'I don't want you to go. Not now, not in the midst of all this. Can't you just stay until they find Brad?'

Nora fought a desire to pull away – from all of it, from Miranda and her agonizing need, from Joe and his implacable mission, from her own confusion about what her life had become.

'He'll never leave me alone as long as I have the trailer.'

'You could hide it somewhere and stay with me until he goes away.'

Nora looked at Miranda's decrepit camper and thought she'd rather stay in a tent like the backpacker who'd just tromped past. 'It's not the easiest thing to hide,' she said quickly.

Miranda straightened, pulling her hand away. Nora feared Miranda had divined her distaste, but Miranda's arm shot up like that of a student who'd just figured out the solution to a particularly complex equation. 'You could sell it to someone and buy yourself a different one, one that he wouldn't want.'

'But I don't want a different one.' She decorated Electra herself, had commissioned the painting on her side. Despite her original purpose as a shared conveyance, Electra somehow felt uniquely Nora's in a way their Denver house never had.

Miranda waved her hand again. 'Oh! Oh! You could sell it to someone who would sell it back to you once Joe leaves.' She gave Nora a smile both triumphant and sly. 'I'll bet Caleb would do something like that for you.'

Nora felt a little leap of hope before logic prevailed. 'I don't know what forest rangers make, but somehow I don't think he could afford it, even for a little while.'

'Nora, listen.'

Nora wondered if Miranda's focus on her dilemma came as a welcome distraction from her own, offering solutions when her life had none. 'You don't have to charge him the full amount. Just make up something. A dollar. Ten dollars. Even a hundred. You know, the way parents sell houses to their kids for a dollar. I always wished I'd had parents like that.'

'Me, too,' Nora said automatically. Even though she and Joe had never needed that sort of help. Well, she needed it now. But she couldn't imagine asking Caleb for such a favor and said as much. What might he expect in return?

Miranda nodded soberly, no words needed. Because there was always an expectation, wasn't there? 'I just wish I could help. I'm all out of ideas, but I've got beer. Want one?'

Without waiting for an answer she climbed up into the camper and returned with two dripping bottles. 'Sorry about the mess. All the ice has melted in the cooler. I'll have to get more next time I go to town. I just don't know when that will be.'

A cooler. So that's how she kept food from spoiling. Nora thought of Electra's efficient little refrigerator, its arctic blast whenever she opened the door. 'I'll bring you some if I get there first.' She wished she'd thought to offer earlier. Miranda could probably use some groceries, too.

They sat in silence, sipping the lukewarm beer.

'I don't suppose,' Nora began, a thought nudging her.

'What?'

'Never mind. It's crazy.' Nora tilted her head back and drained the bottle. She rose to leave. 'You've been a help. Really. With all you're going through, to take so much time with me . . .' She pressed a hand to her heart, unable to continue. Would any of her friends in Denver have been so solicitous? Charlotte had been her friend. So that answered that.

'Nora, if there's something I can do, you need to tell me.'

'Your idea about selling the truck and trailer and then buying them back. That was actually pretty smart.'

Miranda beamed. 'You really think so?' Then, generously returning the compliment, 'But you were right about not going to Caleb. I just wish there were someone else . . .' She clapped a hand to her head and rolled her eyes, signaling idiocy. 'Nora! I'm so stupid! Why didn't you just come right out and ask?'

Maybe it was the beer. Or maybe it was because Nora was still so unnerved by Joe's appearance in this place she regarded as her shelter; maybe gratitude for having found a friend in this most unlikely of places. Or maybe it was just because she didn't have a better idea. But when Nora left Miranda's site and returned to her own, determined to chop enough wood for the campfire Caleb had insisted was essential, a copy of a handwritten bill of sale crackled in her pocket, a duplicate of the one Miranda had carried back into her camper.

FIFTEEN

That first swing of the ax, under Caleb's tutelage, had been lucky.

The final ones, by the time Nora worked her way through the rounds of wood Caleb had left her, landed on target, too. But it took a while, and too often the ax bounced sideways when it encountered a knot, or came down at the wrong angle, sending the wood sailing unmarred off the chopping block, or sank into a soft spot so deeply she had to brace her feet against the log to dislodge it.

But the chore distracted her from a flood of texts from Joe, ones she forced herself not to read, and which stopped only after she sent a single reply: 'I've sold the truck and trailer. So there's nothing else you can possibly want from me. Leave me alone.'

Did she hope for a reply, telling her exactly what he might want from her, a long list of the things he loved about her? The things that made her absence unbearable? If so, she didn't get one. She thought of her reaction the night before, when Miranda conveyed Joe's message. 'He said he'd do anything to get you back.'

Was that what she wanted? Or did she just want a return to the familiar, the comfortable, the reassuring boredom of her previous life? Easy to fling fuck-yous in anger. But the finality that implied – was she ready for that?

She swung the ax again and again, as though the answer might fly up amid the wood chips scattering about her feet. The pile of wood – pieces uneven, of various sizes, but split nonetheless – grew until she'd worked her way through all the rounds Caleb had left and had almost exhausted all of her complicated feelings about Joe.

By the time she was done stacking the wood in a satisfyingly neat pile by Electra's front tire, her shirt clung wetly to her skin and the muscles between her shoulder blades screamed imprecations. She checked the sky. A few stars emerged shyly from a deepening backdrop that was still tinged blue, not the black of full night. She had time.

She'd quickly learned, as long as even a hint of bear-detecting daylight remained, to make use of the campground's bathroom with its two concrete shower stalls. Electra's fat manual contained detailed instructions about dealing with the shower's grey water tank and the black water tank connected to the toilet, warning that mistakes carried consequences both dire and deeply unpleasant. And one of the innumerable message boards loaded with tips about life on the road recommended peeing in the camper's shower rather than the toilet – a hint that saw Nora click hastily out of the site. Despite the considerable charms of Electra's bathroom, the less she used it the longer she could postpone the more onerous housekeeping tasks.

Even the campground shower's lukewarm trickle was restorative, and she hurried back to her site, skin scrubbed raw and hair dripping, eager to enjoy the day's accomplishment by lighting a campfire with her fresh-chopped wood before darkness descended completely. She stepped into Electra, tossed her damp towel onto the table – she'd hang it from the bathroom's clever clothesline later – and opened the kitchen drawer in search of matches.

She stopped, hand hovering above the drawer's meticulously arranged contents. Something was . . . off. Some rearrangement of molecules, almost palpable, as though someone had been in the trailer while she was gone.

She flicked on every light within reach, even the fringed and beaded dinette lamp, and turned a slow circle. Nothing out of place. She pulled out drawers, opened cabinets, examined their contents. Nothing amiss. Same with the fridge, the drawers in the bathroom and beneath the bed. The overhead cupboards. Nothing, nothing, nothing. She even felt about the banquette cushions, reassuring herself that her engagement ring was still safely hidden away.

She was tired, she told herself. Again. All she'd wanted was a few days alone in the campground to figure things out. But then Brad had gone missing, and Joe had shown up and now her imagination apparently had gone into some sort of stress-induced overdrive.

She found the matches in the unmolested drawer and took them to the fire pit beside the picnic table. She'd already arranged a new pyramid of twigs and duff, which flared at the first touch of the match.

She nudged kindling into the flame as it grew and bent toward the long splinters, and one by one added a few pieces of the wood she had split herself that very day, and finally sat back with a glass of the wine that nobody else but her seemed interested in. Which was fine. It was all fine – the wine, the fire, with its warmth and evocative scent, and above it all, the stars that Caleb had earlier promised, no more stray outliers, but an unabashed glittering show, like a woman's sequined skirt swirling across the sky.

She tilted her head back, the wine forgotten, and watched the celestial tango until she woke with a start, the fire nothing but the barest glow, the stars gone cold and remote.

She hurried to the trailer, flicked switches again and left the door open, spilling light across the campsite so that she could see to drown what was left of the fire, stir it with a stick, hold her hand millimeters above the sodden black mess to assure herself it had gone cold.

One more task awaited, her daily text to her mother – 'I'm fine; talk soon.'

She returned to Electra, too tired now to detect the feeling of something awry, that alien presence that had so troubled her earlier, and slept long and – for the first time in days – very nearly peacefully . . . until she awoke to the sound of the dogs leaping and baying at her door.

She'd fallen asleep, again, in what she thought of as her campsite clothes, light sweatpants, a loose, long-sleeved T-shirt and thick socks.

She slid the bedroom window shade up a finger's width and peered out. Saw men. Hooked herself into a bra.

She opened the door a crack. The dogs went wild, surging up the steps, flinging themselves at the fast-slammed-shut door, toenails screeching down Electra's beautiful aluminum flanks. Beneath their howls, shouts eventually resolved into words.

'You can come out now. I've got 'em leashed.' The dogs' howls subsided into a sort of muttering.

Which, Nora thought, was not exactly an incentive to emerge. They must have found Brad. It was one thing to acknowledge that he was probably dead; that Miranda's sad hopes were increasingly futile. Another to have it confirmed.

She called through the door, hoping they could hear over the dogs. 'Just a second.'

She took her time, postponing the inevitable, a few precious moments, brushing her teeth, smearing on some make-up, wetting her fingers and running them through her hair.

She approached the door again. The dogs relapsed into full-on hysteria. There were two of them, not the stubby, sad-eyed Basset Hounds she'd imagined, ears dragging the ground, but leggy, sleek, and impressively strong for such slender animals, nearly pulling their handler off his feet despite the stout leather leashes attached to pronged metal collars. He dragged them back a few steps. The sheriff moved into the space he'd vacated. Behind the men, the reporter hovered. That woman was everywhere.

'Mind if we come in?'

Probably wanted to sit her down, break the bad news easy to the little lady. 'Of course,' she said. 'I'll make coffee.'

'That won't be necessary.' He turned to the handler. 'OK,' he said.

What would the man do with the dogs? Nora wondered if the trees ringing the campground were strong enough to hold them.

'Please stand aside,' the sheriff said. He unclipped the leashes.

'Wait!' Nora cried, too late. The dogs surged into the trailer, knocking her aside, skidding to a halt in front of her bed, sniffing and tearing at the comforter, their renewed bellows bouncing off Electra's walls.

The sheriff brushed past Nora, snapping on a pair of thin rubber gloves, the kind surgeons wore. The handler followed close behind, reaching around him to haul the dogs away from the bed.

The sheriff flung back the comforter, tossed aside the

pillows, rummaged in the tangle of sheets at the foot of the bed. Turned to Nora, something dangling from a palely gloved finger.

A T-shirt.

A man's.

Forest green, with the same pine-tree logo that adorned the sign announcing the campground.

'Whose is this?' the sheriff said. 'And what is it doing in your bed?'

SIXTEEN

Nora actually laughed at the sheriff's announcement that he was taking her into custody, not a true laugh, denoting amusement, but the bark of disbelief.

'For what? Leaving my door unlocked so somebody could dump a T-shirt in my trailer?'

'Is that your explanation?'

Nora knew enough – in her former life, she'd occasionally binged on crime shows and mystery novels – to shut up. She folded her arms across her chest, squeezing tight, holding in a wordless cry of protest as he continued. 'I'm holding you for Brad Gardner's disappearance. Maybe even his death. You have the right to remain silent . . .'

She'd forgotten Brad's last name. Something she was foolish enough to blurt out after the sheriff's bored recitation, despite her vow of silence.

'Do you often sleep with men without knowing their name?'

Nora belatedly clammed up again.

'I'm going to take you on down to the station. You'll get a phone call.'

She had no idea who she'd call. Not Joe. Not any of their friends. And she didn't know anyone in Wyoming, except the wife of the person she was now – unbelievably – suspected of killing. And Caleb, who'd never believed a bear had dragged Brad away.

She didn't want to go anywhere with the sheriff. But with every moment that they stood together in Electra, the space felt smaller, oxygen leaking from the air. The sheriff waited immobile, barely breathing, gone into some reptile-like near trance, apparently prepared to stand there all day. She had to get out into the air.

'Fine,' she said, brushing past him with as much dignity as she could muster. But he caught at her arm. 'Your hands, please.'

'You've got to be kidding me.'

He wasn't.

He assured her of that, sounding almost bored as the cuffs, cold and metallic, circled her wrists with a decisive click, a sound echoed by Bethany's camera as Nora awkwardly emerged from the trailer. Later, she'd think the only reason the sheriff had cuffed her was to provide the dramatic photo that would lead the paper the next day, but of course went online almost immediately. The irresistible image of the chic author of a (suddenly) notorious book about sex arrested on suspicion of killing a ruggedly handsome much younger man, almost certainly after bedding him, in the wilds of Wyoming.

The sheriff's office turned out to be a small frame building in the center of town with a couple of holding cells in the rear.

'County jail's full up now. There was a rodeo in town last night, which always brings in the drunk and disorderlies. They'll take you to county once you're charged. It'll be cleared out by then. You can spend the night here.'

Once she was charged? So she hadn't been? The cop shows she occasionally watched seemed to zoom straight from arrest to courtroom. But they all featured one detail in common.

'I want a lawyer.'

His lips barely moved when he spoke. 'You'll want one licensed to practice in Wyoming. Know anyone?'

Of course she didn't. In that case, he told her, a public defender would be appointed until she could locate one. 'Call it an educated guess, but I don't see you qualifying for one beyond your initial appearance.'

'My what?'

'In court. That's when they set bond and such.'

Court?

'Look, there's been some misunderstanding.' Her shows might have been light on legal procedure, but that particular line seemed to have been uttered by every obviously guilty suspect at some point. Except, in her case, it was true. She soldiered on. 'I have no idea how that shirt got in my trailer.'

'I have an idea.'

She awaited enlightenment.

'Mr Gardner is a nice-looking fella. And if you don't mind my saying so, you're an attractive woman for your age.'

Oh, she minded. She minded very much.

'I don't know who came on to who—'

Curious as she was to hear his little scenario, she couldn't help herself. 'Nobody came on to anybody. Because none of this ever happened.'

He spoke over her. 'My money's on you. Because of how his wife described it. She hears him get up in the middle of the night to check on what he thought was a bear. But it wasn't. It was you, tapping and scratching around outside his camper, trying to lure him out. And then, well. His shirt ends up in your bed. Maybe he gets up after a bit to go back to his wife.' Dropping a little emphasis on that last word. 'And you get upset. Maybe you'd been thinking you found yourself a new man to replace the one you just left, but now here he is, leaving you already. And things go south.'

'That's the most ridiculous thing I ever heard.'

'Is it.' He didn't even bother to lift his voice, make it a question, although he followed it up with one. 'Why don't you tell me where you chased him off to, caught up with him, what you did then? Save us all a lot of time.'

'There's nothing to tell.'

He tilted back in his chair. It groaned a protest.

Nora tried again. 'Did you even remotely consider that Brad – Mr Gardner – might have left on his own? He didn't seem thrilled about the campground host arrangement.'

The sheriff snorted. 'Leave a woman like Miss Miranda? I do not remotely consider that a possibility.'

So it was like that.

He sat a few minutes more, waiting for her to change her mind. An air conditioner blocked the sunlight in one window, but it wasn't turned on. The room was hot and bright and still, but for a fly that buzzed against the other window in a series of small, soft thuds, seeking an escape that didn't exist. She knew just how it felt.

The sheriff reached for a swatter on his desk and reduced the fly to a bluish smear. 'Let's get you set up in here, then.

I'll call the public defender's office. They're usually pretty busy. They got twenty-four hours to get to you and I imagine they'll take all of it.'

He went about the business of the mug shot, warning her not to smile – as if – and the fingerprints, the latter in some way the worse violation, given that it required him to touch her. She'd expected ink and paper, but instead he cleaned her fingers with an alcohol wipe and placed them on a digital scanner, Nora leaning her body as far as possible away from his.

He unlocked the holding cell, guided her inside, and then released her from the cuffs. 'You just make yourself comfortable.' He looked at his watch. 'Looks like we missed the window for lunch. I'll bring your dinner at six.'

She hadn't had breakfast. Until this moment, she hadn't realized she was hungry. Her stomach, gone Pavlovian at the mention of food, stood up and demanded attention with a rolling growl. Six o'clock was a long time off.

She turned away as he locked the cell door. She didn't want him to know that of all the disasters confronting her on this day, it was the missed meal that brought her to the edge of tears.

In her short time at the campground, Nora had gotten used to the absolute blackness of the nights, the cottony soft silence that enfolded her like a quilt.

The sheriff's office was at one end of the main street through Blackbird, a town that stayed busy farther into the night than Nora would have imagined, the air variously disturbed by the hum of passing tires, the scream of Jake brakes as semis geared down on the hill leading into the valley, and the grousing of motorcycles whose riders would clearly rather have been going faster.

A streetlight sent bright daggers through the uncurtained window placed too high in her cell to afford her a view of the free world, even when she stood on tiptoe. It competed with glare spilling from a light from the adjoining office where an occasional, if quickly choked off, snore let her know that the deputy assigned to the overnight shift was getting more sleep than she was.

She lay atop rough sheets worn thin, not wanting to be between them. Despite the eye-watering scent of bleach wafting from their folds, she suspected them of harboring bedbugs at best, and at worst unknown microbes that would leave patches of skin raw and weeping, their fiery itch competing with the blaze of shame over her arrest. Which she shouldn't feel.

She'd done nothing wrong, something she wanted to shout, her protest filling the office, jolting the somnolent deputy awake and . . . what then? He wasn't going to free her. It didn't work that way. And he wouldn't believe her anyway. Perception is everything. How many times had she drilled that into the powers that be at the university?

When three of the school's star basketball players were accused of rape, and a grainy cellphone video emerged that showed them leading the stumbling girl into a bedroom, Nora had argued against shuttling the youths off to an early spring break at a hunting retreat high in the mountains. Dress them up in suits and ties, she told the athletic director, put them in front of a microphone, say they'd removed the girl from the party because they'd been so worried about her safety and that she'd seemed fine when they left, and who knows what might've happened to her after that? The perception of well-dressed, soft-spoken, concerned, young men – live! Speaking directly into the cameras! – would trump that of the furtive video every time. Textbook advice on Nora's part, exactly what she was paid, and paid well, to deliver, even as she queasily tried to comfort herself with the thought that surely no one would fall for such a transparent stunt. But it had worked, the youths strutting free, and she'd later seen online the photo of them celebrating in their lawyer's office, arms around one another, beers in hand, looking directly into the camera, laughing as though at her and at the girl, too, who dropped out soon after the charges against the boys were dismissed.

Dismissed.

Nora sat up so suddenly the thin plasticized mattress beneath her raised up and slapped back down against its metal slab. A sudden attentive change in the silence in the next room told her the deputy was awake.

She stood and paced the cell, aware of his shadow behind the partially open door between the office and holding cells. He was watching her. She didn't care. The movement helped her think.

Why had the charges against the players been dropped? She thought back through the years, the many crises at the university – plummeting enrollment, an embezzler in the provost's office, too many professor-student entanglements to count despite increasingly severe training sessions – that had demanded her attention, leaving her little time to tout the grants and endowments and awards for which the university foolishly expected equal publicity.

She couldn't even remember the players' names. But the case – the details – came back fast. Charges dropped for lack of evidence. The girl – it was suspected her drink had been drugged – woke hours later, disoriented and in pain. But whomever had assaulted her had been smart enough to use a condom, and she couldn't recall a single face, let alone three.

Nora thought of her own situation, the sole piece of evidence, the shirt in her bed. Someone had put it there. She remembered the feeling she'd had the previous night that a person had been in the trailer. So she could pinpoint the time, although she doubted anyone would view her sense of unease as definitive.

But who would want to pin Brad's disappearance on her? Why?

The answers, as obvious as they were painful: Joe. She'd publicly humiliated him at the party, then run off with the truck and trailer he deemed rightfully his. And she'd foiled him with Miranda's cockamamie plan to 'sell' the vehicles. But to engineer this accusation against her, to twist what was obviously a bear attack into some sort of bizarre kidnapping-murder scenario? That was overkill, albeit right in line with Joe's penchant to think big.

How had he done it? He could have slipped into Miranda's camper (she refused to think he might have been invited) as easily as he'd likely entered Electra, grabbed one of Brad's shirts, dragged it along the campground's loop roads, flicking it against the occasional tree or bush in a scent trail that led directly to her door, 'proof' that Brad had been in her trailer.

Which, as with the video of the basketball players going into the room with the girl, wasn't proof of anything beyond that. Now all she'd need was a lawyer, a good one, to make that argument for her. She'd ask her public defender for some names, insulting him or her in the process, but it couldn't be helped. Now was not the time for niceties. That kind of lawyer would cost her. She thought of the ring, tucked within the dinette cushion. She wondered if Blackbird was big enough for the kind of jeweler who'd give her a fair price for it. She needed at least enough to post bail. With no actual evidence beyond the shirt, there'd be no excuse to hold her. Then it would just be a matter of waiting for Brad's grizzly-mauled body to be found before she could put this new nightmare behind her. As strategies went, it wasn't much. But it still counted as a plan.

She stopped in midstep. The shadow behind the door jerked.

'It's OK,' she called, trying to keep the excitement from her voice. 'I couldn't sleep. But I'm going to try.'

She lay down on the slippery mattress, the sheets bunching beneath her, settling herself with ostentatious rustling, until the shadow disappeared. But bright wisps of elation remained, sparked by a realization: her plan, such as it was, admittedly lacked substance. But it was something to build on, to forge into a weapon capable of combatting the helpless confusion of the last few days, the sense that she was spinning untethered through events beyond her control.

New Nora, whoever she was, was starting to Handle It.

SEVENTEEN

The deputy sheriff who'd taken the overnight shift led Nora blinking into the jail parking lot and pointed to a man pacing beside an SUV with Colorado plates. She shaded her eyes against the harsh morning sun, trying to make him out.

'That's him. The one who bailed you out.'

She recognized the car first, the one that on so many weekend mornings had pulled into her driveway, Charlotte waving an arm out the window. 'Come on, girl. Those Bloody Marys aren't going to drink themselves.'

The man turned, and she saw why she hadn't immediately identified Joe's best friend and former law partner, the husband of the woman Joe had so vigorously fucked as a going-away present to himself.

She was used to seeing him in a suit at office functions, or in polo shirt and chinos heading off to the golf course with Joe, in either case supremely confident, his walk the strut of a man who'd made partner young and routinely broke eighty.

The person turning toward her was unshaven, scruffy in a University of Colorado T-shirt and jeans. His shoulders sagged, and when he took off his sunglasses to greet her, his eyes were so reddened with exhaustion she took a step back.

'Artie? What . . .?'

Nora, sleepless from the night in the cell and stunned nearly speechless by the combination of morning sunlight and fresh air she swore she'd never take for granted again, could barely form sentences. She made a supreme effort.

'What are you doing here? And how'd you get here so fast?'

'It hit the news last night. Made a big splash back home, as you might imagine. "Denver woman arrested in disappearance attributed to grizzly." Something like that. I made some calls and got in the car. Drove all night.'

She remembered that drive. Imagined the mixture of

confusion and anger, much like her own, that had launched Artie north.

'I posted your bail,' he said, and she wondered how much that had been. Considerable, she guessed, given his next words. 'I had quite a long conversation with the county prosecutor. The sheriff didn't want to let you out at all, but they made the mistake of setting an initial bail within reason. In addition to posting it, though, I had to personally vouch for you.'

She mumbled her thanks and tried to ask about the cost.

He waved away her question. 'We'll deal with all that later. Hungry? We've got a lot to discuss, and I'd just as soon we both had some energy. We'll need it for your initial appearance.'

'My what?'

'Your initial court appearance. It's where they read the charges against you, decide whether to leave you free on your own recognizance, set the conditions.'

'Wait.' Nora stood in the parking lot. 'But you just bailed me out. You mean this isn't done?'

Artie turned on her a look she remembered from school, the kind of look bestowed by a teacher certain she had explained something so slowly and clearly that only the most stupid student could fail to understand.

'No. It's just beginning.'

The silence that struck the Buckhorn when Nora and Artie pushed through the door went beyond the pin-drop variety. A falling feather would have echoed across the room.

Heads swiveled. Eyes widened. Nora thought she saw someone raise a cellphone. She turned away. The faux-shutter ratcheting sound informed her she'd been too late. She slid into a booth and raised one of the plastic menus in front of her face. Artie pulled it away.

'Get used to it. This is going to be your life for a while. Never hide your face. It just makes you look guilty. Keep your head up. I tell my clients to pretend they're balancing a book on it. One made of glass, that'll shatter if it falls.'

'But I didn't do anything.' Said too loud.

Focus that had returned to food diverted yet again, people

fairly sniffing the air as the tantalizing scent of scandal competed with whiffs of bacon and coffee.

Artie shot her a look. She used the lengthening silence to zip a quick text to her mother, whose calls and texts – outnumbering even those from Joe and her agent – were probably the reason her inbox was full: 'I'm OK. It was all a misunderstanding. Don't worry. I'll call soon.' She wouldn't. But hoped it would mollify.

Abby appeared with a couple of mugs of coffee and a pot of cream, pointedly refusing to meet the eyes of the woman who so recently seemed to have snagged her father's interest, now accused in the disappearance of one man and sitting at her station with another. Nora put her finger blindly at a place on the menu, too cowed to speak, while Artie murmured a preference for poached eggs, wheat toast and fruit. By the time their food arrived – Nora was relieved to see she'd avoided Artie's abstemious choice and dug into a plate of huevos rancheros – conversation once again buzzed throughout the room and she felt safe in speaking. Still, she leaned across the table and lowered her voice to a whisper.

'Artie. Look at me. I didn't do anything.'

He pushed aside a piece of toast, not meeting her eyes. 'I forgot to tell them no butter. And whether you did anything or not, there's no proof, which is all that counts.'

Nora sat back, her relief trumping even her hunger. 'They'll dismiss the charges, then? I won't have to go through that charade of a – what did you call it? – an initial appearance?'

Artie speared a piece of cantaloupe with his fork, studied it, put it down. 'No, you're still suspected of kidnapping. On the flimsiest of evidence, I might add. All they've got is that you slept with the missing man. Nothing at all to prove you had anything to do with his disappearance.'

'But I didn't sleep with him!' So much for whispering.

In the kitchen, a dish shattered. Nora wondered how long it had been since the good citizens of Blackbird had been treated to so much entertainment. Abby scurried from the kitchen with a couple of to-go boxes in her hand. The check flapped beneath them.

'Pie. On the house. It might be best if you go.'

Artie glanced at the check and slid a couple of bills toward Abby. 'Agreed. Keep the change. Can I have that as a receipt?' He looked at Nora and raised his chin. She got the message.

Nora stood up, taking her time about it, and then threaded her way step by deliberate step through the gauntlet of staring faces, head held high the way Artie had just shown her, the look of an innocent woman with nothing more on her mind than the anticipation of a superior piece of pie.

At Artie's insistence, they ate the pie at Electra's dinette.

Nora had suggested the picnic table, within earshot of the creek's burble, but Artie demurred.

'Reporters will show up any minute. You need to be prepared for that. In fact, it might be best if you stayed at the motel in town. I'll book you a room. They'll find you there eventually, but it'll buy you some time. I'd represent you – and I can still be in court with you – but reciprocity here is on a case-by-case basis, and you're better off with someone local, anyway. I've called a lawyer I know up here to represent you. He's good. Here's his card. You've got an appointment to talk with him tomorrow. Ten a.m. Don't be late. I'd like to think they'll have found this guy's body before your initial appearance but if they don't, I'll make sure we get a condition that you can travel back to Denver.'

'But I don't want to go back. I want to stay here.' The words shocked her, and then they didn't. She did want to stay, to luxuriate in the satisfying physicality of chopping more wood, lighting another fire, sitting beneath the stars, soaking in the peace of the place, the stillness within the swirling turmoil that had become her life.

'As your lawyer – as your friend – I'd advise against it.'

Joe, telling her to come home. The sheriff, telling her what he thought had happened. Now Artie, another man, telling her what to do.

'I don't want to go anywhere else. I don't know how to say it more clearly. I didn't do anything. I didn't sleep with that man.'

'Are you sure? That T-shirt. It looks bad.'

'Of course I'm sure!'

Was she?

The night she'd had dinner with Miranda and Brad, the drunkenness that had caught her unawares. Had she somehow blotted out an encounter? She shook her head, aware of Artie's curious gaze.

'I'm sure. Are you going to finish that pie?'

Artie pushed it toward her. Abby had given them two different kinds, the triple-berry and the blueberry-peach, a bit of generosity that Nora took to mean the girl at least hadn't – yet – come to a decision about her. Nora took a bite of hers, then a bite of Artie's, trying to decide which she liked best. Both. She liked both best. 'How long until court?'

'When did they book you?'

It felt like years, eons, since she'd stood in the sheriff's office, leaning away from him as he put his doughy hands on hers, pressing her fingertips against the electronic reader. She hadn't paid attention to the hour. But he'd said something about missing lunch. 'About one o'clock yesterday afternoon.'

'They've got to charge you within seventy-two hours. We're closing in on twenty-four. That gives us two days yet. Nora, did he have a warrant when he found that shirt?'

She shook her head.

'Then how'd he get in here? Did you invite him in?'

'He kind of invited himself. But I didn't stop him.'

'Still. I can go after him on that. But he'll probably be back with one. He'll want to toss this place, looking for more evidence. They won't be able to charge you on what they've got. Just because you slept with somebody' – he held up his hand – 'I know, I know. Just because it looks like you slept with somebody doesn't mean you killed him. They'll be looking for evidence and so will we. Do you know who would want to pin this man's disappearance on you? And why?'

'Joe. I mean, he's the only person I know who's mad at me enough to do this. Other than . . .' She hadn't dared broach the subject of Charlotte yet. She'd glanced at Artie's hand as soon as he'd shown up at the jail. He still wore his wedding band. Now she looked again, more pointedly.

'What's happening with you two, anyway?'

Artie looked as though the single bite of pie he'd had seriously disagreed with him. His face went grey as an overused dishrag. 'She's staying with her sister for a while. But I don't see her pulling something like what you've done. Just up and leaving.'

Nora didn't, either. Charlotte was the collapse-into-hysterics-and-beg-forgiveness type. And Artie? He'd weigh public scandal against career, would contemplate the scenario of walking into an office every day where every person there knew his partner had bedded his wife, and half of them had seen the proof. No wonder Artie had been so quick to head north to her defense. It gave him an excuse to stay away from the office for a few days. But when he returned, Nora's money was on a discreet divorce after enough time had passed for the reek of scandal to have subsided into the occasional unpleasant whiff, like flowers still beautiful in a vase whose water had gone cloudy.

'Artie, you all right? The Airstream has a bathroom if you're not feeling well. And the campground bathroom is right down the road, just around the bend.' She hoped he'd choose the latter.

Artie blotted his face with a paper napkin from the café and slapped the table, a gesture of finality.

'I'm going to call it a day. Head back down to town and get some sleep. You sure you don't want to come back, too? You're a sitting duck up here. That newspaper mentioned the Airstream. My guess is the Denver paper already has somebody on the way up here. It's summer and it's slow. This'll liven up the front page. It'll take them about two minutes to find you here. And don't forget that the sheriff will probably be back with a search warrant.'

As if on cue, they heard a car roll past. At least the site's curved entry meant the interior was screened from the loop road, and Nora had taken Artie's suggestion to clip a new reservation form, using his name, to the post beside the broken stump.

'That won't fool people for long,' Artie warned.

'Fuck 'em,' said New Nora.

Artie blinked. 'Have it your way. But call me if you change your mind. I'd come back up here and get you, drive you back to town. That way, they won't see your truck in front of the motel.'

She thanked him and hoped he didn't see her relief at his departure.

EIGHTEEN

After she heard the third group of looky-loos drive past, Nora filled a Thermos with coffee and took it and her tablet down to the creek where, screened by shrubs, she could enjoy the solitude that was the site's main appeal. This way, even if someone was brazen enough to leave a car and walk into the site, phone held high for a selfie beside a presumed murderer's Airstream, no one would know she was there.

She settled herself on the flat, sun-warmed rock overhanging the water, kicked off her shoes and dipped her feet into the shockingly cold current. She pulled them out so fast her knees bumped her chin. Water splashed onto the rock but vanished almost immediately beneath the strength of the sun. She lowered her feet again, more cautiously this time, just letting the wavelets tickle the soles. Better. Willows surrounded her, their whippy limbs bowing and straightening in the breeze, dropping their slender leaves into the water. They shot downstream in bright-green whorls, dipping and darting like schools of verdant minnows. But for its surface disturbance the water flowed invisible as glass, so clear that every stone on the creek bottom, rounded and polished by eons of flowing water and grit, showed distinct and colorful, aqua and red mixed in with brown and gray.

Still more pebbles littered the rock on which Nora sat and she added them to the collection in the creek bed, idly tossing them into the water whose swirls and eddies were the physical embodiments of her own thoughts, sloshing from Joe's perfidy to her own dilemma and back again.

She balanced the tablet on her lap and tapped away at its tiny keyboard, transcribing headlines. The local paper had gone laconic – *Denver Woman Held in Man's Disappearance* – and she directed a brief charitable thought toward the ubiquitous Bethany. Other news sites were not so kind. She typed in the worst: *Sex-Book Cougar a Suspect in Younger Man's Bloody Disappearance.*

The latter was accompanied by side-by-side photos: the first from her book jacket, airbrushed, professionally lighted, the gentle breeze from a hidden fan lifting her hair from her shoulders. Business-sexy in a blazer over a blouse V'd one button beyond propriety. Lips slightly parted, eyes wide. 'Smoking!' the photographer had pronounced with satisfaction. The other, her booking photo. The sheriff, naturally, had declined her request for a moment in the bathroom before leaving the trailer and although she'd brushed her hair and availed herself of foundation before she'd so foolishly opened the door to him, she'd been unable to apply concealer and eyeliner and shadow and contouring blush that buttressed her ability to face each day; no time to comb product into her hair and blow-dry some volume into it. Eyes wide in this new photo, too, but in terror; lips pressed tight to hold in a cry of protest. Skin wan and blotchy, hair hanging limp, and oh God were those roots? She typed:

> I had it all planned. I'd looked up salons in each town where we planned to stop, checked their reviews, made appointments. There would be no visible roots on this trip. I just hadn't figured on a stop in jail.

She paused at a realization, then typed slowly, ruefully:

> I'm probably on the hook for those missed appointments. I'd better remember to cancel them. And while I'm at it, I'd like to post a review of the Clyde County Sheriff's Office holding cells. The next time you complain about a motel bed, imagine yourself tangled in the thinnest of sheets, sliding around on a plastic-coated mattress a mere three inches thick but flattened in the middle by the weight of bodies much larger than mine. Try balancing over a cold steel toilet with no seat. When Freud invented the term penis envy, he probably didn't realize it had everything to do with women wishing that we, too, could just take care of our business standing up.

The polished metal that passes for a mirror would be inadequate except that the blinding lighting in the cell helpfully highlights every pore. And the smell. Bleach and sweat and stale cigarette smoke still lingering from the days when people were still allowed to smoke. Forget perfume, scented candles, fresh-baked bread. The best smell in the world is fresh air.

So, zero stars to the Clyde County Jail. From which I walked out to find myself notorious. It was one thing to be known as the Middle-Aged Sex Queen of the Mile High City. (Which reminds me that one of the book's big flaws was that Joe and I never joined the mile-high club. But who knows? Maybe Joe saved that particular coup for someone else.)

She hunched lower and lower over the tablet as she typed, the accumulated weight of each individual humiliation almost more than she could bear. Where was New Nora when she needed her?

She lifted her head the way Artie had showed her in the café. Straightened her spine. Gazed into the rushing creek that cared not one whit for her and her problems; indeed, its burble verged on laughter. *Man plans, God laughs.* Well, she could, too.

She picked up a rock, somewhat larger than the others, and ducked away from the splash. 'No more looking back,' she vowed. Time to move forward. Yet still she dawdled, the combination of warm sun on her back and cool water against her feet so pleasant, lulling her into the sort of peace she'd quickly come to expect from the site.

That peace would vanish with her next task: somehow convincing the woman whose husband she was accused of sleeping with – and no matter how improbably, luring him to his presumed and mysterious death – to talk with her.

A stick snapped.

Nora bolted to her feet, belatedly aware she'd left the bear spray in the trailer. Something was moving through the willows, straight toward her. She tossed the tablet away and plunged headfirst into the creek. Later, she'd marvel at the inept workings of her brain, slow-motion punches of realization as she propelled herself toward the bottom.

If I go underwater, the bear won't see me.

Two minutes ago you were marveling at how clear that water was.

Of course he'll see you.

And, finally: *holy shit, this water is* really *cold.*

She burst above the surface, blinking and blowing, feet scrambling for purchase on the beautiful and damnably smooth rocks, backpedaling as fast as she could toward the far bank, away from the apparition staring down upon her from the rock she'd just vacated.

'Hey. Are you all right?'

Nora raised herself by inches into the warm, warm sunlight, dashed the water from her eyes, and beheld the backpacker she'd seen her first night in the campground.

NINETEEN

The woman held out her hand.

Nora splashed back across the creek and took it.

The woman yanked her from the water in a quick, easy move, the strength in her slender arm surprising.

Nora fell onto the rock and lay still a moment, letting the sun bake feeling back into limbs gone numb in just a few seconds in the creek.

The woman gazed down at her. 'Did you know that you're famous?'

Nora's breath caught. 'I'm aware. Infamous, more like.'

The woman stooped and let her backpack slide to the ground. She retrieved Nora's tablet, handed it to her, and settled herself cross-legged on the rock. Nora again noted her scent, a combination of musk and woodsmoke and fresh earth. She wore cargo shorts and a tank top, both worse for the wear. Light hair covered her legs and curled beneath her arms, prompting a mix of revulsion and envy in Nora. What would it be like not to have shave every damn day, rubbing her hands over her legs to make sure she hadn't missed a spot, smoothing in lotion to soothe the inevitable nicks and bumps?

'I'm Joanna. My trail name's Forever.'

'Nora.' She sat up and held out her hand and was again surprised at the strength of the woman's grip, not the bones-to-jelly power clasp inflicted by so many men, but one carrying a don't-fuck-with-me message nonetheless. Which Nora had no intention of doing. 'Forever?'

'It's because I want to hike forever. I've done all the trails – Appalachian, Pacific Crest, Continental Divide, Pacific Northwest. That was my favorite. Appalachian was the worst. People everywhere and too many creeps. Trails are too close to towns. Weirdos wander in, either trying to get away from trouble or looking for it. Which one are you?'

'What?' So much information about so many unfamiliar things. Nora couldn't process it all.

The woman continued unperturbed in a flow of words apace with that of the stream. Nora wondered how long it had been since she talked to anyone.

'My guess is trying to get away. But trouble found you anyway. Because you're in it, big time.'

'Wait.' Nora held up her hands, pushing back against the verbal onslaught. 'How do you know, if you've been off in the woods all this time?'

All those trails the woman hiked. Nora didn't know much about them, other than what she'd read in bestselling movies and books about a couple of them, but she knew it took months to hike them. Years, maybe. She'd taken Forever for a youngster, given her slight frame, but now noticed the wiry strands of silver in her braids, the deep fans at the corners of her eyes, the skin showing the effects of too much sun and wind and too little moisturizer. If she had to guess, she'd put Forever closer to her own age.

Forever grinned, showing a crooked eyetooth that gave her the look of an impish child. She reached into one of the many pockets in her shorts and pulled out an iPhone. 'Just because I don't like to be around a lot of people doesn't mean I don't want to keep up with what's going on.' She pointed to her backpack. A black panel with shiny rectangles rode atop it. 'That's my solar gizmo. Powers up the phone and a GPS locator beacon. I might hike alone, but I don't hike stupid.'

'Have you ever had to use it? The locator, I mean.'

Forever shook her head. The braids swayed, brushing her tanned cheeks. 'Used bear spray on a dude once who thought he'd help himself to a little trail nookie. Then I got this.' She patted her knife. 'The bear spray that day – that was satisfying. Probably the same way you felt when you showed that picture of your husband.' She grinned again. 'Am I right?'

'They put that in the paper?'

'That and a whole lot more. Pretty badass move.'

Was it? Nora had been so busy wallowing in shame and outrage since that initial betrayal that she'd forgotten the flash of sheer furious joy when the photo had filled the screen, Joe's ass front and center; the subsequent exhilaration of careering along the highway, faster and faster as she became accustomed to Electra's weight and maneuverability.

'Yeah,' she said now. 'It did feel good. It felt *great*.'

Forever held up her hand and they slapped five in sisterly solidarity.

Nora had to ask. 'How do you do it?'

'Do what?'

'I mean . . .' Nora fumbled for tact. 'Months on end. Don't you get, uh, lonely?'

Forever threw back her head, revealing a corded throat, and laughed. 'You mean, what do I do for sex?'

She held up her hand in a sort of Girl Scout salute. 'We've all got a slow hand, am I right? Don't need a man's.'

At the look on Nora's face, she laughed some more. 'Given your situation, maybe you'd better get back in practice. Anyhow, I'm not on the trail all the time. I hit town every so often to restock. Sometimes I see somebody I like. When I do, somebody gets lucky.' That mischievous smile again, like a kid who'd gotten to the prize in the Cracker Jack box ahead of a sibling.

Nora wished she'd never asked. Sex was supposed to be her specialty, but Forever made her feel like a schoolmarm. She tried to steer the conversation back into safer territory. 'But how do you live like this? What do you do in the winter? And what do you do for money?'

Forever's gaze slid away. She fiddled with the handle of the knife. 'When the snow starts to fly, I catch a ride south. Plenty of places to explore there. You should check out Big Bend.'

'You mean you hitchhike? Isn't that dangerous?' Nora's mind conjured dire childhood warnings. Lurid headlines. Forced sex. Ax murderers.

'Remember: bear spray.'

Nora imagined a blast of the powerful spray in a confined space, say the cab of a semi. It would incapacitate a would-be assailant, but it probably would leave Forever gasping and helpless, too. She hoped the woman had never had to use it.

Forever stretched her legs before her and touched her

fingertips to her ankles. She turned her head sideways and looked Nora in the eye. 'So did you do it?'

'Do what?' As if she didn't know.

'That guy. The pretty one. Me, I've got a rule. Never sleep with a guy better looking than I am. They're lousy lays. Too many girls throwing themselves at them, never had to work for it.'

Nora remembered Brad's flashing grin. The heat in her face, the catch in her throat. Had he not been dragged off into the forest by a bear would she, given half a chance, have thrown herself at him?

'I didn't sleep with him. I don't know how that shirt got in my trailer, but he was never in there.'

'What about the rest of it? Do they really think you kidnapped him? I mean, you're only about half his size. Hard to imagine, but what do I know? Maybe you've got a gun.'

'I don't have a gun. And you're right. There's no way any of this makes sense. I keep trying to tell them, but no one will listen.'

Forever sat back and flipped one of her braids over a shoulder. 'What do you expect? No one ever listens to a woman. Except that lot lizard. She's got everybody's attention. At least, she did. Until now.'

Nora wished more people would focus on the lot lizard and said as much.

Forever laughed so hard she fell back against her pack. 'Not a chance. I mean, look at you.'

Nora looked over each shoulder, as though somehow expecting to see a version of herself behind her. 'What about me?'

'Think about it. A truck-stop hooker. Usually they're the ones getting killed, but when one turns bad, nobody's really surprised. As stories go, it's interesting until someone like you comes along, a rich bitch—'

'Hey!'

Forever continued undeterred, and Nora thought that if she walked as determinedly as she spoke, it was no wonder she'd conquered all those trails '—coming across a couple that's fallen on hard times, and helping herself to the husband because, you know, she's entitled to all the good things in life, and then throwing him away when she's done with him just like she threw away her husband—'

'Because he cheated on me! Jesus, stop. You sound just like the sheriff.' Nora put her hands over her ears. She'd liked Forever until this minute. Now she felt an overpowering desire to pitch her into the creek although, remembering the strength of the woman's grip, she doubted very much whether she could.

'I'm just saying how it looks. And how it makes a way better story. It's the way of the world for hookers and truckers to get tangled up in trouble. But when somebody like you' – she put her finger under her nose and tilted it upward, signaling snobbery – 'goes off the rails, it means you're no better than the rest of us. People eat that shit up.'

'But I didn't.' Nora stopped. There was only so many times she could say it.

Forever, to her credit, took the hint.

'Cheated, huh? And you just left him? The way the stories said?'

Just. Nora thought of the way she'd flashed the photo that exposed all across the screen at the party, the nighttime drive, learning on the fly how to tow the trailer. 'Yes,' she said, recalling that nighttime drive. 'Threw my wedding ring out the window on the way. Kept the engagement ring in the hopes of selling it someday, though.'

Forever looked at Nora's naked left hand and raised an eyebrow.

'I took it off and hid it.'

'Smart.' Forever touched her fingertips to the knife handle again. 'You know, if you'd killed him, that'd be one thing. Then the sheriff's theory might have made sense.'

Nora forgave her everything she'd said before. 'Exactly! I just need my lawyer to explain as much, and then they can drop this crazy nonsense.'

Forever stood in a single swift motion and hefted her pack, adjusting it on her shoulders.

'You really think that's how it's going to go? You've got way more faith in the legal system than I.'

She nodded a farewell and loped off into the willows, leaving Nora to wonder about Forever's seeming expertise on the vagaries of the legal system.

Nora stood before the map she'd affixed to Electra's wall, red Sharpie in hand, thinking over her conversation with Forever.

She was supposed to have used the map to mark the route she and Joe had planned, taking photos of each new line drawn along its highways and back roads, illustrations for the blog that now only existed in the form of drafts that would never see the light of day. Where would she and Joe have been by now? The Oregon coast, maybe. She lost herself in a brief, wistful daydream of briny oysters and a crisp Muscadet in a campsite on a seaside bluff, a view of haystack rocks looming mysterious from the mist. The man beside her a lifelong companion. They could still have that, Joe had assured her.

She shook her head, summoning reality. If she didn't figure out what was going on, and fast, the only meals in her future would be the baloney-on-white-bread sandwiches at the Clyde County Jail, and her unnervingly stubborn doubts about her break-up with Joe would be moot, their split rendered permanent by default.

She drew a red line along Interstate 25 from Denver to northern Wyoming that represented her trip so far. Then lay down the pen and put her finger and traced the road south, fragments of speech pinging in her brain.

'Looks like she came straight up I-25.'

'A pattern.'

The truckers in the café, talking about the woman who'd killed their fellow drivers.

What had they said? El Paso, Denver, Cheyenne.

She slid her finger all the way down to El Paso on the Mexican border. Looked east, to the words across a large blank spot on the map.

Big Bend National Park.

Minutes earlier, Forever had raised her voice over the creek's babble and urged her to check out Big Bend. Fingers trailing down the tooled leather scabbard as she spoke. Braids brushing her shoulders. Not pigtails. But then, police sketches depended

upon the notoriously unreliable memories of witnesses unaware
at the time that what they'd glimpsed had any importance.

But . . . Forever? A wood sprite of a woman, one who
preferred the solitude of the trail? Impossible to imagine her
in a bustling truck stop. She'd stand out like a semaphore.

Nora stared unseeing at the map, conjuring possibilities.
What if Forever cleaned up, as she'd have to, to ply her illicit
trade? Washed her hair, bound it into loose pigtails instead
of the greasy braids? And for all her professed love of nature,
there was that iPhone, the solar panel on her backpack. Had
she really hiked all those trails? People spent years tackling
a single one in the sections required by most mere mortals.
Maybe she just drifted among truck stops, ducking into the
woods to lie low after each . . .

'Stop it.' Nora rebuked herself aloud. She'd wasted precious
minutes on a meaningless distraction, with only hours left to
deal with her own situation. She turned away from the map
and took the four steps that comprised the length of Electra
from bedside to dinette, where she'd set out her tablet, and
actual pen and paper, too, the better to draw out a plan.

Except that both remained stubbornly blank. She still needed
to talk with the woman whose husband she unbelievably was
suspected of killing.

TWENTY

Miranda wasn't in her camper.

Nora stood before it, hand raised to knock again. She'd done little more than glance at it that first night, about a thousand years ago, when she and Miranda and Brad had shared elk steaks cooked over a flame, a moment of unexpected fellowship. She'd looked at it as an omen, a sign that life would indeed go on, that she'd find new friends, new ways of being. And then things had gotten even worse.

She'd paid little attention to the camper in the tumultuous days that followed. It simply sat there, a silent backdrop to the questionings by the sheriff and the organization of search parties and the impromptu news conferences.

No sleek palatial Airstream, Miranda's abode. The camper sat wedged into the bed of a pickup that looked like the grizzled ne'er-do-well uncle to the model Nora drove. What had Joe called it when he'd bought it? A cowboy Cadillac. Now Nora understood the term. Because Miranda and Brad's truck looked like something an actual cowboy might have driven, red paint faded nearly to pink and streaked with rust, with a long dent in one fender. The camper overhung the truck cab; Nora imagined that sardine-tin space held the bed. Brad had been – *is*, she reminded herself, holding onto a newly necessary shred of hope – a tall man. It must be like sleeping in a coffin. As to the rest of the camper, there was no space for even the most rudimentary bathroom. Maybe a two-burner stove and a narrow dinette that allowed only for two people jammed side by side. The camper afforded Miranda and Brad little more room than if they'd simply put a topper over the truck bed and slung an air mattress inside.

Nora knocked again, a final futile attempt. The camper didn't have that held-breath feeling of someone frozen motionless inside, each of them waiting on opposite sides of the door to see who would give up first.

She headed toward the campground entrance, hoping to find Miranda in the check-in booth. The road bent and straightened, giving her a view of a line of cars waiting at the booth. More curiosity seekers, she guessed. She'd pulled on a baseball cap, tucked her hair up into it, and donned sunglasses. Her legs swam within a pair of Joe's sweatpants. She hoped she looked nothing like the stylish socialite that one story had dubbed her. She thought the socialite part was a stretch, but she'd put quite a bit of time and effort into style, and now she was working equally hard to appear anything but. Still, she stuck her hands in her pockets, averted her head, and slouched as she approached the booth, slipping through its rear door just as one car pulled away.

Miranda jumped down from her stool and felt about for the extra can of bear spray with which Nora had equipped the booth. 'Don't come any closer. I swear I'll spray you.'

'I just want to talk,' Nora began.

A car pulled up. Nora flattened herself against the booth's back wall.

'Tent or trailer?' Miranda called over her shoulder, never taking her eyes off Nora.

'I didn't sleep with your husband.' Nora breathed the words like a prayer.

'We're looking—' said someone in the car.

Miranda cut him off. 'Campsite forty-seven. Take the first right and loop all the way around.'

'And I sure as hell didn't kill him.'

'But we're not staying. We just want to see—'

'Look for the Airstream. It's back in the trees. You can just barely see it from the road.'

'Miranda, I swear. I want him found almost as much as you do.' More, Nora thought. Although saying so probably wouldn't help her case. Under the circumstances.

Miranda's next words confirmed the folly of that particular approach. 'So you can sleep with him again?'

The car pulled away. Another approached.

Nora and Miranda stared at each other. 'Just hear me out. Someone's setting me up for this. But I can't figure out why. I need your help.'

A pickup full of teenagers pulled up to the window.

'Tent or trailer?'

'Neither.'

'Please, Miranda. Whoever wants me in jail for this doesn't want Brad found.'

A sigh came from the direction of the car. 'We're just looking for—'

'I know. The woman in the newspaper. But you're too late. She's already gone.'

'Thank you,' Nora mouthed.

Miranda flipped through a series of signs at her feet, retrieved one that said 'Campground full' and placed it in the window. For good measure, she left the booth, unhooked one end of a chain from the side wall and strung it across the road, ignoring the shouted protests from a couple of the cars.

Nora slid to the floor of the booth and wrapped her arms around her shaking knees. Miranda's acquiescence had been grudging, full of suspicion. Nora still needed her to tear up the fake sale agreement for the truck and trailer. But that could come later. For now, this was enough.

She and Miranda had barely settled themselves in their customary spots facing one another across the picnic table when Caleb's pickup roared up, slewing to a stop in a fantail of gravel and dust.

'Miranda! Are you all right? Why's the campground closed? Because it's sure as hell not full. And what's she doing here? Should I call Duncan?'

'No! No sheriff.' Nora pre-empted whatever Miranda had been about to say and took it as a good sign when Miranda didn't protest.

Caleb joined them without being invited, sitting on Miranda's bench, closer than necessary, a large, protective presence. Together he and Miranda faced Nora like judge and jury.

'She says she was set up.'

'I didn't sleep with Brad.' Nora wondered if she should get the phrase tattooed on her forehead, save the strain of repetition on her vocal cords.

Miranda and Caleb folded their arms across their chests and leaned back, mirror images of disbelief.

'I don't know how that shirt got into Electra – my trailer. When I came back after my shower that night, I felt like someone had been in it. I know' – she held up a hand to forestall the obvious questions – 'it sounds crazy and there's no way I can prove it. But somebody put that shirt there.'

The breath she drew came ragged and voluble. 'Don't you see? If someone is trying to pin this on me, it means a bear didn't get Brad.' She sensed Caleb's sudden attentiveness. He'd hated the idea of having to kill the bear.

Nora looked at Caleb, who refused to acknowledge her gaze, and laid down the closest thing to a trump card she had.

'If we can figure out why someone would want to set me up, maybe we can save the bear.'

She hadn't sold either of them, not completely. The arms remained crossed, brows drawn tight, judgment banging down on her like a gavel. But maybe the blows were a little bit lighter.

'Who would do such a thing? And why?'

Nora drew circles in the dirt beneath the bench with the toe of her running shoe as she answered Miranda. 'I've been trying and trying to think, and all I can come up with is Joe.'

Miranda shook her head, quick, decisive. 'No way. He wants you back. He told me so.'

'You going back to him?'

Nora took some satisfaction in the fact that Caleb was no better at faking casual than she was. His question hung in the answer. The answer, unknown, even to her. Was she?

Nora had spent years putting lipstick on the pig that was a failing university. If there was one thing she knew, it was the non-answer.

'I'm in no position to make decisions about anything right now. I just need to find something that keeps me from ever going back to that jail. Caleb, are you sure it wasn't the bear?'

'About as sure as you are that you didn't sleep with Brad. And I've got just about as much proof as you do. Which is to say, none.'

A rebuke of sorts, but oddly comforting too, acknowledging the shared impossibility of their situations. Their eyes met, finally. A connection, one Nora decided not to analyze beyond an appreciation of the steadiness she sensed there.

A connection broken by Miranda's voice, so wan and sad of late but now infused with the optimism Nora remembered from their first meeting.

'If a person did this, whatever it is, maybe Brad was kidnapped.'

'Is there any reason to think anyone might want to kidnap him?' Nora bit her lip, wishing she hadn't asked the obvious, especially as the silence lengthened. The muscles in Miranda's face tensed, relaxed and tensed again as she puzzled over and apparently rejected possibilities.

'No.' Miranda shook her head, almost as though she were trying to convince herself of something. 'Well. No. No.' She shook her head again, apparently rejecting whatever she'd been about to say.

Nora and Caleb leaned in. Miranda shrank away from them. 'What?'

'Miranda.' Nora tried to get her voice under control. 'If there's anything, *anything* at all, you have to tell us.'

'It's nothing. It's too . . . I just . . . can't.'

Nora watched Caleb suppress the same impulse she herself felt, to grab Miranda by the shoulders and shake the idea out of her.

'There's nobody here but us. And we're just spitballing. So lay it on us.' Language deliberately casual, belying the intensity in his eyes.

Miranda curled into herself. 'Promise you won't tell.'

'If you've got information, you have to tell,' Nora said, sharper than she'd meant to be. Caleb kicked her under the table. 'Sorry. Of course we won't tell. Your crazy idea might be what finds Brad.'

Miranda perked up. 'Do you really think so?'

'No way to know without hearing it,' Caleb urged.

'OK. But remember, you said you wouldn't tell.' A child's retort. But there was nothing childlike about the scenario she outlined.

'After we lost our jobs and went through our savings, we got into debt. Really bad debt. We maxed out our credit cards and got new ones and maxed them out, too.'

You and half of America, Nora wanted to say. But Caleb continued to administer preemptive kicks every few seconds.

'Somehow Brad came up with some more money. But he'd gone to some bad people. Really bad. And when he couldn't pay them back, all the interest. Oh, my God.'

'The vig,' said Caleb.

Nora looked at him.

'Cop shows,' he shrugged. 'Not much else to do in the cabin in winter.'

'Go on,' said Nora.

'They told him if he didn't pay them back, they'd hurt him. Maybe even kill him. Same if he went to the police.' She gulped back a sob and squared her shoulders. 'So I got us out of there. Took the money that was left, bought this wreck of a camper and came up here.' Handling It, just as Nora did. Why did that always seem to fall to the woman?

Miranda swiped her sleeve under her nose. 'I thought we were safe here. That nobody could find us in such an out-of-the-way place.'

Have you never heard of the internet? Another thought – kick, kick – Nora kept to herself.

Caleb jumped in. 'Have you told the sheriff this?'

'N-n-no. I mean, everyone is so sure about the bear. That seems so logical compared to this.'

'Not everyone thinks it's the bear. And you're right. It sounds farfetched. But you have to tell him.'

'But those guys said they'd kill him!'

Nora floated a possibility largely driven by self-interest. 'Why would they kill him? He's worthless dead. They probably just kidnapped him. I mean, if it's really them and not the bear.'

Caleb came to her assistance. 'If there's any possibility he was kidnapped, it'll go to the FBI. They know how to handle these things. Nothing will happen to Brad. But the first thing you have to do is tell the sheriff.'

Miranda nodded solemnly. 'I will. I should have before.

Because if someone took Brad, it means he might still be alive!'

The woman was relentlessly hopeful. But, under the circumstances, what choice did she have? A single tear slid down her cheek. Nora found some tissues in her pocket and offered Miranda one. Her eyes met Caleb's.

He didn't believe a bear killed Brad. And despite Nora's suggestion that Brad might have been nabbed by loan sharks, she could tell that neither she nor Caleb believed he was still alive.

TWENTY-ONE

Caleb walked her back to her campsite in the soft darkness that precedes true night.

Edges blurred, the pines blending into a single inky mass, the road visible only as a gap between them. Nora drew her phone from her pocket and clicked on the flashlight app.

'Turn it off.'

'Why?' But she complied.

'Let your eyes adjust. Just give it a few minutes. You'll see.'

They stopped walking and stood in the middle of the road, which gradually came into focus, its potholes patches of black against a grey background, treetops standing like spikes against the sky.

'You use a flashlight, all you can see is what's in the light. That's clear, but everything else is just one big black mass. With your own eyes, maybe it's not as clear, but you can see so much more.'

Nora took a slow, uncertain step. 'What do you think about what Miranda said?'

He offered his arm. 'Sounds pretty wild to me. But not impossible. I have to think, though, that if those kind of characters were prowling around here, somebody would have seen them.'

She took his arm for a few steps, then dropped it as their surroundings, just as he'd promised, came into black-and-white focus.

'I know. And murder seems so extreme.'

'Agreed. And don't those guys hurt people first? Kneecap them, kill their pets, something like that?'

'I don't know. This stuff is way out of my league. In my world' – her former world, she reminded herself – 'we just destroyed people's reputations.' Nora thought again of the university basketball players accused of rape, of their victim.

The young woman who the university – under Nora's tutelage – had quietly let it be known, was just shy of blind drunk, something that would have labeled her legally incapable of consent. Who'd been partying with the guys. What had happened to that young woman? Would she, like Brad's loan sharks, someday come after Nora with murder in her heart? For sure, she deserved it. Because 'just doing my job' reeked of 'just following orders', an excuse generally accepted as a nonstop ticket to hell.

Thoughts of murder and retribution toyed with her psyche. Nora cast a nervous glance around. The fact that she could see was not necessarily reassuring. The trees loomed close, only a few steps away. Anything lurking there could close the distance in a heartbeat.

'I know you said it's better without the light. But wouldn't the light help scare away any bears?'

His chuckle was as quiet and enveloping as the darkness. 'Remember what I said. Given all the activity around here, no self-respecting bear is going to come within miles of this place. Besides, bears are diurnal.'

'Di-what?'

'They're like us. They sleep at night, are awake during the day.'

Nora took a few more steps before a thought occurred to her, one that stopped her so suddenly that Caleb nearly bumped into her.

'Wait a minute, wait a minute.'

He took a step back. 'What?'

'If bears sleep at night, then a bear probably didn't grab Brad.'

He tapped her head, the briefest of touches. 'Here, genius resides.'

'How come you didn't say anything earlier?'

'About your genius?' He was teasing her. Maybe he didn't completely trust her denials about Brad, but at least he'd suspended disbelief.

'About how it couldn't possibly be the bear.'

His sigh tore a hole in the good feeling surrounding them. 'Because it's not impossible, especially with bears that have become food-habituated. They're really, really smart. Say our bear has figured out that campgrounds are basically a buffet. But all day long, they're swarming with people, and people are trouble. So why not wait until nighttime and cruise the campgrounds then? Somebody's sure to have dropped a Pop-Tart somewhere, and then our bear can snack in peace. Besides.' He stopped.

'Besides what?'

'There've been nighttime attacks. Not many, and a long time ago, but it's not unheard of. There were those two girls up in Montana who got killed by different bears on the same night.'

Nora mentally crossed Montana off her places to visit, ever.

Caleb's next words made her think she'd been too hasty.

'But that was a long time ago, back in the sixties, and those bears were beyond food-habituated. It was back before we'd learned how dangerous it was, and the parks literally set up bleachers around garbage dumps so people could watch the grizzlies forage. We've gotten smarter since.'

A half-century ago. Nora wanted to relax. But she couldn't help but wonder: maybe people had gotten smarter, but what if the bears had, too?

She'd left a light on in Electra. It shone through the window, casting a bright stage on the ground beside the picnic table. They stood just outside it.

'So?'

Now that her eyes had adjusted to the darkness, Nora kept her back to the light. She could just make out Caleb's expression, the raised eyebrows punctuating his question.

'So . . . what?'

'What are you going to do?' The tightness in his voice hinted at his meaning.

She stalled. 'About her theory? Wait for the sheriff to weigh in, I guess. I'm supposed to meet the lawyer tomorrow. I'll run it by him. Seems pretty thin to me, but I'll take anything I can get right now.'

'That's not what I meant.'

She waited for him to spell it out.

'Your husband. You going back to him?'

She moved to the picnic table and sat. The breeze lay down at night, but cold arose, swift and certain. She craved the warmth of Electra's heater, but she was too embarrassed to ask Caleb inside, lest he harbor lingering suspicions about possible murderous intent. And the turn their conversation had taken was too intimate for bright light. Better to talk in darkness, even as she rubbed her arms against the chill.

'I don't know.' Startling herself with the honesty of it. She couldn't imagine forgiving Joe for Charlotte, the way he'd helped himself to what he'd carelessly dismissed as a 'one-off', heedless of the consequences to all concerned. But the idea of setting out on her own at fifty . . . 'How did you decide? Was it quick?' Aware that she was poking at the rawest of wounds. Or maybe, after so many years, a betrayal scabbed over, turned into scar tissue, smooth and tough and impervious to new pain.

'God, no. It was awful. Still is, some days.' So much for scar tissue.

'We hung on for months. I mean, we had Abby. She was just a little girl. And my wife swore she'd give the guy up. I swore I believed her. But I never really did, and she could tell. I don't know if she kept seeing him all along, or if she finally went back to him because I was being such a dick.'

'Sounds like you were entitled.'

The movement beside her suggested a shrug. 'You know how it is. Fault on all sides and all that. I like the woods. She likes town. It's probably just that simple. There weren't many things we enjoyed doing together, other than . . .'

She was glad for the delicacy of his silence, Abby being the evidence of exactly what they'd enjoyed together.

'More to the point, she fell in love with someone else and loves him still. It happens. They're better together than she and I ever were. No use trying to hang on, hoping things will change.'

Nora sucked in a breath. She'd never considered the possibility that Joe might be in love with Charlotte. No, he'd sworn it was just the one time. A 'mercy fuck'. Would you talk that way about someone you loved?

More to the point, did she still love Joe? Even as she tried to shove her own mental question away, Caleb gave voice to it.

'How about you? Still in love with him?'

She'd spent most of her professional life putting a positive spin on things, terming the most egregious fuck-ups 'challenges', wielding force fields of say-nothing phrases, so many over the years that they rose smoothly, assuredly to her lips. One hovered there now. These-are-difficult-times-but-I-have-the-utmost-respect-blah-blah-blah. She shocked herself by opting for honesty.

'I don't know. I mean' – the words came slowly as she thought it through – 'after so many years – twenty! – you just sort of assume love. Our lives were really busy, just getting through all of our day-to-day work obligations, and then the social stuff on weekends. Now that I think about it, we'd been going on automatic pilot for a long time. Love? Sure. The way you love family, friends. But *in* love? Until now, I thought that's what the long-term thing was. You had choices – everyone does – but you choose to stick with that person.' She stopped. 'I'm babbling. Clearly, I have no idea what I'm talking about. That's why I wanted to stay here awhile. Just take a little time, think things through. But things keep happening.'

Her voice broke on her last words, teeth chattering.

He stood. 'Time you got inside. You'll freeze out here.'

She rose and stood before him. 'Thanks for hearing me out. Not just about this, but about Brad. Even though I can't tell if you believe me.'

That soft chuckle again, in keeping with the night's hush. 'I can't either. But I don't disbelieve you. Come here. I think we both need this.'

He held out his arms and she stepped into a long hug that felt like the most natural thing in the world.

She puzzled a long time over what sort of photo should accompany her latest draft on the never-to-be-published blog, a continued bittersweet private indulgence.

Maybe it was the wine she'd poured after Caleb left. Or the

humming tension over the pending meeting with the lawyer. She found a pair of pliers in Electra's toolkit, clamped one end around a fingernail, and snapped a suitably macabre photo. She typed:

> **We're in thriller-novel territory.**
> The latest theory, if you can elevate it to the level of actual theory, is that pissed-off loan sharks kidnapped Brad to get the pennies on the dollar that comprised all that was left of what he owed them. That they somehow figured out where he was and drove up here from . . .

She realized she had no idea where Brad and Miranda had lived before showing up at the campground. Their camper had Wyoming license plates but they might have bought it when they'd become campground hosts.

> I can't help but imagine a squad of musclebound tattooed guys in black creeping through the woods, hauling Brad off to some rural lair where they'd torture him until he coughed up some cash. (See inappropriate photo, for which I suppose I should apologize, especially given that it sounds as though I'm mocking what very well might be a dead man.)
> As potential perpetrators go, they're no more – or less – convincing than the bear. But the sheriff will have to look into it, and if the lawyer is as good as Artie says, he'll use this as an argument to keep me out of jail until they find Brad.

She stopped typing, not wanting to admit even to herself that it would also leave her free to explore whatever might happen next with Caleb, whose hug had ended with an abashed parting, each of them backing away, laughing a little in embarrassment and pleasure. The long-forgotten electrical charge of possibility. She'd been so focused on Joe, looking backward. Now she wondered what it might be like to look – not forward, necessarily – but at what was right in front of her. To simply live in the moment, to borrow a phrase from the self-help sort of advice Lilith had hoped would tinge the book that Nora would never write. She clicked off the tablet and fell asleep with the feel of his arms still around her, an unexpected comfort that let her drift into oblivion with the sense that just maybe, things would work out.

TWENTY-TWO

Caleb's grip grew uncomfortably tight.

Nora twisted within it, no longer enjoying the half-dream within which she'd fallen asleep, the enjoyable musing about what it might be like to actually go to bed with Caleb. Now it seemed as though the dream was turning dark. Next thing she knew she'd be plunging from a precipice. That old nightmare.

She twisted again, trying to rouse herself before she slipped fully into the fall.

A hand across her mouth, something cold and hard and round to her neck. A muffled voice.

'Not a sound.'

Nora came fully awake with a brief, sharp moment of longing for the nightmare she'd feared. Because no matter what might have haunted her dreams, this trumped it.

'Caleb?' she said against the hand.

The thing – her brain refused to accept *gun* – jammed against her windpipe. She tried to jerk her head away but the hand across her face held it immobile.

'What did I just say? Are you going to be quiet?'

She nodded.

'You got shoes?'

Another nod.

He removed his hand but kept the gun to her throat.

'Get up. And put them on.'

She swung her legs over the edge of the bed, feeling about with her feet for her running shoes. She put them on without socks, hands shaking so hard she could barely tie the laces, questions slamming like sledgehammers inside her head. Who was he? What did he want? And the one drowning out all the rest – was he going to kill her?

A tiny small part of her threw up fists against the hammers. No. Not if he was making her put on her shoes.

The hammer came down hard. Probably because he was just going to take her somewhere to kill her.

Another feeble punch. So, maybe on the way she could escape.

Slam! Sure. Since when could you outrun a bullet?

He yanked her to her feet, ending her crazed internal monologue, and shoved her ahead of him through the trailer, nearly wrenching her arm from her socket as she almost fell through the open door (which she'd locked, she was sure of it; if she survived this, the salesman who sold her Electra would hear from her). He jerked her around so that her back was to him. She got a glimpse of a bit of face, just the eyes and nose visible between a pulled-low watch cap and a bandana tied bandit-style across his face, explaining the muffled voice. She waited for a jolt of recognition, but none came, and besides, there was that gun against her neck again, driving all thoughts from her head except don't shoot dear God don't shoot.

The gun disappeared with a rustle, as though he'd tucked it into a pocket. He fitted a band around her skull. Something hard pushed into her forehead. He pressed the top of it and light, blessed light, flooded the ground before her. A headlamp.

'We've got a long way to go. You'll need this so we can move fast. Turn around, try to see me, and—' The gun again, this time with a rap against the side of her head, so abrupt and hard her ears rang. 'Get moving.'

Caleb had told her how a headlamp would blind her to everything but what was directly before her. Is that why this person had given her the lamp? And was it possible that Caleb was just playing some sort of pervy game with her? He didn't strike her as the sort of man who believed women liked to be overpowered. Although, at this very moment, she would welcome that scenario. He could reveal himself; she could give him a piece of her mind and for sure that was the only piece of her he was ever going to get.

Or was this one of the loan sharks of Miranda's half-baked scenario? But if so, what would they want with her?

A hand on her shoulder swung her toward the road. The gun poked the small of her back. She took a hesitant step, then another. A poke. 'Faster.'

Her feet followed the slash of light, blinding against the darkness, as they passed one campsite after another. She knew them to be deserted but cursed the headlamp anyway. Without it, she'd have been able to see if by some unlikely chance, someone had checked into the campground, occupied one of the sites. Maybe Miranda had taken down the 'campground full' sign, welcomed people in again. But it wouldn't have mattered. By the time a scream for help had left her lips, a bullet would have splattered her brains into the trees.

Which was where he steered her next, off the road that wound between the sites and onto a trail leading deep into the forest, the purview of hikers like Forever and the wild creatures whose cries and mutterings would be the only sounds, other than her own stumbling footsteps and the considerably easier strides of her captor, she would hear for the next several hours.

Hours? Really? That's how it felt to Nora. Long enough to cycle through several stages.

First, fear. Except this went beyond fear. This was death-in-your-face, guts-turned-to-water, brain-screaming-no-no-no terror. Fear such a gentle emotion by comparison. The last-minute swerve as the other car blew the stop sign. The knife-edge section of a high-altitude hike. The scariest part of a scary movie, the shark's head thrust voracious from the churning sea. 'We're gonna need a bigger boat.'

Fear was rush and ebb of adrenaline, the relieved laughter afterward, the extra-generous splash of whiskey into the glass.

But in all her fifty years, she'd never experienced this bargain-with-God-please-let-me-live-I'll-do-anything state so all-encompassing that it took a root across the trail, her toe caught, her body pitching forward, hands flung out but not fast enough to prevent a full face-plant, to short-circuit it.

She lay for a brief, blessed moment of relief, the terror knocked out of her along with the wind. She spat dirt. Then: the hand on her arm, the gun to her neck.

She clambered to her feet. Started to dust herself off. Habit. Because who was going to see her out here?

'Move.'

She moved, paying more attention to the ground before her

this time. Other realities began to intrude. For starters, it was fucking cold. She'd tumbled from Electra in just the T-shirt and light sweatpants in which she slept, and oh what she would have given for the silk long johns she donned under her ski gear, and her fleece-lined winter running tights, and a quilted nylon jacket. A hat. Gloves. Wool socks. Because the cold wrapped itself lovingly around her bare arms and ankles, crept insinuatingly up her calves and upper arms, slithered in around the neck of her T-shirt and washed across her breasts and back. The yellow shirt was her favorite, one of a line sold in outdoors stores, depicting happy stick people skiing, hiking, kayaking, or in the case of hers, waving from the door of a camper trailer. The same brand made sweatshirts and why, oh why, hadn't she bought one of them, worn it to bed, maybe with a couple of layers under it? She walked faster, swinging her arms, trying to work up a sweat, her pace earning an approving grunt – 'Better' – from her captor, which was bullshit because she wasn't better at all.

At some point, far too late into her ordeal, it occurred to her to pay attention to her surroundings. If, through some miracle she managed to escape, she'd need to find her way back. She turned her head the slightest bit to one side, then the other, her gaze desperately seeking a strangely shaped stump, a notable rock. Nothing – just the monotony of blackness, the trees distinguishable only by their vertical pattern of deeper black, unnerving as the bars of a cell. She thought about Hansel and Gretel tactics, leaving signs that she could follow back. But when she reached to break off a twig from a trailside shrub, the gun rose from her back and conked her on the side of the head.

'Knock it off.'

Same thing when she tried shuffling her feet, hoping to leave drag marks in the duff and the dirt. That merely earned another growl. 'Pick it up.'

She rubbed her arms vigorously and emitted a few loud 'Brrrs' conveying the innocently obvious – she was freezing – as a way to provide an excuse for shoving her hands into the sweatpants' pockets. What were the odds she'd stocked them with matches, a granola bar, her cellphone?

Exactly zero.

Her fingers closed around the shreds of a tissue, the one she'd offered to Miranda. She spread them wider, seeking something else, anything.

Nothing.

She rolled a bit of tissue between thumb and forefinger, forming a tiny tight ball, and pulled her hand slightly from the pocket, letting it fall to the ground. Then again. And again.

No idea if they were dropping on the trail or if she'd flicked them into the brush beside it. If her captor's footsteps immediately ground them into the earth, rendering them invisible. If birds would swoop down in the morning, mistaking them for food, scoop them up in their beaks, foiling her hopeless plan as completely as that of poor Hansel and Gretel.

And who was her captor, anyway? Joe? Maybe his big boohoo-take-me-back speech had been little more than a ploy, something to lull her into complacency so that . . . what? He could frog-march her off in the woods and kill her? To what end? She'd humiliated him, sure, but seeing her arrested had surely evened the score. Besides, this person evidently was familiar with the campground and the trails leading into the backcountry.

Caleb? He'd been her first thought in her confused half-sleep and indeed she continued to wonder. But search their conversations as she might, she could divine no reason he'd want to hurt her.

Her mind kept returning to a possibility that she pushed away again and again. Maybe Miranda's theory was right and at this very moment, for some unfathomable reason, she was in the clutches of whomever had taken Brad, who she'd assumed dead, but now – despite the many days gone by, despite the splotch of blood on the ground and the shred of shirt – most fervently hoped was alive.

In the ensuing hours, Nora learned more about the nature of terror. That, over time and distance, it can very much turn into something akin to boredom; that as weariness sets in, a deep and abiding desire for sleep can replace the mental metronome plea for life. She counted those hours as best she could: at least one wasted unproductively on sheer terror. Another as the realization of cold seeped in, followed by the knowledge that she would only grow colder still. And now the hour of hopelessness, where exhaustion dragged dominant, the burning in her legs and lungs in competition with the frozen numbness spreading from her fingers and toes.

She stumbled, this time catching herself before she fell. But careened again a few steps later. The gun again, in the small of her back. 'Wait,' she said. 'Wait.' She angled her head and caught a tree trunk in the lamp's glare. She staggered toward it and slumped against it, futilely seeking a scrap of daytime heat in its rough bark, finding none but welcoming its support. She leaned her head against it and thought it a perfect pillow. If she could just sleep for a few minutes . . .

Her captor said something that sounded like 'Fine'.

Good. She'd just take a little rest and then they could continue their Bataan death march. He said something else.

'This is as good a place as any.'

She started to come awake, a little and then fully with his next words.

'Take your clothes off.'

'No!'

She whirled on him then, the light full on his masked face, before she turned to run, throwing up her hands as though to somehow ward off the shot that never came. He caught her easily, jerking her to face him, tearing away the headlamp and stroking the gun once, twice across her face, stepping aside as she fell.

She lay in the dirt, blood pouring hot from her nose and flowing down the back of her throat. She choked and spat.

He nudged her with a toe. 'Fucking bitch. Clothes. Off.'

She worked her jaw, stuck her tongue against her teeth. A couple wobbled. She touched her fingertips to her nose, her hand leaping away as she detected the unnatural angle.

He leaned over her and pressed something sharp against her side – not the gun, this was different – and then he drove it in and down and she screamed and screamed until he grabbed the hem of her T-shirt and ripped it over her head. She shut up then, but it was too late. He drew back his foot and casually kicked her over, pulling off her shoes, then her pants and underwear. She rolled onto her side, clutching her knees to her chest, her 'no, no, no' gurgling indistinct through the blood filling her mouth.

'Get up.'

What?

Nora had never obeyed a command more quickly in her life. Later, much later, she would think that 'get up' from what she presumed until that moment to be her would-be rapist/killer would ring sweeter than any 'I love you' she'd ever heard. 'Get up' meant deliverance. Maybe even meant life.

A thought to which she clung for the few seconds it took for him to drag her to the side of the trail, slide something cold and slick over her torso, and then shove her into the blackness beyond through which she fell, hands clutching at the unresponsive air, as though in the dream that had begun her night.

TWENTY-THREE

Nora Best woke to the scent of bacon.

Ahhhh, bacon. She inhaled again, more deeply, hoping for the sensory overload of pancakes, butter, maple syrup. And coffee, sweet Jesus, coffee because she had the mother of all hangovers, pain sawing like a serrated knife behind her eyes, even as the rest of her jerked as though at the hands of a crazed puppeteer in a violent reaction to cold.

So cold. Because she was – she ran an experimental hand down her side – naked. And – she rubbed her fingers together – sticky, too. She held her fingers to her nose, breathing in bacon fat. Her hand fell as memory returned.

The stranger at her bedside. The forced march through the woods. A long fall. Thank God she didn't remember landing. She flexed her fingers, then slowly, slowly stretched each arm and leg. They protested, but then, her whole body was one pulsing protest. She tried to take visual stock, but darkness cloaked her and besides, it hurt to raise her head. She ran her hands over the wrecked landscape of her body. Something had gouged deep scratches across her arms and legs and torso. Her fingers encountered dampness, warmth, a few still oozing blood. Others were beginning to crust over. What she'd remembered as a fall through open air must have, at some point, turned into a rough tumble down a steep slope. Still, everything appeared to be working. Albeit, so horribly cold. She lifted her gaze and was relieved to see treetops feathering black as raven's wings against a backdrop of slate sky. That meant dawn and, soon, the warmth of the sun. All she had to do was get up and keep moving. People froze to death because they lay down, gave up. And true light was probably still a couple of hours away, plenty of time to freeze. She blew an experimental breath and damned the vapor that hung momentarily before her face. Yes, it was that cold. She had to get up.

Easier said than done.

Just because nothing appeared to be broken didn't mean anything in her body particularly felt like working. Her back screamed at her when she rolled onto her side; her left wrist gave an angry throb when she tried to push herself up. She examined it. It was swollen and – she touched her right hand to it – hot, but she could turn it. Probably just a sprain. She leaned on her right and rose to her knees, which let her know how unhappy they were with this new arrangement, which was nothing compared to what happened to her head when she reached out, grasped a nearby tree and pulled herself to her feet. Her vision spun and darkened, and she bent and vomited, nearly losing her tenuous balance in the process. She wrapped both arms around the tree, the vanilla scent of its rough bark denoting a Ponderosa pine, and held on until the landscape stopped tilting and blurring around her.

When it did, the trees stood sharper, the sky lighter. Colors began to emerge. Sounds. Somewhere nearby, the babble of water, triggering a Pavlovian realization of her tremendous thirst. A whisper of wind, something she'd have welcomed on any other day, but now serving only to drop her body temperature another crucial degree. Branches creaked overhead. Closer, a stick cracked.

A deer, maybe, and Nora's heart warmed at the thought of another creature close by, the knowledge that she wasn't alone. She turned her head very, very slowly, bargaining with the pain, which rewarded her by holding steady, and searched the woods for long legs stepping daintily through the trees, the flash of a white tail, a glance from dark, liquid eyes.

Her brain caught up with her heart a moment later. Deer weren't the only creatures in the forest. What was the word Caleb had used about bears? Diurnal. 'They're like us. They sleep at night, are awake during the day.'

Daylight was fast approaching and – she reached around to her shoulder, felt the stickiness there, raised her hand to her face and again breathed in – that asshole who'd marched her through the forest had inexplicably smeared her with a slab of pungent greasy bacon. Why? To keep her warm? She clung briefly to a memory of childhood adventure stories, cowboys-and-Indians stuff; the Indians, always smarter, smearing themselves with – hah! – bear grease to fend off the cold. But why not just leave her with her clothes?

She had no idea whether a bear had attacked Brad Gardner, but if she wandered around the woods naked, smelling like a whole frying pan full of bacon, for sure that's what would happen to her. It took her another two seconds for the obvious to penetrate her poor, clanging brain – that's just what her captor *wanted* to happen to her.

Her breath came fast and ragged and audible, heading toward hyperventilation. Her head spun anew, the reek of bacon vanquishing all her other senses. She had to get that shit off. She released the security of the pine and staggered toward the sound of the water, grabbing at skinny, unreliable willow branches to keep from falling. Her handholds ended at an overhang, one that appeared so abruptly she nearly lost her footing.

A few feet below, the creek appeared like a mirage. But this was no desert oasis, blue water pooling serene and sparkling at the edge of golden sand, overhung by date palms, their fronds clacking gently in the breezes.

Here the creek was wider than the stretch beside her campsite, deeper, angrier, its rushing dark water slamming black against rocks and boiling up white. And almost certainly frigid. She remembered her brief dip at Forever's appearance, the icy shock. She'd been clothed then, and beneath a benevolent sun.

Hypothermia killed people and did it fast. She turned her head to her greasy shoulder and sniffed. But so did bears, and not nearly so fast.

She briefly considered her choice: the hard bite of cold, followed by the slow, spreading warmth of approaching death, one that involved – so she'd heard – a benevolent departure into sleep? Or a primordial roar, slashing fangs and claws, soft organs exposed, flesh peeled from bone?

Just a few hours earlier, Nora had been pushed into midair. This time, she jumped on her own.

TWENTY-FOUR

She was lucky enough to splash down into a deep spot instead of smashing against a rock.

Just as she was congratulating herself on her good fortune, the water surged beneath her, tossing her midstream and carrying her along like a chip of balsa wood, thwacking against what felt like every single rock in the stream. She tried to remember the long-ago lessons from river trips, imparted with great seriousness by their guides in case a raft flipped. But she'd been outfitted with a flotation device then, and it was easy to bob along on her back in a stretch of rock-free baby rapids, feet first, arms curled around her head for protection, in those practice runs.

She folded her elbows beside her ears and held her breath as the water sucked her under, bounced her off a rock, flung her briefly into the air and sent her sideways into yet another rock. She wasn't going to have time for the lovely slow hypothermic death she'd imagined. She was going to drown first. Either that or be battered to bits. The creek had the last laugh, lifting her with a final great aquatic heave and depositing her in a shallow pool, rushing away in a great hurry as she dragged herself with her one good arm across the pebbled bottom and fell gasping onto a patch of gravel lit golden by an utter miracle: the sun.

Nora lay still a very long time, shifting only as the sun inched along its path, letting its warmth seep through the layers of dermis, through fat and muscle and sinew, into her very bones. At one point, she supposed she should worry about sunburn. A moment later, she decided she didn't care. She'd take blistered skin any day over the killing cruelty of cold.

But with the return of warmth came more pain – from the cuts and scrapes on her body, reopened as the creek had battered her against the rocks, and new bruises from said battering. The sprained wrist, the worrisome banging in her head. And the fear that her brutal baptism hadn't entirely eradicated the scent of bacon. Once again, she went through the painful contortions that involved sitting up. She scooped up handfuls of gritty earth and scrubbed them against her skin. That couldn't be good for the cuts – but getting sniffed out by a bear would be even worse. Finally, when she'd coated every part of her body she could reach, including rubbing dirt into her hair, she tried standing again, even taking a few steps. Her legs, already blackening with bruises, at least appeared to work.

Which left the question: now what?

She was naked, covered in dirt, beset with injuries, many of them no doubt even now working their way toward infection. She almost certainly had a concussion. She didn't know where she was.

And, not to put too fine a point on things, some asshole had kidnapped her and tried to kill her; or at least, set her up to be eaten by a bear.

Why?

She forced her mind away from the question that had bothered her in some form practically since her arrival at the campground: why? Why had Brad disappeared? Why had someone tried to tie her to his disappearance? And now, why did that person want her dead?

Because, as compelling as all those whys were, the crucial issue now was *how*. As in, how the hell was she supposed to get herself out of here, when she didn't even know where she was?

First things first. She had to get back to the trail. Which was easy, sort of. All she had to do was get to the top of the rockface from which she'd been pushed.

It loomed above her, a foreboding slab of limestone, nearly vertical, cut by outcroppings on which small pines had managed to take root. Not the smooth cliff she'd feared when she'd first considered the idea. This part, at least, would be difficult, but not impossible.

A quarter of the way up, she changed her mind. The rocks cut into her bare feet, and scraped her stomach and breasts. Her left arm was useless, the wrist assertively swollen and throbbing a call to attention. Rivulets of sweat cut a delta through the dirt encrusting her torso.

The summit hadn't seemed that far. After all, the fall hadn't killed her. Now, she feared the climb back up just might. She cried out as a sharp stone bit into her instep. The sudden heat there told her the skin was broken, blood released. She wondered if bears were like sharks, drawn to the scent of blood just as they presumably were to bacon. If so, her damn-near-fatal dip in the creek and subsequent dirt bath had been for naught.

She wouldn't have been surprised to see a whole family of bears assembled atop the outcropping, dinner napkins tied around their necks, knives and forks at the ready, awaiting her arrival.

Instead, when she finally hauled herself over the lip of the cliff and fell gasping onto the ground, she beheld Forever, sitting cross-legged, one heel tucked in her lap, wrists atop knees, palms up, thumbs to fingers in a lotus pose.

Forever opened her eyes and smiled beatifically.

'Oh, hey. You made it. How's it going?'

TWENTY-FIVE

Nora spoke past the stitch in her side, the fire in her lungs, the pain in her feet and her wrist and her head. 'How long have you been there? And why didn't you help me?'

Forever unfolded herself, stretching her arms over her head, lacing her fingers together and bringing her hands slowly down to her lap.

'I was afraid I'd startle you, and that you'd fall. You seemed like you were doing just fine. Slow, but fine. And seriously, there's not much I could have done. I've got some cord in here that maybe I could have used to haul you up, but I don't think it's long enough. Now that you're here though, I have all sorts of things that can help you.'

She dug in her backpack as she spoke, pulling out packets sealed in zip-lock bags of varying size. Nora crossed her arms over her breasts, hands in front of her crotch. She hoped Forever had clothes in her pack.

'Let's see. Fluids first, I think. You're probably dehydrated. You didn't drink any of the creek water, did you? It's probably lousy with giardia. You think you feel bad now, wait until that hits you.'

She handed Nora a water bottle. 'Sips. Nothing more. Seriously.'

Nora thought she'd probably swallowed about a gallon of the creek water but thought it best not to mention that. Besides, the idea of cool, cool water down her throat – to hell with sips. She took the biggest swallow she could. Then spat it right back out again. 'Gahhh!'

'Yeah. I brought some electrolyte drinks. Figured if I found you alive, you'd need them. Small sips. It'll go down easier.'

Nora spoke between swallows of the vile stuff. 'You were looking for me?'

Forever dove back into her bag and came out with a handful

of palm-sized packets. She tore one open with her teeth. The tang of alcohol cut the air.

'Give me your arm. Let's get these cuts cleaned up before they get infected. How'd you get so dirty, anyway? That's not just from falling down.' She wielded the alcohol wipes over and around the cuts. It stung like a motherfucker.

'I was trying to get rid of the bacon smell.' It was all she could manage.

Forever paused, started to ask, and then came to the slash in Nora's side. 'What happened here? You didn't get this from a tree branch. Jesus.' She tore open a fresh packet of alcohol wipes and dabbed around its edges. 'You're lucky. It's not deep. But you'll probably need stitches. I've got some butterfly bandages. They'll do for now. And I'll put Neosporin all around it.'

'He stabbed me,' Nora started, but her throat closed up. A long shudder rocked her body.

Forever pulled her into a quick hug, then released her and went back to her work, fingers swift and sure, drawing the edges of the cut together, pressing the bandages across it in a neat little row. She sat back and admired her handiwork. 'Looks like the tail of a kite.' She shrugged out of the button down shirt she wore over a T-shirt and handed it to Nora.

'Here. Put this on while I work on your legs. Don't want you going into shock on me.'

Nora thought she was nowhere near going into shock but admired the woman's tact in her unspoken acknowledgment of the dignity that returned with being even partially clothed. She reached for the shirt, but Forever forestalled her.

'Wait.' She untied the bandana that swung from her pack and splashed water – real water, not the nasty electrolyte stuff – from her bottle onto it and gently rubbed it under Nora's nose and around her chin, cleaning away the blood crusted there, apologizing as Nora flinched. 'You've got some world-class shiners. They're going to get really, really colorful over the next few days. I'm just warning you now, so you don't have a heart attack when you look in the mirror. And my guess is, just looking at you and seeing the kind of person you are, the way you live with that nice trailer, you'll probably want to see a plastic surgeon about your nose.'

Nora put a tentative finger to the side of her nose. It wasn't where it used to be.

'No judgment,' Forever said. 'But for my money, what most people might call an imperfection will make your face way more interesting.' She turned her attention to Nora's feet. 'These are bad. Walking out's going to be a challenge. Who did this to you?'

'I don't know.' Her voice suddenly unreliable. Just the mention of her captor brought it back to her, the hand across her face, the rough grasp. The head-to-toe terror. 'I've gone through all the possibilities about a thousand times. Joe, loan sharks – never mind, I'll tell you later – even Caleb.' A thought occurred to her, one that somehow had failed to push its way through the night's horror. 'I suppose it could even have been a woman. A really tall one.'

'Good thing I'm short. Otherwise I'd be on your list. Miranda's tall,' Forever observed.

Nora considered the possibility. When her captor had jerked her close, had she brushed breasts, the curve of hip? She couldn't remember, and it seemed like the sort of detail that would have caught her attention.

'No. It didn't seem like anyone I know.' But she knew, and Forever probably did, too, the odds of a stranger making his way to a remote Wyoming campground and singling her out for – what, exactly? Death by bear? – were off-the-charts unlikely. 'There's some detail I'm missing. Something.' Almost palpable, hanging just out of reach, competing with the stabbing pain in her head.

She groaned and pulled the shirt closer around her, wrapping herself in its protection, summoning just enough strength to push back against the memory with a question of her own.

'You were looking for me? Why? And how'd you know where to find me?'

Forever said she'd returned to the campground from one of her local rambles later than she'd planned and ended up pitching her tent a little way off the trail, preferring a final night in the peace of the backcountry to the comparative bustle of even a mostly deserted campground.

Middle-of-the-night footsteps brought her upright in her sleeping bag. The quivering sense of something wrong. Not the usual forest sounds, the scurrying of squirrels overhead, small rodents rushing about the forest floor. The cautious, halting footsteps of deer, the lumbering progress of a bear, easily avoidable during the day and never before heard at night. These were different.

She listened a moment more and relaxed. People, two of them by the sound of it, the footsteps of one shuffling and uncertain, the other's a purposeful stride. She dug out her phone, charged during the day by her solar device, and angled it away from the trail so its light wouldn't reveal her presence. A little before three in the morning. Not exactly the time anyone chose for a hike.

Still, a nearby summit attracted climbers, who sometimes set off well before dawn so as to begin their ascent in daylight. These two were probably newbies, overeager, she thought, even as sleep overcame her.

'But when I got back to the campground, the whole place was in an uproar because you were gone. Here. Put these on.'

Socks emerged from the backpack. Forever worked them over Nora's feet.

Nora luxuriated a moment in the surprising comfort, so warm and soft and protective, another layer between her and the horrors of the world and tried to digest what Forever had just told her. Something didn't jibe.

'But if they thought I'd left town, why'd you coming looking for me up here?'

'Because— Hey, hold still.'

Nora forced herself not to jerk her knee away as Forever cleaned grit from a particularly deep scrape.

'Because I thought about what I'd heard in the middle of the night. And because some people said a bear got you.'

Forever's steps had slowed as she approached the campground, the final reluctant half-mile slower than the eager first mile of setting out, a familiar pattern.

The forest worked to quiet the jangle in her head, always too many thoughts and emotions scrambling for expression that never came out right. She talked in a flood of words and ideas, speech tumbling forth as though from a breached dam, followed by even longer silences as she tried to tamp down the emotions stirred up by interactions with people. She was accustomed to the excuses, the urgent task that demanded attention, the clumsy escapes from her one-sided conversations. Except for sex. Guys didn't care how much she talked as long as they were getting what they wanted; never mind that she'd wanted it, too, because of the way all of her thoughts slowed down and merged into a singular thrilling focus. But otherwise she'd gotten the side-eye her whole life until she fled, discovering that the rhythm of walking smoothed things, turned her attention outward, toward the wonders of wildflowers that revealed themselves like delightful secrets, peeping out from under rotting logs or swaying cheerful beside a stream; the trees whose branches rubbed together overhead with a reassuring creak; the animals who moved away at her approach with a respectfulness she'd never found in people. Often, once they'd achieved a safe distance, they stopped and turned, regarding her with the same sort of curiosity with which she viewed them. She'd wait, crouching to make herself smaller, less threatening, until they'd determined she posed no danger, and then they'd resume nibbling at foliage or scrabbling for grubs or whatever it was they'd been doing when she invaded their space. She viewed their regard as the highest of compliments, worth more than any paycheck, a roof over her head, a lover or spouse.

So when she heard the hubbub in the campground, she very nearly turned around and went back into the forest, thinking to bushwhack away from the trail and make her way to a high cirque she'd glimpsed from various vantage points, above the treeline, craggy and cold, just the way she liked it.

But she was nearly out of food and a quick trip into town – she'd catch a ride with Caleb – would set her up for a much longer sojourn on the trail. Her plan was to spend another week or so with this campground as her base and then move on, hitching a ride north to Montana to explore the Crazy Mountains, or backtrack south and west to the Wind River Range.

Encounters with people were always jarring, even after just a few days in the forest. They were so loud, so clumsy, so heedless of the world around them. Even now, some of the group at Miranda's campsite had stepped beyond the circle of packed earth and onto the surrounding vegetation, crushing it beneath the ridged Vibram soles of their big boots. Forever flinched, the death cries almost audible. It was too much. She turned to flee.

But it was too late, they'd seen her, and they rushed her, questions coming so hard and fast they all ran together, so that it took her long moments to sort out their words.

Miranda reached her first, wrapping a hand around Forever's wrist and tugging her toward the group. 'Nora's gone. Have you seen her? Or even any sign of her? Because I saw that bear last night, and now she's gone and all we have is this.'

She dropped Forever's hand and pointed to the bloody yellow shirt dangling from the sheriff's hand, and as Forever processed Miranda's words and the stained shirt and the footsteps she'd heard on the trail the night before, she knew it all fit together but she just wasn't sure how, only that her response was imperative.

'No,' she said. 'I didn't see anything.'

TWENTY-SIX

Forever swiped the last alcohol wipe over the palm-sized scrapes on Nora's haunches. She hesitated.

'Is that the last of it? He didn't . . .?'

'No.' Nora knew the question at the forefront of every woman's fear. 'He didn't rape me. I thought he was going to when he made me undress, but he just . . . just!' Her own weak laugh shocked her. 'He just stabbed me and then pushed me off the bluff. He didn't have to undress me to do that.'

'He wanted to leave you helpless.'

And he did, Nora thought, even as Forever moved to quash the notion. 'But he didn't. You were resourceful. Stabbed, all beaten up by the fall, and look at you. You climbed right back up that bluff again.'

Nora hadn't thought of it that way. A spark of pride sizzled within her, igniting a filament of strength.

Forever sat back on her heels, turning a critical eye on her handiwork. 'I'm all out of Neosporin, but those scrapes don't look too bad. Here. I don't have another pair of pants with me, but these long johns should do. They're really light but they're silk. They're warmer than they look.'

Forever turned, giving Nora a bit of privacy as she pulled on the long johns, grateful to the point of tears to have this most personal vulnerability vanquished. Forever's voice reached her.

'What was that business about bacon?'

'It's OK. I'm dressed now.'

Forever turned around and handed her something new from the seemingly endless reserves in her magical backpack. 'Sit down. Put this around you. I'll find us something to eat. But not bacon.' A gentle prompt as Nora lowered herself onto the ground and wrapped the crinkly metallic space blanket around her shoulders.

'I think he smeared me with a slab of bacon. Right before

he pushed me off the bluff. He ran something slippery over me, and when I came to, I was all sticky and I smelled like bacon. I think he wanted a bear to eat me.'

Just saying it aloud sounded crazy. She wished she'd kept her suspicions to herself.

But Forever, busy unwrapping a power bar, nodded as she spoke. 'I think he did, too. Here.' She broke off a bit and handed it to Nora. 'It's nuts and dates and peanut butter, I think. More protein than a steak. You need to get your strength back.'

'You believe me?'

Another nod, another scrap of power bar. Nora thought that whatever else she ate for the rest of her life; the airiest lemony souffle, the darkest bittersweet chocolate, the tartest pie with the flakiest crust, nothing would compare to the protein bar fast dissolving amid a rush of saliva. She sat on her hands to keep herself from grabbing the whole bar from Forever and stuffing it into her mouth.

'Makes you think, doesn't it? Brad disappears, they find a bloody shirt, bear gets blamed. Wait, was his shirt bloody? Anyway, it doesn't matter. Then they find his T-shirt in your bed, you go missing and they find your bloody shirt, bear gets blamed. There must've been a fire sale on shirts, the way they're being spread all over the place.'

'Wait.' Nora put a hand to her head. Now that Forever had attended to her other injuries, the flashing pain there assumed dominance. 'If they found my shirt, how come they didn't find me? And how come you did?'

The gathering around Miranda's picnic table had come to seem familiar. The sheriff. Caleb. Miranda. Joe. And, a little apart from the others, that reporter. Bethany.

The sheriff: 'Damnation. The judge never should have listened to that lawyer. I knew something like this would happen if they let her out on bail.'

Her not-quite-ex-husband had rushed to her defense. 'Nora wouldn't do that. She wanted to stick around, prove her innocence. Besides, where'd she go? The truck and trailer are still here.'

'He had a point there,' Forever told Nora.

'The bear.' Miranda's whisper came so soft that no one but Forever, her ears attuned to the smallest forest sounds, heard it at first. Miranda's eyes went wide with fear, and she said it again, louder. 'The bear.' The men finally stopped and looked at her. Bethany edged closer.

'It was here last night. I'm sure of it. I heard something banging around. But after what happened to Brad' – no mention, Nora noted, of the recent theory, the one Miranda had so eagerly adopted, that the bear had nothing to do with Brad's disappearance – 'I was afraid to go out.'

The sheriff and Caleb snapped to attention, entirely different expressions on their faces.

'Where was it?'

Miranda closed her eyes a second and thought. 'I was in bed.' She walked to the pickup and stood by the hood, looking up at the camper's overhang, and closed her eyes again, longer this time.

'There.' She pointed, swift and sure, toward an eastbound trailhead, and Caleb and the sheriff took off without a word. Joe started to follow them, but Bethany shook her head.

'Wait here. If they find her, you won't want to be there.' Leaving unsaid, but far too easily imagined, the brutality that might greet them.

Joe, half-risen from the bench, sank back down and dropped his head into his hands. 'Why didn't they just shoot the goddamn thing when they had a chance?'

Tears washed Miranda's eyes, turning them a deeper blue. 'Exactly. I like Caleb. He was so helpful to us when we first came here, setting us up as campground hosts. "He's saved our lives," I told Brad over and over again. If I'd known he cared more about bears than people, I might have kept going. But we were out of money and out of gas and nearly out of food. We were desperate. And look where it got us.' Openly sobbing now, words escaping in bursts. Joe moved to the other bench and put a comforting arm around her. Forever caught a sidelong glance from Bethany and pressed her lips together, words already piling up behind them, thoughts caroming off the shell of her skull, all of them variations on the theme of 'this doesn't make sense'.

She heard it before the others, the slight vibration in the atmosphere that signaled footsteps, the sudden, quivering silence of the birds and squirrels, those forest sentinels.

Miranda's sobs subsided. Joe ceased patting her shoulder. Bethany pulled out her phone.

The sheriff led the way, something in his hand. Caleb trailed, his eyes looking anywhere but at them.

The women sat frozen as Joe rose, pulled toward the sheriff by an invisible elemental need to know. The sheriff held out his hand, the shirt swinging stiff, shingled with dried blood. The awful tear in its side.

All the various sounds – Miranda's cry, Caleb's curse, Bethany's urgent questions and Joe's agonized moan – came to Forever from far away as her own thoughts pushed forward, shouting to compete with the din in the campsite.

'They found your shirt on the eastbound trail, and just a little way in, given how fast they got back. But the people I heard last night were on the trail to the west, and I was at least three miles out. I knew right then the whole thing was bullshit. I just don't know why.'

She looked a question at Nora, who shook her head sorrowfully in response.

'Me, neither.'

TWENTY-SEVEN

Shadows swept the clearing where they sat, the wind kicking up, trees agitated.

Forever cast an eye skyward. 'Sun's going down soon. It's going to get cold. If I activate my locator beacon now, they'll still have time to get to us before dark.'

'No!' It came out as a shout, Nora shocking even herself with the vehemence of her refusal. She tried to think of a way to explain her sense that somehow, someone in that campground had betrayed her and until she figured out who, she didn't want to see any of them.

Forever pointed out the obvious. 'Given the shape you're in, we've got a good two-, three- or maybe even four-hour walk back. Think you're up to it?'

Before Nora could respond, she answered her own question. 'I don't think you are. You keep touching your head. Are you OK?'

Nora started to shake it. A burst of pain stopped her. 'I'm probably concussed. Maybe when he hit me with the gun—'

'He had a gun?' Forever's face went very still, in a way that both raised a question and warned Nora not to ask.

'Yeah. Or maybe when I fell. And I tried to protect my head when I jumped into the creek but I clocked it pretty hard on a couple of those rocks.'

'You went into the creek? On purpose? You're lucky you didn't drown or die of hypothermia.'

'Bacon,' Nora reminded her. 'I figured either one of those was better than getting eaten.'

'Point taken. And if you survived both of those things, I'm not going to worry about a concussion. Still, after everything you've been through, I don't think a walk is the best idea, especially given the shape of your feet. You up for a night in the tent? It's a one-person, so it'll be snug. But that'll keep us warm.'

The prospect of a few hours of oblivion, with someone as capable as Forever watching over her, was more enticing than the most exotic vacation Nora had ever planned.

'I'm in,' she said. 'Do you have any more of those power bars?'

Forever traveled light. The tent was as tiny as promised; her sleeping bag the slenderest of tubes; the pad equally narrow, an abbreviated model meant to cushion only from shoulder to hips.

She laid it crosswise in the tent, urged Nora to lie down, then unzipped the sleeping bag and squeezed in beside her, tugging the sleeping bag over them, and pulling the crinkly space blanket atop that. 'Our legs are going to get cold, lying directly on the tent floor like this. But our core will be warm, and our feet and heads. That's what counts.'

There'd been an extra watch cap, along with the spare socks, within the depths of the backpack. 'There's some things you can't afford to be without. If my socks get wet, or I lose a cap – little things like that can spell real trouble in a bad situation.'

They lay spooned, Nora's back to Forever's flat stomach, one of Forever's arms around her, more reassuring than she would have thought possible.

'Have you ever been in a bad situation?'

'Yeah. Now.'

Nora surprised herself by laughing. 'Besides now.'

'Some. Especially early on, when I was still learning. I didn't realize how fast weather could turn in the high country. Got caught in some pretty gnarly snowstorms, lost the trail, almost went off a cliff in a blizzard. Now, when the snow starts, I stop. I just dig in and wait for it to be over.'

That explained the backpack, seemingly equipped for any emergency. Nora said as much.

'Exactly. I figured I'd need every bit of it today, and I was right.'

Nora had started to drift toward sleep. Her mind snagged on a detail. 'Why did you figure you'd need it?'

'Nothing added up. The way everybody was so sure a bear had gotten you. Except Caleb.'

'What do you mean?'

'He said that rip in your shirt was too clean, that if a bear had bitten or clawed you, it would have been all ragged and shredded. They brushed him off – said it was time for him to quit worrying about the bear and start giving a shit about people.'

Both of them breathed slow and deep through a long silence.

'But you believed him.'

'Sure. He was right. And I'd heard those people on the trail, one of them walking funny. I figured that might be you, and that if someone was with you, something was really wrong. So I waited awhile, and when they were all distracted, I went out looking for you.'

Another silence, longer than the first, Nora's brain taking longer and longer to process things as the events of the day and previous night caught up with her. 'But why didn't you tell them? Find that guy with the dogs, have them search for me?'

Forever's reply came swift and sure, jolting Nora from her almost-sleep.

'Because something's off here. I don't trust them. And neither should you.'

The night was, if anything, longer than the previous one. She woke screaming, twice, three times, each time soothed back to sleep by Forever's shushing. Somehow, finally, she did sleep.

And woke to a motherfucking miracle.

Which is how she termed it when Forever's face appeared in the tent's opening, her hand extended inside, holding a steaming cup of coffee.

'You got that right. Credit Starbucks. Complain all you like about big, bad corporations, but their instant coffee packets are genius. Hope you like it black.'

Nora loved it black. And hot, so hot it burned her throat as she gulped it down, holding out the mug in a silent plea for more. Forever exchanged it for a water bottle. 'Drink this first. The coffee will just dehydrate you all over again. I'm going to head down to the creek – turns out the bluff really levels out just a couple hundred yards away. Go figure – and filter some more water while you pee and get yourself together. There's oatmeal for breakfast. Eat it. The more hot food and drink you get into yourself, the better you'll feel.'

Nora slid feet-first from the tent and stood, taking a moment to be sure of her balance. Her breath hung before her, blending into the fog that floated through their impromptu campsite, brushing her face like soft, damp feathers. A tiny fire crackled at her feet, the orange flames a startling flash of color in a dripping grey landscape. It must have rained in the middle of the night. Forever had positioned a small rock in the middle of the fire. A tin pot perched on it. A spoon lay on another rock, off to one side. *Food.*

Nora hastened behind a shrub to pee – as if there were anyone to see her – and doubled-timed it back to the fire, pulling down her shirtsleeve over her hand to snatch the pot from it, digging the spoon into the instant oatmeal that, if possible, tasted even better than the previous night's power bars. Warmth spread throughout her body, stiffened from the cramped night in the tent. She stretched her limbs, favoring the sprained wrist, luxuriating in the return of flexibility. She didn't feel good – she couldn't imagine ever feeling good again – but the morning was an improvement over the previous night, and that was something.

'Leave any for me?'

Nora jumped.

Forever emerged silently from the pines, a full water bottle in each hand. 'Relax. I was just kidding. I already had some. Figured I can't take care of you unless I take care of myself first.'

Nora held out the scraped-clean pot in silent acknowledgment.

Forever poured in some water and sat it back in the fire. 'Hope you don't mind if your next cup of coffee tastes a little like oatmeal. But it's the caffeine that counts, right?'

Nora nodded, not trusting her voice yet.

'We're going to need all the caffeine we can get, given what we'll be up against today.'

She bustled around as she spoke, extricating the sleeping bag and pad and space blanket from the tent, rolling them into

small tight packets and stowing them in her pack. She snapped
the poles from the tent, which collapsed into a square of nylon
that looked no bigger than a large kerchief.

'You mean the walk? How far is it?' Nora lifted a foot,
warm in Forever's sock, and favored it with a dubious glance.
She took a step and winced. She'd had to pee so badly when
she woke up that she'd barely given a thought to the pain in
her feet when she'd hustled behind a bush, but now wondered
exactly how far they'd carry her.

'Not far. Two, three miles.'

As far as Nora was concerned, it might as well have been
ten. Twenty. She looked at Forever's tiny feet, safely encased
in sturdy hiking shoes. No way could she jam her feet into
them.

Forever followed her gaze. 'I already thought about that.
You're stuck with just socks. We'll take it really, really slow.
You can lean on me. Or' – she considered the pack, already
a considerable burden, and slid her knife from its sheath on
her belt – 'just a minute. I'm going to cut you a walking stick.'

The stick she brought back a few minutes later was nearly
as thick around as Nora's forearm, which gave her new respect
for the lethality of Forever's knife. She'd once imagined
Forever drawing it across a truck driver's neck. But given the
woman's multiple kindnesses, that now seemed ridiculous.

'I'll be fine,' she said. She was clothed and fed; her cuts,
cleaned and bandaged, no longer in danger of suppurating and
spreading infection throughout her body. Even her head felt
better, although for that, she credited the caffeine.

'That's not what I meant,' said Forever. 'Are you ready for
what you're going to face when you walk back into that
campground?'

How bad could it be, Nora had wondered when Forever posed
the odd question. Several slow, shuffling hours later, she found
out.

She'd ended up leaning on Forever after all for the last
half-mile, so exhausted and hurting she barely caught the
woman's low, whispered stream of encouragement. 'One foot
in front of the other, that's the way, step a little higher now,

over that root, I can see the clearing ahead, we're just about there, you're going to make it, you really are.'

But until the trees parted, until she stepped into the sunshine that suffused the clearing with a golden hue, until she saw the circle of faces turning toward her, Nora hadn't been sure.

Forever slid from beneath her arm. She nearly fell, the walking stick wobbling in her hand, balance beginning to fail. Strong arms wrapped her, pulled her close.

'Babe. Oh, babe.'

Joe.

Tears started. She fought them. Abandoned the fight.

Joe patted her back. Kissed the top of her head. Pulled back to look at her, gaze still tinged with disbelief. 'Dear God. What happened to your face?' He drew her close again, and spoke through tears of his own, such an urgent mixture of care and fear in his voice that she immediately crossed him off her too-short list of possible assailants. 'I thought you were dead.'

She turned her head to one side, rubbing her damp face against his shirt. She blinked hard. Caleb stood a few steps away, arms folded across his chest. Shaking his head.

She closed her eyes and let Joe half-carry her to the truck. Her new caretaker, much as Forever had been, but more assertive, voice louder, looking to others for what was needed, where Forever had provided it herself.

'Let's get you to town. To a doctor. And then to the sheriff. He'll want to call off the searchers.'

There'd been searchers? Then how come they hadn't found her?

'Wait,' she said. 'I need my phone.'

'I'll get it.'

'No.' She couldn't explain why she didn't want him in Electra. She didn't really know herself. He drove her to the trailer, helped her up the steps. She closed the door in his face, ignoring the look that crossed his face. The phone sat on the tiny nightstand where she'd plugged it in to charge. She tapped the *de rigeur* text to her mother. 'I'm OK. Don't worry. I'll call soon.' Someday, maybe in a decade or two or three, her mother would forgive her for not calling. Maybe.

It took all of her remaining energy, even with Joe's help,

to walk the few steps to the truck. Joe boosted her in. As he fastened the seat belt around her, she remembered Forever saying her shirt had been discovered along an eastbound trail, far from where she ended up. Maybe some animal had carried it there.

Her head lolled back against her seat. She closed her eyes. The truck rumbled to life beneath her. She'd worry about all of that later.

She didn't get that luxury.

The sheriff met them at the clinic, crowding in behind Joe and the nurse practitioner as soon as Nora had donned the hospital gown they'd insisted upon. She sat on an examining table in a curtained alcove barely big enough to contain all of them while the nurse jabbed her arm and got an IV going.

'Mind if I come in?' the sheriff asked, even though he was already in. Joe said yes before Nora could open her mouth. The nurse peeled off her bandages, repeating the same sterile-wipe-and-Neosporin routine Forever had applied, along with a shot of antibiotics, the sheriff documenting Nora's wounds with a small camera.

'Evidence,' he said.

The nurse also gave her an ice pack for her face, which a quick check in the truck's rearview mirror had displayed all the technicolor bruising Forever had promised. 'Given what you said about dizziness, you're probably concussed,' he told her. 'You'll want to get plenty of rest. Avoid bright lights. Stay hydrated.'

'You say a bear did this?' The sheriff's skepticism was palpable.

'No. I didn't. There was no bear.'

The sheriff edged closer.

'Somebody kidnapped me. Came into my trailer in the middle of the night with a gun and forced me into the woods and made me take my clothes off and rubbed me all over with bacon and left me there.'

The nurse paused, Steri-Strips hanging loose from his hand. Glances shot among the men.

The sheriff cleared his throat. 'This person. What did he – or she – look like?'

'He. At least, I think he. I suppose it could have been a tall woman. But I never saw a face. It was dark. And he wore a bandana, which made it hard to make out his voice.'

'Tall? Short? Old? Young? Fat? Thin?'

She studied the sheriff, thinking to use him as a benchmark, but finally shook her head. 'Maybe taller than you, but I just can't say. He was behind me most of the time. And when he stabbed me' – she paused to collect herself, the memory a renewed assault – 'he was bending over. Not fat. As to age – no idea. Not old. Could have been anywhere from twenty to forty.'

'So, a tall, not-fat man with a twenty-year age range. I'll get a sketch right out.' The sheriff didn't bother to temper his sarcasm. 'What about the gun? What kind was it?'

'I never saw that, either. Just felt it.'

'Then how do you even know it was a gun? Could've been anything. I've seen guys get away with playing stick-up men by jabbing a finger in somebody's back.'

Nora held out her injured arm so the nurse could wrap her wrist. 'A finger didn't do this to my face. It was a gun. Oh, and this is where he stabbed me, in my side. That's why there was blood on my shirt.'

'That's not a stab so much as a slash,' the nurse said. 'It's not very deep. At first I thought it needed stitches, but the butterfly bandages are probably a good way to go.'

Nobody asked you, Nora wanted to say.

The sheriff put his camera away. 'Walk me through this again, will you? Some guy breaks into your trailer in the middle of the night?'

'Yes.'

'Just like some guy broke in a couple nights earlier and planted a T-shirt in your bed.'

Nora didn't like where this was going. 'Maybe. I mean, I suppose it's possible it's the same guy. I have no idea who put the shirt in my bed. And I don't know who this guy was, or why he kidnapped me, or why he left me out there for a bear to get me.'

'That's right.' The sheriff had switched out his camera for a notebook and scratched away at it with a cheap ballpoint pen. 'That business with the bacon. But you don't appear to have any bacon fat on you now. Would we find any on the clothes you were wearing? Although' – he paused, pen poised high above paper – 'you said he stripped you, but you were dressed when you got back to the campground.'

'I jumped in the creek to wash it off. And then I rubbed dirt all over myself.'

'She's still pretty dirty,' the nurse interjected. 'All the parts that we didn't clean off.'

This time, the no-one-asked-you look came from the sheriff.

'And the clothes came from Forever. She found me. Fed me, cleaned me up, gave me the clothes, kept me warm. She saved my life.'

The sheriff snapped his notebook shut. 'Your opinion of Miss – what did you call her? Forever? – certainly has changed.'

The paper covering the examining table crinkled as Nora shifted. 'What do you mean?'

'Why, just a few days ago, you were thinking she might be our Lot Lizard Killer. Now you're making her out to be some sort of Florence Nightingale.'

Nora had mentioned her suspicions only to Miranda, who must have passed them on to the sheriff. Damn her.

'It was just a passing thought. I don't think that anymore.'

'Uh-huh. That cut.' He pointed to her side. Nora pulled the soft cotton hospital gown closer around her. 'Any chance it was self-inflicted?'

'Of course not!'

He turned to the nurse, who shrugged. 'Anything's possible.'

With the painkillers kicking in, indignation asserted itself. 'You keep blaming things on me. You haven't even considered the possibility that it's one of the same guys who were after Brad. Though why they'd be after me, I don't know. Isn't it your job to find out?'

'What guys?'

'The loan sharks who were after Brad.'

The sheriff's heavy-lidded eyes widened a fraction. Given

his typical impassivity, she thought, it was as though he'd shouted his ignorance into a bullhorn.

'Miranda didn't tell you about that yet?' Nora didn't wait for an answer. 'Then you'd better go and talk with her right now. Because you don't seem inclined to believe a single thing I say.'

He turned to Joe. 'My apologies for upsetting your wife. And my deepest apologies to you for raising what is obviously a painful possibility.' The sheriff spoke to Joe in that hearty man-to-man tone that decisively excluded the only woman in the room. 'But given what we already know about the circumstances under which your wife left Denver, her – ah – tendency for, let's call it, dramatic actions, is it possible she could have staged this so-called bear attack to get attention? Maybe get your sympathy, try and win you back after what she did to you?'

'What *I* did to *him?*'

Nora came up off the table, nearly ripping the IV from her hand. He hadn't paid attention to anything she'd said.

'Steady there.' The nurse stepped in front of her with the calm, practiced moves of someone who routinely worked a weekend night shift, on duty when the bars closed and the fights began.

'A way to deflect attention from the fact that you're under suspicion in the disappearance of Brad Gardner?'

'I'm not making this up. Ask Forever. She heard me go by in the middle of the night. Well, she didn't know it was me. But she heard two people pass on the trail.'

The sheriff rubbed a thumb along his jawline, stopping at a patch of stubble he'd missed. The room went so quiet Nora could hear the soft sandpapery rasp as the meaty part of his thumb moved slowly back and forth across the bristles.

'Two people.'

'That's what she said.'

Disbelief met anger in the space between their gazes, opposing force fields so charged the room fairly sizzled with intensity.

'Your version: some man took you off into the woods.'

'It's not my version. It's the truth.' Nora folded her arms

across her chest, foiling the nurse's attempt to reinsert the IV needle, now dangling crookedly from the back of her hand, the tape half torn away.

'Hold still,' he ordered. 'You need fluids.'

'Or maybe you disappeared into the woods with a woman who's suspected – *by you* – of possibly killing a number of truck drivers. The two of you on the run together. Cooking up a so-called kidnapping as a way of avoiding a court date. Something, by the way, that allows me to take you into custody right now.' He quit bothering his chin and gave the handcuffs on his belt a shake.

'No!'

Only hours after escaping her kidnapper, Nora couldn't face the thought of another type of captivity. 'Ow.' The nurse found a new spot for the needle.

'Now, hold on.' Joe stepped in. 'Whatever happened last night, Nora's had a hell of a shock. Maybe she has gone a little crazy' – *Murder*, Nora's glare promised, *as slowly and painfully as possible* – 'and I hold myself to blame for it. It's no reason to put her in jail. Set a new court date. She'll be there. I'll guarantee it.'

'How?' Nora had had just about all she could take of two men playing footsie with her immediate fate. 'Are you going to take charge of me now? Don't I ever get to just be on my own?'

'Honey—'

'And don't "honey" me.'

Another one of those man-to-man exchange of glances.

'She's had a shock,' Joe said again. 'However she ended up out in the woods, she was out there for a long time, and she's got some significant injuries. Give her a day or two to rest up, recover. She'll be back here right on time.' Smart enough, this time, to remove himself from the equation. 'Won't you, h—?' Smart enough, too, to stop himself from letting loose another *honey* into the charged atmosphere.

The men waited in identical postures, arms folded, legs slightly apart, something Nora and her women co-workers had once derided as the testosterone stance. Nora had no doubt that if the nurse were standing, he'd make it a triad.

She was exhausted, she was hurting, she was outnumbered. And, she was afraid.

'Of course,' she said.

Joe, as had Artie earlier, tried to talk her into checking into a motel in town.

'No.'

She couldn't explain why she felt safer in Electra, already twice invaded by a stranger.

It had something to do with the fact that the Airstream, if even for just a few days, was the first space that had been hers and only hers in more than twenty years. So when Joe finally pulled up in the campsite, and started to follow her from the truck to the trailer, she turned and put up her hand, policeman-style.

'No.'

'But where am I supposed to stay?'

Without making a conscious decision, she'd limited her answers to monosyllables – or no syllables at all. She shrugged. He had, after all, just offered to pay for a motel room for her. He could damn well get one for himself.

'C'mon, Nora. I just saved your ass back there. You'd be sleeping in a cell tonight if it weren't for me.'

'You saved my ass by calling me crazy.' She'd have to get over it someday, this repeated habit of breaking her own vows of silence.

'I was playing to the crowd,' Joe defended himself. 'I would have said whatever it took to get you away from that man.'

So Joe saw the sheriff's skepticism, too; something to add to the small – very small – tally of chits in his favor, tiny shims as yet inadequate to stave off the crashing topple of twenty years of marriage.

She forced a grudging 'thank you' and hurried to Electra before he could say or do anything that might soften her resolve still further. She closed the door behind her and locked it, not that locking it had done anything to keep her kidnapper out. She found the canister of bear spray and put it beside the bed. She checked the window. Joe stood beside the picnic table, his relaxed, confident posture at odds with the irritation on his face, seemingly waiting for her to change her mind.

She pulled the curtain closed, turned on the fringed lamp on the dinette table and took a moment to appreciate its warm glow, so different from the harsh lights of the jail, and the absolute blackness of the night sky during her interminable hours in the woods. She washed her face, brushed her teeth, and checked again. Still there. Fine. He could damn well sleep in the truck.

But a few moments later, the sound of the truck's motor revving brought home a third possibility, when the rush of relief at Joe's belated departure was replaced with the realization that, with the truck gone, she was effectively stranded in the campground.

Which, she told herself, was just fine. Almost. She looked at the flimsy lock, then again at the canister of bear spray. Wished, for the first time in her life, for a gun. Something along the lines of a cannon.

Then had a thought.

She drew back the curtain a half-inch, scanned the campground, and darted outside as fast as her wounded feet would let her, returning with the ax that Caleb had brought her.

She dragged it down Electra's four-step hallway and propped it against the nightstand that held the bear spray.

Thus armed, she took a moment to recall the last three nights – the previous one, beneath the inadequate warmth of the sleeping bag and space blanket; the one before, the endless terrified walk with her captor; and the one before that, tangled in the jail's scratchy bedding – then slid between the miracle of sheets and awoke hours later, shocked by the realization that, improbably, she'd slept like the proverbial baby.

TWENTY-EIGHT

S he'd pulled Electra's light-blocking curtains tight across the windows facing the road and any potential curiosity seekers who might tiptoe up the entrance into the camp-site, but left the ones on the creek side open. Morning sunlight glinted on Electra's shiny curved ceiling and spilled across the bed like a blessing.

Nora, tucked beneath the duvet and an extra wool blanket, bundled in flannel pajamas, was warm. She was dry. She glanced toward the front of the trailer. Electra's door was closed. The books she'd stacked against it as a sort of crude burglar alarm sat undisturbed. She was safe.

In a few minutes, she'd rise and make coffee – not the instant Starbucks packets with which Forever had restored her brain to functionality, but real coffee from just-ground beans, with a dash of cinnamon to smooth the jolt. She'd slice open the melon she'd bought just a few days earlier – it felt like years – in Blackbird and arrange chunks around the edges of the plate that would hold her scrambled eggs. With cheese and mushrooms and onions, thank you very much. She was alive and all the aching stiffness from the various insults to her body did nothing to detract from the fact that it was very, very good.

But first.

She reached for her phone and, without looking at the blinking lists of texts and emails, typed her now-daily message to her mother: 'I'm OK. Don't worry.' She slid the tablet from the nightstand where it had charged beside her phone, propped herself up on the pillows, and began to type into her faux blog.

Back from the Dead
Because it appears I was supposed to be. Stabbed. Pushed over a cliff. And, in case none of that did the trick, smeared with bacon, presumably to draw in the bear that would finish the job.

She stopped, rubbing her hands together until the shaking ceased.

> I don't know who did this to me. I don't know why. But so help me God, when I find the son of a bitch, I'll . . .

She'd what? And how would she find him, given that she'd never seen his face? And, especially given that no one believed she'd been kidnapped, except Forever. And Joe.

She tapped the delete key, erasing the paragraph, thinking about Joe as the letters vanished from the screen, the way he'd stayed beside her through the ordeal with the sheriff, had shut down any talk of jailing her until her court appearance.

As if her very thoughts had conjured him, his voice sounded outside the trailer.

'Nora? Are you up?'

She jumped. The tablet tumbled from her lap. She'd been so lost in her thoughts she hadn't heard the truck. She leaned across the bed and pulled the curtain back. He stood at the door, cradling a large paper sack in his arms.

'Just a second,' she called faintly.

Time to go to the bathroom, brush her teeth. No make-up – and anyway, the concealer hadn't been invented that could deal with the bruises from the pistol-whipping. Besides, Joe didn't deserve the effort, she thought, summoning the spitefulness that had sustained her ever since that nighttime rush from Denver.

She nudged the books away from the door with an aching foot and opened it a crack.

He held up the bag. 'I brought breakfast.'

She thought of the meal she'd mentally planned, the espresso, the lovely just-ripe melon, the eggs folded over the cheese.

She didn't invite him in. But she stuck her feet into slippers, wrapped herself in a fleece jacket, and sat at the picnic table with the husband who, until a stranger had made her confront the ghastly fact of her own vulnerability, she'd been on the verge of breaking with forever.

It's wasn't much. But it was a start.

*   *   *

'I brought crullers,' he said. 'I know we don't eat this stuff, but I thought you deserved a treat. And coffee.'

Two insulated go-cups emerged from the sack. He must have bought them first, mindful that the coffee would cool on the drive. So thoughtful. The first tentative sip was still hot enough to burn her tongue, syrupy with milk and sugar. His thoughtfulness had not extended to recalling she drank hers black, something that after twenty years of marriage he might have remembered. She told herself that the previous days had left them all rattled.

She turned her attention to the cruller, spongy and crusted with sugar, and unkindly labeled it a convenience store variety rather than anything from a real bakery.

'Good, huh? I'd almost forgotten.' Joe had already devoured one and started on another.

She hadn't forgotten. And when it came to baked goods she suppressed a thought of the Buckhorn's pie.

At least he hadn't asked to come into the trailer. He'd respected that. Give the man credit, she told herself, even as she wondered if this is what life would be like if she ignored the stirrings Caleb had triggered and succumbed to Joe's blandishments. If that life would involve a daily drumbeat of self-imposed internal reminders to look beyond the bad – the clanging, unforgettable bad – to the small, good things. Is that how people got beyond twenty years of marriage to thirty, forty? By fifty were they too worn down from the constant effort to make a final break?

She choked down another swallow of the godawful coffee.

He winced in misplaced sympathy and reached across the table for her hand. She forced herself not to pull away, letting her hand lie passively in his. 'How are you today? Are you all right? Your face . . .'

She avoided the bathroom mirror after that first glimpse of eyes lost somewhere within wide, purple rings that spread down her cheeks, her nose a swollen, pulpy mass.

'Don't remind me.'

'It's good, though. It'll help in court.'

For a few blissful minutes, she'd managed to forget that she still faced a court appearance – and the uncomfortable fact that Artie, whose last interaction with Joe had been at the party where Joe had fucked his wife – would be there, along with the local lawyer he'd hired.

She mentioned the lawyer, leaving Artie out of the equation.

'I know,' Joe said.

He did?

'I fired him. You don't need a lawyer. One look at that face – no one in their right mind would believe you'd done that to yourself.'

'You fired him?' How had he even known about the lawyer? He must have run into Artie. The cruller churned in her stomach. 'But who's going to represent me?'

'You're going to represent yourself.'

She jerked her hand away. Everybody, even people who weren't married to lawyers, knew the saying: 'The person who represents himself has a fool for a client'.

He didn't push his luck by taking her hand again, merely patting it benevolently. 'Don't worry about it. You won't be on your own. I'm not licensed to practice here, and besides, I couldn't represent you anyway. But this case is so cut-and-dried a kindergartner could argue it. I'll be right beside you, coaching you through.'

But Joe's legal specialty was contracts. He hadn't done criminal defense since mock trials in law school. She ventured as much.

Again, he waved away her concern. 'If it were something serious, I'd have kept the guy on. But this part is pretty pro forma. You'll be out on your own recognizance fifteen minutes after we go in.'

'But it is serious. Joe, they think that guy might have been murdered.' Not that anyone had come out yet with the m-word. But 'held in connection with the disappearance and possible death of Brad Gardner' was about as close as it got.

'Nobody murdered him. Once you're out, it's just a matter of waiting for them to find wherever that bear left his body. They'll drop the charges, and we can go on with our lives. Where would you like to go? I know we were heading for wine country, but what about changing things up? You've already headed north. Let's just keep going, all the way into Canada. British Columbia is supposed to be beautiful . . .' And he was off, the old Joe, spinning a seduction of turquoise lakes rimmed by snow-capped mountains, island-dotted fjords with seals basking on their beaches and orcas frisking offshore, cities with sidewalk cafes and flower gardens famous the world over.

'A new place. A new start,' he finished.

'A new court date.' It had always been her job to bring him back to reality. Nothing new about that.

Her face, despite its ruination, must have adequately conveyed her fear, because he said hastily, 'We can always go with the public defender if you'd prefer. Unless you sold the truck and trailer for what they're worth. Then you won't qualify for a PD. How is it you still have them if you sold them?'

'Oh, that.' She was glad to turn the focus away from her legal issues – not to mention their future – for a minute. 'I didn't really sell them. Miranda and I just drew up a fake bill of sale. I thought—' She stopped. Probably best not to tell him the idea was to keep him from claiming the truck and Electra for himself.

'Are you sure it was fake?' The airiness with which he'd dismissed her worries about her court appearance vanished. Concern creased his face.

'I mean – it was just on a couple of scraps of paper. Handwritten.'

'You'd be surprised at what constitutes an official contract. You signed something, right?'

She didn't bother to answer.

'Shit, Nora. We could be in trouble.'

At least he said *we*. 'I've got my copy. And I can ask her for hers.'

'No, I'll go have a talk with Miranda. She seems like a nice person. I can't imagine she'd jam us up over this. I just hate to bring up business, given everything she's going through.'

What about me? Nora was getting tired of reminding herself that Miranda's situation was so much worse than her own. Because, given the events of the last couple of days, was it really? Granted, Brad was probably dead. But someone had tried to kill her, and that someone was still out there. If Miranda's situation ranked a ten on a scale of awful, hers was pushing eight. That had to count for something.

A breeze slid through the campsite, lofting the bits of waxed paper that had been folded around the crullers, scattering sugar across the table.

'Oh, no!' Nora ducked into Electra and emerged with the spray cleaner and paper towels. 'Bears,' she said by way of explanation. 'There can't be any traces of food.'

'Which is why I can't believe you want to stay up here. You'd be so much safer in town.'

Nora chased down the fluttering bits of waxed paper and squeezed them tight in her good hand. Better not to answer at all, she thought, knowing that no explanation would suffice. She didn't even have a good one for herself.

He turned on the bench to face her where she stood. She didn't move to rejoin him at the table, and eventually he got up and left, saying something about going to straighten things out with Miranda.

She stutter-stepped on her aching feet across the campsite through the willows to the flat rock by the creek and collapsed, staring for a long time at the rushing water, trying to decide how she felt about the encounter with the man who was still her husband.

She was learning, in her brief time in this new environment, to distinguish human from animal sounds. So while the sound of steps through the willow, sticks cracking at ground level and no higher, jerked her from her reverie she felt no urge to repeat her leap into the icy creek. She perked up at the thought that it might be Forever. She owed the woman a visit, and readied an apology for not stopping by her site.

But it was Caleb.

The gut-thump of mingled anticipation and fear was so strong she grabbed at a branch for support. It dipped traitorously in her hand.

'Steady.' Caleb crouched beside her, a hand on her shoulder, removing it as soon as she regained her balance, even inching away to give her more space.

She took a breath. 'Thanks.'

Forever always pretzeled herself into a lotus position whenever they sat together, but Caleb remained in a crouch so comfortable it proclaimed the elasticity of the cartilage in his knees. Nora patted her own knees, trying to remember the last time they'd bent so easily.

Other people – Joe, the sheriff – had averted their eyes at the sight of her face, but Caleb studied her openly. 'Wow. That's impressive. Hurt?'

'When it happened, sure.' She watched for a reaction. Had he done this to her? 'Now, only when I smile. Or talk. Or chew. Or breathe.'

He winced. 'You using ice packs? They give you painkillers at the clinic?'

'Yes to the icepacks.' Electra's little freezer had come through, hardening new trays of ice by the time the packs melted. 'I've got painkillers, but I haven't used them.'

She'd feared the sort of knockout sleep that had struck her the first night in camp, one that would plunge her too deep into oblivion to hear anyone breaking into the trailer before she could wield her bear spray or ax against him. Which wasn't anything she wanted to say to the man who just might have been that intruder.

'Any idea who it was?'

At least he didn't seem to subscribe to the theory that she'd faked the whole thing.

'None. You?'

'No. But the whole bacon thing really pisses me off. I mean, in addition to what happened to you.'

Nora, who'd slumped back onto one elbow, sat up straight. 'How do you know about that?' Forever knew, of course. But other than that, the only people she'd mentioned it to had been in the cubicle in the clinic with her.

He grimaced and rose, taking his phone from his pocket and holding it skyward, walking back and forth across the rock. 'There. Just got a signal.' He clicked a few buttons. 'Take a look.'

Still holding the phone high, he extended his other hand and pulled her to her feet, lowering the phone inch by inch, checking the signal, until it was before her face. She beheld the *Mountain Messenger*'s logo. The story beneath it. The headline.

Sheriff: Alleged victim spins lurid kidnapping tale.

'Alleged? Alleged my ass! And – tale? That makes it sounds like it wasn't even real. Just look at that photo.'

Bethany had snapped a picture of Nora and Forever stumbling into the campground, Nora leaning heavily on the smaller woman, her sprained wrist held away from her body. She'd raised her head at the sight of the group awaiting them and Bethany's photo had caught her face in all its multihued glory, features beginning to crumple with the sobs too long held in. Her mother would have seen that photo. At some point, she was going to have to have that conversation. In the meantime, she'd increase the frequency of her texts. She finished her rant. 'That's about as real as it gets.'

'But read what the sheriff says.'

She turned her head and squinted, trying to bring the tiny print into focus.

'Here. I'll read it for you.' He offered his hand yet again, helping her ease back down onto the rock.

'We're investigating all angles,' the sheriff had told Bethany, 'including the possibility that there was no kidnapping. When Miss Duffy—'

'That must be Forever,' Caleb interjected.

'—found her, she was alone, babbling that someone had smeared her with bacon. Ms Best is still a person of interest in the disappearance of Brad Gardner, and has already missed one court date—'

'Because I was kidnapped! Put that damn thing away.' Nora started to push herself up again, forgetting about her bad wrist. 'Owwwwww.' She fell back onto the rock.

Caleb crouched again. 'May I?'

He waited for her nod and took her wrist carefully in two fingers. It was still swollen, the skin below the wrapped fabric bandage taut but no longer hot, which Caleb noted. 'That's good. You'll be swinging that ax again in no time.'

'I wish,' she said. 'But I don't see me sitting by a fire at night anytime soon.' She stopped, the image of her assailant returning, creeping through the shadows beyond the circle of firelight, too vivid to verbalize. She looked at the sky, then the creek, going fast to shadows, the willows on the far bank already a blurred black mass. 'In fact, I should be getting back.' She longed for the safety of Electra, the locked door, the books stacked against it, the bear spray and the ax and her phone set to ping 9-1-1 with a single tap. Not that anyone could get to her in time all the way out here.

Joe and Artie might not be on speaking terms anymore, but they'd both been right that town was the safer option. How to justify the fact that – no matter the fact that each, in his own way, had swooped to her rescue – she didn't want to be in prolonged proximity with either of the men whose presence reminded her of the humiliation that she herself had made so very public?

What if she'd just walked away from that bathroom, pretended she'd never seen anything? None of this would have happened. She never would have found herself hauling a trailer without the slightest notion of how to do so; wouldn't have ended up a witness to one (possible) crime and a victim of another, and no doubt it was a crime, no matter what that damned sheriff said.

She and Joe would be sitting beneath Electra's light-strung awning somewhere in wine country, sipping the day's purchase, drinking just enough of it to allow her to plead a headache, that classic excuse, when they tumbled into bed, where she'd no doubt have lain tense and resentful, biting her lip against the knowledge she longed to reveal, until she was sure he'd fallen asleep. How long would it have taken her to forgive him? Or, if not forgive, for the anger to become wearisome, for it to become easier to look to the next day's adventure, and the one beyond that, as distractions? Had her agent envisioned the story of her travels as catnip to people just like her, in flight not just from jobs-turned-grind, empty nests too echoey, but as a way to avoid – or at least postpone – divorce in marriages long gone stale? Had hers been that stale? Joe must have thought it was. As for herself – in hindsight, she'd done her best not to contemplate its condition.

'Whatever in the world is going on in your head?'

Nora had counted on her bruises hiding her emotions. Caleb, though, had looked past them.

She turned her palms up and voiced the best kind of lie, the one that was partly true. 'I miss the fire.'

A smile spread across his face, rearranging its odd angles into something far more pleasing. 'Come on. I can help you with that.'

Flames shot high and hot by the time she carried the corkscrew and wine bottle in her right hand and two glasses gingerly in her left to the folding chairs set up by the fire ring.

'I just found out I can't manage a corkscrew one-handed.'

He took them from her. 'Real glasses. Fancy. I usually drink mine out of my coffee mug.' The cork slid from the bottle with a muted pop. She held out the glasses and he poured, then took one from her and clinked it against hers.

'What should we toast?'

'To finding the asshole who did this to me,' she blurted, wishing it weren't too dark to see his expression.

But his voice was all equanimity as he agreed: 'To finding the asshole.' And then: 'Any ideas at all about who it might be?'

Maybe that first sip of wine emboldened her. 'I thought it might be you. The person was really comfortable in the woods. Seemed to know where he was going.'

'That's smart,' he said. 'You should consider everybody. But it wasn't me. I was texting with Abby. Some sort of teenage drama, which normally I wouldn't care about but she's at an age where I'm just glad she wants to talk with me about anything. So unless your guy was stopping every few minutes to text, it wasn't me.'

If the first sip brought boldness, giddiness swept through her with her decision to believe him. 'Good. Considering I'm sitting here with you.'

'There's another good thing. At least, for me. Besides your being safe, I mean.'

'What's that?'

'It's looking less and less like a bear's to blame. Brad going missing, then you – and that business with the bacon. My only fear is that before we get to the bottom of this, somebody's going to shoot a bear who never took a bite out of anyone.'

The bear, the bear. The man was obsessed. His next words confirmed it. 'And speaking of bears.' He pointed to the Big Dipper, tilted on its handle – or, as Caleb told her, the bear's tail – directly above them. After which she sank back into the chair and forced herself to focus on the wine and the sky and Caleb's voice as he murmured the names of the various constellations, following the black line of his arm silhouetted against the firelight as he traced the patterns above them and told her the Indian names and stories of the stars she'd long associated with Greeks.

The wine gurgled into their glasses again, and then again, and at some point he shed his jacket and wrapped it around her and the warmth and the wine lulled her nearly to sleep, too tired and tipsy to protest when he lifted her from the canvas chair and carried her into Electra.

Panic flared when he laid her on the bed and tugged at her shoes, and her hand darted out, seeking the bedside bear spray. But he merely pulled the duvet across her and tucked it in around her neck and shoulders, smoothing her hair away from her face and touching his lips so gently to her forehead in a kiss more reassurance than erotic.

'Sleep well,' he whispered. 'Abby's mom and I traded weeks. I'm going to pitch my tent outside. Nobody's going to bother you tonight.'

And if she pulled him back to her as he straightened to leave, drew him close and kissed him on the mouth?

Maybe that was a dream. Even though she knew it wasn't.

TWENTY-NINE

I n the morning, he was gone and she wondered again if she'd been dreaming, not just the kiss, but the whole encounter.

But when she stepped out of Electra, she saw the tiny flames in the fire ring, a stack of kindling and bigger pieces of wood beside it, ready for her to build it into a proper fire, and so she poured her coffee – real espresso, not that sugary gas station shit – into the insulated mug Joe had brought the previous day, grabbed her tablet and hustled out to greet the dawn.

Clouds of salmon pink scrubbed the sky and birdsong increasingly competed in volume with the creek. She inhaled coffee and pine and woodsmoke and thought she was beginning to understand why Caleb might have left behind life as a short-order cook in a crowded café.

Although, as the caffeine increasingly permeated her senses, she thought that she wouldn't mind a visit to the Buckhorn. Her food supplies, never lavish, were dwindling and the idea of a plate piled high with, say, buckwheat pancakes swimming in butter and syrup, maybe even followed – oh, luxury! – by a slice of pie, brought her stomach fully awake.

But Joe had driven off with the truck and Caleb was gone to do whatever it was he did during the day. And with that unpleasant realization came others – that she faced a day in court. That her assailant was still out there. That her mother was probably still frantic. That she and Joe were still . . . what?

He said he wanted her back, and she'd taken the help he'd offered the last couple of days and drunk his awful coffee and considered what life together might look like going forward, and then she'd turned around and kissed another man. And, while the recollection was hazy, she did remember that she'd liked it.

She fired up the tablet and tried to make sense of it all.
He loves me. He loves me not.
Nothing within view seemed to make for a photograph to illustrate her latest post on her blog-turned-diary of sorts, so she downloaded a stock image of a daisy and kept typing.

> That's how we figured things out when we were kids. We mutilated flowers, scattering petals like confetti in search of answers. Or we wrote our name and his and then crossed off the letters in common. Then we counted the crossed-off letters: an even number meant love; odd, not. Or was it the other way around? We read horoscopes, saved fortunes from cookies. 'It's a four-star day! Step out of your comfort zone.' 'The love of your life is right in front of your eyes.' Even then, I knew better. But what about now? A horoscope, or an insipid saying on a scrap of paper makes as much sense as anything else. Is Joe the love of my life? Or do I need to step out of my comfort zone? What if that just means letting go of my anger and sticking with Joe? Or might stepping out of my comfort zone mean a fling with someone like Caleb?

She thought of the long hug, the chaste kiss; the way, despite his love of the woods, he spent every other week in town to be with his daughter, and added: 'Although, he doesn't strike me as the fling type.'

She stopped typing and tried to imagine a life in this place, suits and pumps traded for jeans and hiking shoes year-round. Which, of course, had been the idea with Electra, but that plan had involved being on the move, not settling down in some backwater. Places like Blackbird were only charming in limited doses, knowledge hard-won from her small-town childhood.

She pushed the tablet aside. She was restless, nerves still jangly. Under normal circumstances she'd go for a run, but she still couldn't walk without discomfort. But she *could* walk.

The crude walking stick Forever had cut for her sat propped against the picnic table. She stowed her tablet and coffee cup back in Electra, steadied herself with the stick, and set off for Miranda's campsite to find out whether Joe had managed to settle things about Electra. She could have just called Joe. Or, for a bit of emotional remove, texted him. But she rather liked this new balance of power, Joe as supplicant, herself as beneficent granter of forgiveness.

Or not.

Joe could wait. Newly energized, she thumped the stick with each step and told herself she really, truly wasn't imagining whacking Joe with it instead.

Miranda stood before a bucket on the picnic table, her blonde hair backlit by the sun's strengthening glow, twisting something in her hands.

Water dripped back into the bucket. She jumped when she saw Nora, a turquoise silken scrap dangling from her cold-reddened hands.

Nora belatedly recognized it as a thong. She looked away.

'Nora. I didn't hear you walking up. You caught me doing laundry.' She clothespinned it to a cord strung between two trees, where it fluttered unabashed in full view next to other tiny undergarments, bright as jewels against the black-green of the pines, all of them looking out of place and impractical in their rugged surroundings.

Nora wondered if there'd been a similar display when Joe had stopped by the previous evening. She herself was running low on clothing. But she'd thought to make a trip to town, where surely there was a laundromat, rather than finding herself up to her elbows in fast-cooling sudsy water on another see-your-breath morning.

Miranda glanced around the campsite, as if seeking someone else. She looked back to Nora, then away again. She'd probably read the same stories everyone else had. Or maybe she'd even been there when the sheriff told Bethany of his doubts about Nora's account of her kidnapping. She came at the subject obliquely.

'Are you all right? Your face.'

'Right now, my face is the least of my worries. The sheriff doesn't believe me.' Putting it out there, letting it sit.

Miranda bit her lip. 'You have to admit, it does sound

strange.' She plunged her hands back into the water and scrubbed something furiously between them.

'No stranger than a bear dragging off your husband but leaving almost no sign of an attack. Or thugs working him over for whatever money he has left.'

Was that mean? She didn't care. It was a fact. 'What did the sheriff say about that, anyway? Because when I asked him about it at the clinic, he said he didn't know what I was talking about.'

Miranda lifted a lavender bralette from the bucket and stared at it as though she'd never seen it before. 'I'm sorry. I'm sorry. I just couldn't.' Her shoulders shook with the onset of sobs.

Nora tried to remember whether, beyond that first night, she'd ever talked to Miranda without tears being involved. An entire waterfall gushed forth.

Nora knew she was supposed to hug her, but feared Miranda would detect the anger in her embrace. Lacking the capture of a bear, whose stomach contents would presumably indicate guilt, Miranda's tale of vengeful loan sharks was the only half-plausible theory so far that directed suspicion away from Nora.

She sat and gestured for Miranda to do the same, a successful hug-avoidance maneuver. 'Miranda, why not?'

'I know Caleb says the FBI knows how to deal with things like this without anybody getting hurt, but what if he's wrong? And besides . . .' She dropped the bralette back into the bucket.

Nora ground her teeth. 'Besides?'

Nora marveled at Miranda's ability to speak clearly even as tears rolled down the planes of her cheekbones, clinging like tiny crystals along her jawline before falling in a steady patter to the tabletop.

Miranda lowered herself to the bench. She nudged the bucket aside with her elbow. Soapy water sloshed onto the table. In the bucket, her underthings bobbed to the surface and floated briefly, a harlequin island, before sinking modestly from sight.

'It was illegal, his getting mixed up with those guys, wasn't it? What if, when they find him, they arrest him?'

'I'm pretty sure it's not illegal,' Nora said, even though she was pretty sure it was. 'The people who make those kinds of loans, they're the ones doing something illegal.' That, at least, was true.

Miranda covered her face with her hands. But she'd stopped crying. Her voice floated sorrowful and muffled between her fingers.

'Nobody believes either of us, do they?'

'Caleb thinks the sheriff wants to believe it's the bear.'

'But I don't want to believe the sheriff. If he's right, that a bear took Brad, then Brad's probably . . .'

Nora didn't blame her. She wouldn't have said the word out loud, either.

'But if what happened to you is the same thing that happened to Brad, then maybe he's still . . .'

She seemed likewise unable to bring herself to say the word *alive*. Nora wondered if she feared a jinx. She rubbed her hands together.

Miranda pointed to the fire ring, where a blaze much like her own threw cheerful sparks skyward. A pot sat on a metal rack above it. 'Coffee? I could use a break from laundry.'

'You don't need to go to any trouble.'

'Water's already on. It's no trouble.'

Miranda clambered up into the camper that sat in the back of the pickup and came out a few moments later with two mugs and a spoon. 'It's just instant. I hope you don't mind.' She splashed water into them, stirred, and handed Nora a mug of pale brown liquid.

Nora minded and wished she didn't. What kind of person complained about coffee from a probable grieving widow?

'Do you have to cook everything over the fire? I thought maybe you had a stove in there.'

'I do. Do you want to see?'

Nora didn't, not especially, but nor did she want to jump right into the reason for her visit; namely, finding out what Joe had discovered about Electra.

'Go on,' said Miranda. 'Climb on up. We could both fit in, but it's crazy crowded with two people.'

And yet, she and her husband apparently had toughed it out in that tiny space for weeks before Nora arrived. Nora grabbed a railing with her good hand and pulled herself up the three steps that led to the truck's bed where the camper perched.

She'd guessed right. A two-burner stove and sink whose surface area was barely bigger than her tablet sat in a shelf on one side; across from them, two narrow seats faced one another at a briefcase-sized table. The bed was wedged into the space that overhung the cab, so confined that Nora wondered if Brad had scraped a broad shoulder against the ceiling each time he turned over.

'It's very . . . efficient,' she called to Miranda.

'Here, let me give you a hand.' Miranda, who'd been looking at her phone, shoved it back into her pocket and helped Nora down from the camper. 'Want to go for a walk? I'm going crazy sitting around here all day, nothing to do but wait for news, and no news ever coming. Except for you. Wow – now that was some news!'

'Speak for yourself.' Nora didn't care if she was never the subject of news again. And she didn't particularly want to go for a walk. But it would be easier than posing difficult questions to Miranda across a table. 'Where to?'

'Let's go see if that backpacker's still around. What does she call herself? Forever?' They set out from Miranda's site in the center cloverleaf loop and headed for the western loop, and then farther still on an offshoot that led away from the main track, the companion to Nora's isolated site on the other side of the sprawling campground. Miranda shortened her steps to match Nora's slow ones, chattering to fill the time. Mostly, she asked questions: Where was Nora from? Didn't she miss Denver? And didn't she wish she'd stayed there, given the fix she found herself in now?

Nora, who'd sought to answer in monosyllables, surprised herself with her response. 'No. I wish all these things hadn't happened, but I'm glad that's behind me.'

That life had been a lie. She just hadn't known it.

'Are you taking about Denver? Or Joe?' Miranda asked shrewdly.

'Both.'

After Forever had rescued her in the woods, their interminable walk back to the campground had been made mostly in

silence, companionable and focused. Nora was glad Miranda
hadn't discovered her instead. Nora thought she might have
crawled back into the underbrush rather than face hours of the
sort of empty jabbering that drowned out the forest noises
she found so comforting. At least, until this moment, Miranda's
queries had been inoffensive. But Miranda had managed to
dig beneath the surface to what really mattered. Was she really
glad she'd put Joe behind her? And, had she?

Leaving a husband because he'd fucked her friend – that
made sense. But making a final decision based on a single
kiss from another man?

Miranda nattered on again, and for a moment Nora was
grateful, especially when Miranda changed the subject.

'Her campsite's right up here. Do you still think she might
be the lot lizard?'

Nora's denial was lost in the rush of Miranda's
conjecture.

'Don't you think it's weird the way she showed up for you?
That she just happened to be in the woods?'

'But that's what she does,' Nora said. 'She lives to hike.'

Miranda raised her eyebrows and lowered her voice. 'So
she says.'

'No.' Nora thought of Forever's battered, well-stocked
backpack. 'I'm pretty sure she spends most of her time on the
trail.'

'What about the times between?' Miranda persisted. 'She
can't stay out there forever. She needs food, money.'

Thoughts Nora herself had once harbored, crowded out by
the memory of the gentleness of Forever's hands as she cleaned
and bandaged her wounds, of her comforting arm around her
in the tent, of her calm reassurance when Nora woke screaming.

'I've changed my mind. Not that I ever really thought it,
anyway. I just wondered. But there's no way she could have
done those things. She's too nice.'

'It's the nice ones,' Miranda intoned, 'you've got to watch
out for.'

Anyone else would have coated the words with the fine
sheen of irony, but Miranda exuded sincerity.

Nora nodded and tried not to smile. Had she herself ever

been so young? Of course she had. But never, she was sure of it, that naïve.

Forever was gone. *Gone* gone, the site swept clean with a pine branch that lay to one side of the clearing, the little paper tab with which campers marked their sites when they checked in gone from its clip on the site's signpost, the ashes in the fire ring cold and dry. Forever hadn't just doused them a little while earlier. She'd left hours ago, maybe in the dark of night.

Miranda's mouth hung open. 'But the sheriff wanted to talk to her.'

'Maybe he already did.' Nora felt obligated to come to her friend's defense.

'No. He stopped by last night.'

'He did?'

'To update me on the search for Brad. He doesn't have to. He could just send a deputy. Even before this happened, he'd check on us every so often, make sure we were adjusting OK. And now that I'm on my own, he comes by every day. Isn't that nice of him, to drive all the way up from town like that?'

The same sheriff who'd made a point of talking about his wonderful marriage? In Nora's experience, people who proclaimed marital bliss rarely were in its throes. (She suppressed the squirmy thought that her own book had been the most public proclamation possible of marital bliss.) Maybe the sheriff's daily visits involving a two-hour round trip, allowing time for a chat, the cup of coffee that inevitably would be offered, were a welcome break for whatever awaited – or didn't – at home. Maybe the sheriff wasn't entirely upset by Brad's disappearance. Maybe the sheriff . . . Nora wondered when her imagination had taken such a dark turn, first picturing Forever as the lot lizard, now the sheriff as capable of removing an inconvenient husband.

'Very nice.' She turned to go, scanning the site one last time as though Forever might step from behind a tree, bent beneath her pack, braids swinging forward, crooked-tooth smile lighting her face. She'd rather have spent an hour in Forever's silent company than the fifteen-minute walk back to Miranda's site.

Her annoyance with Miranda's prattle nearly drove from her mind the original reason for her visit, until Miranda's site with its aging camper came into view.

'Look at that old thing,' Miranda sighed. 'It's on its last legs. Your trailer is so much nicer. Would you show me the inside sometime?'

'Sometime, sure,' Nora said. Thinking, but not today. She was eager to relax in the solitary peace and quiet of her own site until Joe brought the truck back from wherever he'd been with it. And then what? Would she have to drive him back to town, drop him off at his motel? Which would involve spending far more time with him than she was prepared for and would leave open the uncomfortable question of whether to accompany him into the motel.

'Speaking of Joe. And of the trailer.'

Miranda spun on her heel and faced her, hands in pockets, face suddenly closed. 'What about him?'

She was probably used to women asking about her interactions with their husbands. Nora herself knew a little about that, about the defensiveness it could engender.

'That bill of sale we drew up. You know, the fake one.' Had she overemphasized the word fake?

Miranda looked about the campsite, as though expecting to see the bill of sale lying atop a rock or fluttering from a twig. She turned back to Nora and the taut muscles in her face relaxed into a smile.

'Oh, that. Joe explained last night. That, with you two getting back together, there was no need for it.'

Nora bit back a retort that she'd made no such decision. No need to complicate things further. 'So I can have it? The bill of sale?' She'd feel better with it in hand.

But Miranda shook her head, so hard her ponytail lashed her cheeks. 'I'm so sorry. Once Joe said you didn't need it, I tossed it.'

She pointed to the fire ring. 'I used the trash to start the fire this morning. It's all gone. You've got nothing to worry about.'

Nora limped back to her site in considerably better spirits.

Joe's worries about that silly contract had been for naught.

Electra was hers, along with the truck. And of course, if she took Joe back, there'd be no further worry about him laying claim to them. But if she stuck by her original impulse to call it quits?

She'd heard enough tales of friends' divorces to know some of the details. Divisions of property; complicated and usually divisive negotiations over money. On the one hand, their aborted plans had made things easy. They'd gotten rid of most of their property but for a storage unit with a little furniture, kitchen essentials, some books and art. Electra and the truck were their only significant possessions, and they were safely in her name. The money part would be problematic, especially when she braced herself for the necessary phone call in which Lilith would ask how the hell she planned to pay back her advance. Or, maybe the fact that there wasn't any money would simplify things.

A distant thwapping high above jerked her thoughts from the future back to the present. The first couple of days after Brad's disappearance, the helicopter had flown near-constant searches. It was equipped with infrared devices to detect heat, Caleb had told her, so as to be able to spot Brad if he lay wounded somewhere. 'Problem is, it also detects every deer and bear and bighorn sheep and mountain lion. The pilot told me this whole place is crawling with them. Which is good news for me – my whole job is to manage this forest for the benefit of the animals as well as people – but I can see where it's a pain for him.' Nora hadn't pointed out another obvious problem, which was that the fancy infrared equipment would be useless if Brad were lying cold and dead somewhere.

It seemed as though the helicopter flew over only once or twice daily now, enough to reassure Miranda the search hadn't been called off, but not so often as to waste valuable time and fuel on a lost cause. But it had the effect of reminding her that before she dealt with the looming decision of how to live the rest of her life – solo? Or in a mended marriage? – she'd have to show up in court and convince a judge it was in his best interest to either drop the charge, such as it was, or at least let her continue to walk free until things were resolved. Joe had promised to coach her through the hearing, or help her with the public defender. No matter what she decided about him in the long term, she needed him for the moment.

Newly purposeful, she raised her head, expecting to see Electra. But she must have misread the landmarks. There was the broken stump at the entrance to her site, but her paper tab indicating occupancy was gone. The signpost stood empty, just like those at all the other nearby sites. She must have gotten turned around. There must have been another stump, nearly identical to the one at her site.

She started off again. Stopped. Looked at the number. Forty-seven. Her number. Her site.

But the lane beyond the post led into an empty clearing.

She tossed the walking stick aside and pain in her feet be damned, ran into the clearing, turning a slow circle once, then again, speeding up, familiar sites flashing past – the ax leaning against the tree, the stack of split wood, the shiny spot on the picnic table where she'd scrubbed the grease away.

Everything just as she'd left it, except for Electra.

Electra was gone.

THIRTY

'**A** robbery,' she gasped to the dispatcher who'd picked up on the first ring when she hit 9-1-1.

'My trailer. An Airstream. It's been stolen. I took a walk and when I got back it was gone. I was only away for about half an hour. If you hurry, you can catch whoever took it.'

The dispatcher broke in with a series of tedious questions. Who was calling? Could she spell that? Her phone number and home address?

'My home address was that trailer! Can you please send somebody after it? Whoever took it is probably headed straight down into town. You'll run right into them if you head out now.'

'Or,' the dispatcher pointed out, maddeningly laconic, 'they could have gone the other way. In which case, we'd have to alert the authorities in the next county over.'

'Then alert them! Alert everybody! Put out one of those things – what do you call them? APBs?'

'We're not on TV, ma'am. You're in the campground? Someone will stop by soon.'

'Stop by?' She made it sound like a social visit. Nora didn't want anybody stopping by to see her, especially when that 'soon' meant at least a half-hour drive from town, assuming they did that lights-and-siren thing. She wanted them on the road, chasing down Electra, prying her loose from whoever had taken her, and bringing her back safely. She hated the idea of thieves putting their grubby hands all over her, hastily hooking her up to who knew what sort of inferior vehicle, speeding as they drove away, sending Electra careening around curves, maybe banging into guardrails, denting and scraping her beautiful aluminum flanks. She'd have chased them down herself if only Joe hadn't taken the truck.

'Dammit!' She wanted to hit something.

She eyed the ax leaning up against a tree.

A few minutes later found her wielding it one-handed against the already-chopped pieces of wood, whacking them clumsily into kindling, each wallop a blow against everyone and everything that had gotten her into this situation.

For starters, Joe and Charlotte, defiling her bathroom vanity. The bastard who'd kidnapped and nearly killed her.

The idiot sheriff, who refused to believe someone had abducted and stabbed her, and who persisted in thinking she might have had something to do with Brad's disappearance.

And even poor Brad. If he hadn't gone missing, she'd probably have spent a day or two in the campground, recovering from the shock of discovering Joe and Charlotte, and coming up with a plan on how to live the rest of her life.

She ran out of wood before she exhausted her fury. To keep chopping would be to end up with a stack of toothpicks. She replaced the ax against the big pine, although around the back, out of sight from whoever might drive by, given that it represented – beyond the clothes she wore, the phone in her pocket – the sole item in her possession.

She didn't even have a charger for her phone. She hurried to type the daily text to her mother – 'I'm fine. Will call soon. I promise.' – in case the phone died before Electra was found, when the rattle of a diesel engine broke the silence. The sheriff's white pickup rolled up to the site.

'About time,' she said as he swung down from the truck.

He patted his hands along his duty belt – handgun, taser, radio, flashlight – and touched the tiny camera affixed to his breast pocket. 'That wasn't the greeting I expected,' he said. 'But I'm glad you're ready.'

'Ready? Have you found it? Do you have some news?' Her heart leapt. About time something broke her way.

But the sheriff wasn't listening to her, looking past her with a puzzled gaze that swept the campground once, twice, much as her own had a little while earlier.

'What happened to your rig?'

'What do you mean? Don't you know? Isn't that why you're here? I called 9-1-1. Didn't they tell you?'

'Didn't anyone tell *you*?'

'Tell me what?' Nora didn't like the circular nature of the conversation. Things should be linear: Electra was gone. The sheriff should find her.

'They found something in the woods. I was almost up here when I heard you'd called in. I thought it might have something to do with what they've found. I've got a couple of deputies already out in the woods right now, so I figured your call lets me kill two birds with one stone.'

Nora understood each individual word, but overall, they made no sense. What did something – or someone – being found in the woods have to do with Electra being gone?

'If you didn't know about my trailer, then why are you here?'

By way of answer he unhooked the cuffs from his belt, motioned her to hold out her hands and gave a wholly unwelcome repeat recitation.

'You have the right to remain silent . . .'

On the way to town, he told her she'd missed her second court date and he was taking her into custody as required by law.

The first time she'd ridden to town with the sheriff, she'd sat in shocked silence.

This time, her protests began as soon as he started the white pickup with the leggy black star on its rear door.

'But I didn't know it was today! My husband was supposed to tell me. If he had, I'd have been there.'

But he hadn't. And now Electra was gone and Joe was . . . where, exactly?

'No,' she said. 'Oh, no.' The nurse had said she was probably concussed. He hadn't warned her that said concussion had effectively knocked all common sense right out of her.

The truck sounded its repeated ding until the sheriff found his seatbelt and buckled himself in. 'Oh, yes,' he said, misunderstanding. 'I don't care what your husband was supposed to do. The responsibility was yours.'

Nora finally shut up, which was a good thing. Because if she'd given voice to her thoughts, the sheriff would have had ample cause to lock her up for intent to murder.

*   *   *

Her public defender was a woman, as was the judge.

Nora thought it was about damn time she got a break.

If it was, indeed, a break. Sometimes women could be harder on each other than on any man. She uneasily remembered her college days, when the news of a fellow student's rape at gunpoint had flown through their dorm. 'She must have led him on,' Nora's roommate had insisted. 'She could have gotten away.' A stranger. With a gun.

The judge was a small, severe woman, almost lost in the robes surely designed for a man. She glared down at some paperwork before her as though it contained a personal insult.

Nora turned to her public defender. 'Can we get a different judge? I can't go back to that jail.'

Her lawyer didn't look old enough to have graduated college, let alone law school. She had a high, breathy voice that did nothing to dispel the impression. 'She's our only judge. And besides, you wouldn't go back to the holding cell. You'd end up in county. It's way better, though. An ACLU lawsuit forced them to build a new one last year.'

At which point, Nora fought an impulse to hold her breath until she passed out, a two-year-old's response but the only one she could think of that would remove her from the situation.

The prosecutor, barely older than the public defender, went first and Nora, who'd held her breath after all, heard only a few words – failure to appear, the apparent liaison with Brad Gardner the night of his disappearance, the subsequent bizarre kidnapping claim. The sheriff sat in the front row, hands clasped on his stomach, nodding and unable to escape the occasional smile. Bethany sat a few rows back, scratching away at her notebook, raising a camera every so often to click a photo. Worse yet, a camera crew stood at the back of the room, accompanied by a woman who matched Former Nora in the blow-dried, business-suited, matching-pumps department. Nora recognized her as a reporter from one of the Denver television stations.

She clenched her fists and opted for oxygen after all, short shallow breaths that threatened to become audible until the lawyer whispered, 'Settle down. Let me do my job.'

She rose. Tiny as she was, she wore flats, not even trying to make herself taller, more imposing. Nora dipped her head toward her hands, forcing it back up just before lapsing into visible despair.

'Your Honor.'

Nora sat up. What had happened to the little-girl voice? The lawyer had shoved it down into a deeper register, one powered by a hot wire of anger, its sizzling glow barely detectable but there nonetheless, an implicit warning that a full conflagration was just a spark away.

The judge raised her head.

'Let's take these things one by one. My client's failure to appear: how was she supposed to appear when she was recovering from being kidnapped and thrown from a cliff? She's lucky to be alive.'

She rushed to her next point, neatly sidestepping the fact that Nora had missed not one, but two court appearances. 'As to having made up the kidnapping – Ms Best, would you please raise your head a little more? The judge needs to see your face.'

The black bruising around her eyes had gone yellow, a startling lemony shade, oddly festive, her cheeks still puffy and swollen, the nose an unmentionable purple mess in the midst of it all.

The judge flinched. Nora's lawyer gave a satisfied nod.

'The sheriff' – she made it sound like an epithet – 'thinks she did this to herself. These, too. Your Honor, may I approach?'

Given permission, she lay a file on the high bench. 'These are photos of our defendant's injuries, taken at the clinic. Nice work, sheriff. Take particular notice of the stab wound despite the fact that our defendant had no knife – no clothing at all, in fact – when she was discovered. We don't know if a knife was found in that location because the sheriff never sent anyone to look for one.' She gave a little cough, as though clearing something unpleasant from her throat.

Nora turned her head just enough to see, from the corner of her eye, the sheriff's expression gone apoplectic.

'As to our' – she kept using that word, bonding the judge with herself and Nora in a neat grouping – 'Ms Best's allegedly, *allegedly*, having spent time in her trailer with Mr Gardner, she has consistently maintained no such encounter ever happened and once again, the sheriff did nothing to shore up the veracity of his ridiculous assumption. To the best of my knowledge, no one ever checked for Mr Gardner's finger-prints or any other evidence of his presence in the trailer other than a shirt that appears to have been planted to throw suspicion on my client. I'd argue that until the county can come up with even a shred of actual evidence, my client is owed an apology, not a stint in our new jail. At the very least, this hurry-up hearing should be rescheduled. My client needs medical attention. And her home – the trailer where she's been staying – has just been stolen.'

At the word 'stolen', the sheriff emitted an audible snort. The lawyer continued unperturbed. 'She needs to find a place to stay. Get her affairs in order. I'd argue for at least a month.'

She'd wound up her argument without mentioning Brad's having pissed off the men seeking payback of their loan. Nora wondered if she even knew. 'There's something else,' she whispered, but the woman elbowed her into silence.

The prosecutor was on his feet but fired only the same tired shots as before. The judge waved them away.

'I've heard more than enough. A postponement seems reasonable.'

'A month, Your Honor?' Nora's public defender lapsed into a child's squeak of optimism.

'A week.' The judge tapped her gavel once. 'And Ms Best. Miss this next one, and I'll take you to jail myself.' She turned away. The bailiff called another name.

Nora stood but remained rooted, not trusting what had just happened.

A heavyset man reeking of cheap beer brushed past her. Her public defender shuffled files on the desk and reached to lay a hand on his arm. 'How are you doing today, Mr Sanderson?' She looked to Nora, her smile discreet but triumph blazing from her eyes. 'You're free to go. Congratulations.'

'Thank you,' Nora gasped, and got out of the courthouse as fast as she could.

THIRTY-ONE

The courthouse was one of those granite piles dominating the centers of small towns all over the west, erected to proclaim the arrival of white people's version of 'civilization'.

Nora stood on the sidewalk in front of it. She'd given Bethany and the TV reporter a decisive 'no comment', standing her ground, folding her arms and shaking her head until they finally gave up and chased down the sidewalk after the prosecutor instead, leaving Nora to herself. The public defender was still in the courtroom, working her way through the pile of cases on her schedule that day. Her brain buzzed *now-what-now-what-now-what*, uncomfortably reminiscent of the same panicked fury that had driven her from the house in Denver. Except then, she'd had Electra.

She was exhausted, wrung out, afoot without a vehicle and, to top it off, suddenly, ravenously, hungry. She'd consumed nothing but her morning cup of coffee hours earlier. She glanced up and down the street. Saw a familiar sign. Felt hurriedly in her pocket to convince herself that the neat packet of cash, license and credit cards was still there; that it hadn't somehow vanished along with the truck and Electra and everything else she owned.

Thus reassured, she set off at a lopsided, limping trot for the Buckhorn.

She fell into a booth, trying not to weep at the mingled scents of coffee and toast and bacon. She looked around for a clock. Her phone had long since gone dead.

Two in the afternoon. The Buckhorn must have been serving up BLTs. Which she decided was exactly what she wanted as Abby arrived, a mug of coffee already in hand. Good girl.

'Two sandwiches,' she specified. 'And please, for the love of God, don't let the coffee in my cup go below half.'

'Got some pie already saved. Two slices of that, too?'

Nora could have kissed her. For whatever reason – she decided not to question it – suspicion had been lifted. Either that, or people had gotten used to her as the husband-stealing, kidnap-faking hussy from the campground and had woven her as one of the eccentric threads into the fabric of their day. The tears made another run, shoving at her eyelids, demanding freedom. Nora waited until the girl was gone, took a long pull of coffee, and dabbed at her eyes with the napkin. With the lunch rush long past, only a few other booths were occupied. But while the now-familiar hush had briefly fallen over the room, soft conversation soon washed it, underscored by the clinking of cutlery and the occasional tumble of ice cubes melting their way through a glass.

The sandwiches arrived, the toast crisped golden, a satisfying snap to the bacon, and a burst of tomato against the roof of her mouth. She'd already decided the intense pleasure delivered by a slice of the Buckhorn's pie surpassed that of sex any day of the week, but their BLTs weren't far behind. At some point, she was going to have to start eating like a normal person again, at least if she still wanted to fit into her jeans. But she needed her strength for whatever came next, she convinced herself as she dispatched the first sandwich and started in on the second.

Abby arrived with a single slice of pie.

'Keeping the other one warm for you,' she said. 'Didn't want it to sit here getting cold while you were eating this one.'

Nora's reply, a fast-gulped sob.

Which turned to a gasp as Caleb slid into the seat across from her.

'Abby called me soon as you walked in. I'd have been there in court, but Duncan talked them into putting the case on the docket too fast for me to make it down into town after I heard he'd picked you up. What's going on? I went by your campsite and saw the trailer gone. I thought you'd checked out.'

'Who told you I'd been picked up?'

He waved his phone in her face. 'Who do you think? Our resident sees-all, hears-all, tells-all. Bethany tweeted it out. Where's your trailer?' He glanced through the Buckhorn's picture window as though expecting to see it parked at the curb.

'That's what I was hoping the sheriff would find out. Somebody stole it. He seems disinclined to care.' Her hunger vanished as quickly as it had come on. 'Want my other piece of pie?'

He pulled the plate across the table. 'Duncan's not a bad guy.' He caught her look. 'Really. It's just that you're a major inconvenience to him. He's supposed to be dealing with a dead trucker. Now he's got another dead man, a kidnapped woman and a stolen trailer all piled high on his plate of shit. If you made up your kidnapping, he can forget about all of this and go back to figuring out who cut that man's throat.'

'But I didn't make it up.'

Sadness suffused his smile. 'And I still don't think a bear ate Brad. Despite what they found today.'

She looked up from her pie. 'What are you talking about?'

He waved his phone again, clicking at it first to display the *Mountain Messenger*'s website, a red 'breaking news' banner nearly obscuring the newspaper's name.

'Human remains found.' A map showed a dot north of the campground.

Nora's hand went to her mouth. 'They found Brad?' No wonder she'd ceased to be an object of such curiosity in the café.

Caleb grimaced. 'What was left of him. One of the search and rescue guys went into shock. We see all sorts of things up here. People with compound fractures – now that's a truly gruesome sight. People who've frozen to death or drowned. You'd be surprised how many people fall into that creek and don't come out.'

Nora recalled the malevolent force of the water as it sucked her under, slamming her against rocks, rushing her downstream. And the icy cold, turning her limbs rubbery, useless. She wasn't surprised at all.

'But bears go for the soft parts first. Well, any carnivore does. Anyway, he was pretty well shredded, and the magpies had had their way with his face.'

A bit of pie remained on Nora's plate. She left it. 'Poor

Miranda. Can you imagine, knowing that's how your spouse died?'

The remains of his own pie sat likewise untouched. 'And now the bear's going to die, too. At least there's no doubt anymore. Not that it makes things any easier.'

She resisted an impulse to reach across the table and take his hand. 'What do we do now?'

He rubbed his hands briskly together, perhaps suppressing the same impulse. 'I don't know about you, but I'd just as soon avoid the inevitable. The campground's still closed. If for some reason the bear's come back – which they tend to do, eventually – I can track it and kill it later. Let's find you a place to stay. Unless we find your trailer first. Want to take a drive?'

They drove for nearly two hours, up and down the main road from town, turning off and jouncing along gravel tracks whose entrances she hadn't even noticed, and into the looping layouts of other campgrounds. They saw Airstreams a-plenty especially in the other campgrounds, but none with a distinctive prop plane painted on its side – or a telltale scar or fresh design where the painting of the original Electra had been.

'I didn't know there were so many people who could afford these things,' Caleb said after the fifth or sixth one.

'Only way we did was by selling the house. Thank Denver's economy. We'd lived there long enough that the boom worked in our favor.' She had to give Joe grudging credit for that. The real estate agent he'd found had done her job well, selling the house for a shocking amount within a week of putting it on the market.

'Hope you had it insured.'

She did. But she didn't want a pile of insurance money. She wanted Electra back.

'It's hard to explain,' she said, and then decided not to try. How to convey what Electra, the one thing from her old life that could carry her into this new one, had come to mean to her?

But he nodded into her wordless silence. 'It's how I feel about the cabin. A wildfire blew through a couple of years ago and I didn't know for a few days whether the cabin had survived. I mean, I could have rebuilt. But it wouldn't have been the same. You're welcome to stay there, by the way. Until we find your trailer.'

She loved the confidence of his statement, false reassurance though it may have been. But she'd become nearly as enamored of the campsite as she had of Electra, its whispering pines, its murmuring creek. The idea of being surrounded by stout log walls, a stranger's things – 'Thanks, but no thanks. I think I'd miss the campsite too much. That's hard to explain, too. I'm not doing very well in the explanation department today.'

Caleb tapped the brakes and hauled on the wheel, pointing his pickup down another gravel road. Stones struck like shots against the truck's undercarriage. They saw a trailer, not an Airstream but a rusting mobile home, tires atop its roof as anchors against a grabby wind. A dog leapt and howled at the end of a stout chain, glistening ropes of drool swinging beneath bared teeth. The truck picked up speed.

The road narrowed, climbing through scrubby trees. Long fingernails of underbrush squealed against the truck's side panels.

'Somehow I don't see Joe in a place like this.'

Caleb shot her a quick glance, then returned his attention to wrestling the truck through a series of ruts.

'You think Joe took it.'

'Duh.'

'You sound pretty sure.'

Was she? In a way, she hoped so. 'The unkindest cut,' she murmured. 'Or maybe in this case, the kindest.' No more dithering, no need to wonder whether he was worth a second shot.

'What's that?'

'Nothing. I mean, yes. Joe probably took it. Who else? Oh!' She slammed a hand to her forehead, then yowled in pain. She'd forgotten about the damage to her face.

'Jesus. Are you all right?' The truck slewed to a stop. Caleb turned to face her.

'She told me she tore it up.' She spoke between breath coming hard and fast as the realization hammered her consciousness. 'And I believed her. Stupid, stupid, stupid.'

'Who tore what up?'

The abrupt stop had stalled out the truck. They sat in silence but for the ticking of the engine, in time to her pounding pulse.

'I thought he might try to take Electra.'

'Take who?'

Embarrassment settled her racing thoughts. 'That's what I call the trailer,' she reminded him. She took a breath.

'I told Miranda that. She offered to help by drawing up a fake bill of sale. That way, I could say I'd sold the trailer, and once Joe backed off, we could forget about it. I figured no way was something like that legal, so I did it. I mean, the thing was practically written on paper napkins. Then Joe showed up being so sorry and supportive. He said the contract could actually be legal and he'd take care of it. I believed him when he said it. Same way I believed him when he said he'd help me with the court stuff. I mean, that's his specialty. Contracts. She told me she'd tossed it, and I believed her, too. But what if she didn't? Joe had been to see her and maybe he persuaded her I'd been lying, that the trailer was really his. I thought maybe . . .'

She stopped. She didn't want to tell Caleb she'd worried that her husband had strayed again, and that this time, maybe he'd done so with deliberate intent, to charm Miranda into transferring 'ownership', no matter how shaky, of the truck and trailer to him.

'When the sheriff told me I'd missed another court date, I said I hadn't known about it, and I didn't. Joe said he'd take care of everything. He was probably hoping they'd throw me in jail again for missing it, give him more time to get away. My brains are so scrambled from everything that's happened that I couldn't even see the obvious. Christ! When I drove away from Denver, I should've just kept going. Driven all the way to the Arctic. Someplace far enough away from my own monumental stupidity.' She whacked her head again, no longer caring about the pain.

'Hey, hey.' He grabbed her hand and pulled it away. 'No sense in adding to that display you've already got. Not to mention you don't want to mess up the one good arm you have left.'

She flexed her left wrist. A fierce throb reminded her not to do that again. 'It's getting better,' she said. 'Not quite healed, but almost. But I see your point.'

He started the engine.

'Good. Because it's time to focus on what comes next.'

He executed a five-point turn in the truck, missing trees by fractions of inches.

'What's that?'

He pointed the truck back downhill and gave it some gas, gravity and momentum sending them aloft over the worst of the ruts.

'We're going to go have a talk with Miranda.'

'Now? But she's just lost her husband. I mean, she's just found out he's really, truly gone. We can't possibly intrude.'

He took his eyes off the road long enough to catch her gaze. 'Can you think of a good time? We'll pay our respects, offer sympathy, see if she needs any help with anything, and clear this thing up, too. The quicker it's done, the quicker both of you can get on with your lives. If she really got rid of that agreement, then Joe can be charged with theft. That trailer – it stands out. It won't take them twenty-four hours to find it.'

He took his eyes off the road just long enough to meet hers. 'You're going to get . . . what do you call it? Electra? You're going to get Electra back.'

THIRTY-TWO

Caleb cut the truck around the post holding the chain that blocked the way into the campground, the 'closed' sign swaying as they passed it on their way to Miranda's campsite.

No surprise: Miranda was gone.

Not just Miranda, but her rig, the clothesline with the sexy undies, and the hand-lettered sign reading 'The Campground Hosts are IN'.

'First Forever. Then Electra. Now Miranda. Has the whole world up and left this place?' Nora purpled the air with curses.

'Impressive,' said Caleb. 'Unfortunately, not very helpful. Smart money says she's probably just gone to town. Now that they've found Brad, there'll be paperwork. And, somehow, an identification.'

Nora, for lack of anything better to do, climbed out of the truck and kicked at the picnic table. He joined her but sat atop the picnic table and stuck out a leg to block her.

'Hey, take it easy on that tree.'

Nora had grabbed a slender branch from a young pine tree and was stripping the needles from the twigs. They fell around her feet in a shower of green slivers. She released the branch and it sprang reproachfully away.

'Now what?'

'We can go to town and look for her.'

Nora looked at the sky, which had begun its daily lowering, nearly imperceptible. But it would quicken fast, shadow lengthening, birds falling silent, even the wind resting from its daily romp through the treetops.

'I'd rather stay here. Goddammit!' she yelled. 'I want Electra back!'

'Easy, easy.' He came up from the table and approached but didn't touch her. 'A break might be a good idea. We can probably catch Miranda in the morning at the Buckhorn.'

'Sure. Fine. But I'm going to finally have to get a place in town. The thing everybody but me seems to want me to do.'

'You don't have to go to town. You can stay in my cabin. Or even right here.' His smile offered the first genuine warmth of an otherwise-grim day. It knocked her off balance. She tried to regain her equilibrium with the logic of her next query.

'And sleep where? Under the picnic table? Or on top, to make it even easier for that bear to eat me, too?'

'First of all, let me remind you for about the three-hundredth time that I don't think that bear is even in the area. And if he does come back, he'll go to wherever he left Brad, which is several miles north of here. Besides, I've got a tent set up in one of the sites in the next loop over. Given how much time I'm spending up here, it makes it easier than running back and forth from town, or even the cabin. You can sleep there.'

The rush of gratitude nearly knocked her to her knees. She grabbed at the pine branch, then released it lest he fear more mayhem on her part. Common sense delivered another blow.

'I'd love that. Understatement of the century, in fact. But that guy who took me is still out there somewhere. It was one thing for me to stay in Electra. I could lock the door, even though it didn't seem to keep people out. I have to think I'd hear a bear fumbling around, though. And I had bear spray and –' she smiled – 'that ax you gave me. But a tent seems a little too risky. You said the bear would probably come back.'

She cast a regretful glance around Miranda's empty site, which even though it lacked the charm of 'her' creek and giant ponderosa, nonetheless offered the scent of pine, the utter stillness. And soon, the stars.

'If it does, I'll be there. I can sleep in the truck,' he added hastily.

She looked at him, her eyes traveling his height, and then to the truck bed, and started to shake her head. He forestalled her.

'I've done it before. The tent's great, but when it rains, there's a lot to be said for having a hard shell over your head. Come on. I've got some pasta and even a little something for a nightcap. It won't be the Buckhorn, but it won't be half bad.'

'When you put it that way . . .'

She let him walk ahead of her to the truck so he wouldn't see her smile.

With a nod to her wrist, improved though it was, he built the fire, splitting the wood in half the time it would have taken her, even with two good arms.

He retrieved a plastic jug of water from the back of the truck and sloshed some into a pot and set it over the fire. He went back to the truck and opened a cooler. Another pot joined the first. 'Spaghetti sauce. I freeze it in chunks and thaw it out over the fire while the spaghetti's cooking. Settle in. It'll be awhile. It takes water forever to boil at this altitude.'

Nora settled. He had wine – a nice surprise – and gave her his mug, taking an occasional swig from the bottle until she offered to share the mug. When the pasta was done, he drained the water around the edges of the fire and then dumped the spaghetti into the sauce pot. They shared it as they had the mug, passing the pot and single fork between them. 'Sorry,' he said. 'I've never had company up here.'

Had he had 'company', as he so euphemistically called it, in town? And did it matter? She decided it didn't. What mattered was the sauce, rich and flavored with chunks of sausage, the spicy kind that gave it a nice bite.

'You're quite the cook,' she said.

He pushed the last piece of sausage to her side of the pot. 'All yours. I'd love to accept the compliment, but truth is, I get it by the gallon at the Buckhorn.'

'Don't suppose you also got some pie.'

He shook his head vehemently. 'Please tell me you wouldn't eat day-cold pie. Crust gets soggy, and then what's the point of pie?'

She clinked the mug against the bottle in a makeshift toast.

'Damn straight.' On that one point – a not insignificant point! – they were soulmates.

Later she sat beside the fire in a canvas chair, something else that had also come out of the back of the truck that she was starting to think of as the vehicular equivalent of Forever's backpack.

Caleb sat on the ground beside her, leaning against the chair, presenting a nearly irresistible urge to run her fingers through that unruly thatch of hair. He tilted the wine bottle over the mug and handed it to her. 'That's the last of it.'

It was the perfect amount. She felt tipsy, but not drunk, relaxed and warm, the horrors and betrayals of the last few days receding into the darkness beyond the wavering circle of light cast by the fire.

'I should be coming up with a plan,' she murmured. 'It's what I do. I plan things. Prepare for every contingency.'

He took the mug from her and drained it. 'How's that been working for you lately?'

She started laughing and couldn't stop. He joined her. A burning log broke in two and collapsed into the fire, showering them with sparks. He got up and poked it back into place with a long stick. This time, when he sat, he reached up and took her hand.

The tent stood at the edge of the firelight, a beckoning shadow.

They sat in silence. Her move.

She released his hand, stood, and stretched. 'I think I'll turn in. That tent big enough for two?' She didn't wait for his answer. 'I'm going to grab a quick shower.' Either he'd be in the tent when she got back or he wouldn't.

He rose to his feet and returned to the truck. She was no longer surprised when he presented her with a towel.

'Here. Take this, too,' he said, handing her a canister of bear spray.

'I thought you said you didn't think a bear got Brad.'

'I don't. But that doesn't mean I don't think one won't get you.'

He danced across the campsite, jumping to and fro to avoid her snapping towel, yelling 'Joke! Joke!' – a ruckus that, along with her laughter, was loud enough to scare away any bear within earshot.

THIRTY-THREE

A bathhouse was just a few sites away, but Nora walked past it and made for her old loop, which had its own bathhouse where, because she used it daily and no one else did, she'd felt free to leave a cake of soap and her razor.

If she and Caleb were going to end up in bed – well, sleeping bag – she wanted the legs she wrapped around him to be sleek and smooth. She'd neglected them lately, along with everything else, the many steps of her make-up routine, and the interminable moments in front of the mirror with hair product and blow dryer. As for clothes, she was fast becoming addicted to sliding into jeans and a T-shirt every morning, topped with a fleece that could be shed as the sun rose high, so much easier than coordinating suits and shoes and scarves and jewelry each night before she turned in.

Darkness had fallen by the time she left the shower. A full moon hovered, so bright its light obliterated that of the stars. There'd be no lesson in the constellations on this night. No need to let her eyes adjust to the darkness. The whole campground might as well have been floodlit. She slung the towel over her shoulder and, even though she could have seen a bear coming at thirty yards, popped the safety off the bear spray, holding it at the ready as she headed back to Caleb's tent and the first sex she'd had in . . . she decided not to do that particular calculation. Once she'd finished that damn book, the frequency of her lovemaking with Joe had declined precipitously. At the time, he'd seemed as grateful as she to end each night in the blue glow of the phones that fell from their hands as they clicked their way toward chaste sleep. *Joe.* She brandished the bear spray as though to clear him from her brain, returning her thoughts pleasurably to Caleb. Because, after everything she'd been through, a little uncomplicated fun seemed in order.

What would he be like? Slow, if that initial hug, the lingering kiss were any indication. Slow was good. In keeping with that thought, she took the long way back, continuing along the far side of the loop, letting the anticipation build. The day's warmth lingered and the night air was soft on her arms. A rush of love for the forest enveloped her, its casual magnificence, its utter indifference to her presence. All the outdoors adventures in her previous life had been done in groups, someone or other always nattering on, explaining the ecological importance of what they were seeing but never shutting up and letting them simply *be* within it, feeling its quiet power.

Caleb got it. That much she knew. And if he understood the forest so well, what else might he intuit? She picked up the pace.

She rounded a corner almost at a trot and stopped so abruptly she almost lost her balance.

She ducked behind a tree. Peeped around it.

Squeezed her eyes shut. Opened them again.

There before her, firelight flickering on her silvery sides, was Electra.

Even without the big black pickup still hitched to the trailer, Nora knew it for Electra.

The fire leapt high, briefly revealing the aircraft painted above the wheel, removing any doubt.

Nora grasped the tree to keep from falling. Of all the places she and Caleb had looked that day, it had never occurred to either of them someone might simply have towed Electra to a different campsite, assuming – correctly – that with the campground closed, no one would think to search there.

'Sonofabitch.' It was a slick move. She peeled her gaze away from Electra just long enough to note the other vehicle at the far edge of the site, one she'd half-expected even before she noticed it, a black blocky outline against the fragmented darkness of the trees.

Miranda's camper.

Nora crept closer, cursing under her breath, a new curse for each silent step. Oh, they'd played her like the proverbial fiddle, those two. And now Miranda was partying it up with Nora's husband in Nora's trailer, just hours after Miranda had learned of her own husband's death.

She remembered how Miranda had urged her to explore her camper, how the woman had been busy with her phone when she emerged. Probably letting Joe know she'd be luring Nora away for a bit, so that he could steal Electra.

A pounding bass line thumped louder the closer she got. Light shone diffuse from the curtained windows. Miranda's laughter rang out above the music, raucous, drunken. Laughing at her, no doubt, about how easily they'd fooled her. Nora moved closer still, to the edge of the campsite, then to the picnic table. A few steps closer and she'd be able to touch Electra, stroke her shining flanks, reassure her that everything would be all right.

Shadows passed across the window, the curtain reducing those within to silhouettes, a man and woman, their outlines separate, dancing with arms above their heads, now melding for a long kiss. They weren't fucking – yet – but somehow this was even worse than when she'd caught Joe and Charlotte.

'You bastards! You absolute rat bastards!'

She didn't realize she'd spoken aloud until the music cut off. Miranda's voice rang into the silence.

'The fuck was that?'

A male mumble, low, unintelligible.

'No, really. I thought I heard something. Maybe that bear is back. Oh, wait. I forgot there is no bear!' More laughter, both of them this time. Then another long kiss and a sound that sounded like a slap to Miranda's round little – and, from the sharp sound of it – bare bottom.

Nora muffled the resulting curse but couldn't prevent a groan from escaping.

'There it is again!' They cut the lights.

Nora shrank back. Belatedly held her breath.

'Where's the gun?'

Oh, *shit*.

The trailer door opened.

Nora ran.

She'd hoped to make a quick escape, get back to the campsite, just enough time to call the sheriff. No way could he ignore this one.

Heavy footsteps behind her mandated a more immediate concern. She needed to get back to Caleb *alive*. Because apparently, sometime in the last few days, Joe had acquired a gun. Should she hide behind a tree, zap him with the bear spray as he passed? No. What if she missed? And he didn't?

She glanced over her shoulder, hoping to catch a glimpse of her pursuer. A mistake. A rut sent her sprawling, the bear spray flying from her hand, off into the darkness. She scrambled to her feet and ran empty-handed, her only defense gone.

The footsteps gained on her, the rigors of the past few days dragging at her body, her own strides heavy, uneven.

At least she knew her way around the campground. That was one advantage she had over Joe. All she had to do was make it back to the campsite and . . . what? She'd have to scream, somehow warn Caleb. Pain flashed through her feet, cuts scabbed and healing breaking open afresh as she headed down the hard-packed dirt loop. Agony raked her side. Never mind, never mind. She should be there any second. She gulped a lungful of air, preparing a mighty scream.

It fizzled at the sight of the broken stump. The sound of the creek.

In her panic, she'd gone the wrong way, instinctively running back to her old campsite. Caleb was an entire loop away.

She was all alone with her pursuer.

She darted behind the big pine and held her breath, thinking of her plan to zap him with the bear spray, seemingly so crazy moments before. Now it felt like a genius move. Because bear spray would have been better than no weapon at all – which was what she had now.

The footsteps slowed, her pursuer so close she could hear his ragged breathing. Good. So he'd gone slack, too. But he was still taller, heavier, stronger. And, given the condition of her feet, far faster.

She turned away from him, flattening her back against the rough bark, closing her eyes, clamping her mouth shut against another damning whimper. See no evil, speak no evil, and she couldn't hear a damn thing over the slamming of her heart. Shame there wasn't a way to think no evil.

Because her thoughts were laser-focused on evil, specifically, the sort of evil that might be perpetrated upon her already battered body by a vengeful ex-husband who'd just realized she'd discovered his little scheme.

She pressed her hands tighter over her ears, to no avail. She could still hear his footsteps, blessedly fading away. She let out a long breath. How long should she wait before she dared move?

He knew she was here now. He could get in the truck and go looking for her. If that happened, he might shoot first and ask questions later. Was Joe capable of that? Did she want to find out? She had to get back to Caleb. They could drive like hell for town, calling the sheriff on the way.

She sucked in her breath again and listened hard, straining past the sound of her heart, the blood roaring in her ears. Nothing.

She'd have to keep to the shadows at the edge of the road, where the footing was more treacherous. But she couldn't risk being seen. She wondered if Joe was already back at the trailer, unhitching the truck, gun in hand, now fully immersed in the macho persona he'd adopted when he bought the pickup. A predator, like the grizzly who'd been – falsely, she was now certain – blamed for Brad's disappearance. And she was his prey.

She took a tentative step. Then another. The twig cracked beneath her foot on the third.

The low laugh sounded only a few yards away, followed by words she barely heard over the fear roaring in her ears.

'Got you now.'

She spun back to the tree, wrapping her arms around it, as though its solid bulk could somehow protect her. She had a vision of herself and Joe going round and round, the tree always between them, him trying to get a shot. If she screamed, would Caleb hear her? Could he get to her in time?

She sidled a step to the left, then another. Stubbed her toe on something sharp and metallic.

'Ow.'

It didn't matter if he heard her now. In fact . . .

She reached down, verifying her first reaction. Almost smiled.

'Got *you* now,' she called into the clearing.

Spread her feet apart. Bent at the knees, bouncing a little to set her balance. Apologized to her sprained wrist that was probably going to end up sprained all over again. Opened her mouth in a mighty shriek as she raised her arms high.

He came at her at a run, spewing curses, at the last minute his eyes shining wide and white in the moonlight as he beheld the ax swinging down upon him in a single, vicious chop.

THIRTY-FOUR

Nora Best didn't kill her husband.
'Holy shit. It's Brad.'
She whirled.

Forever stood panting behind her, for once minus her heavy backpack.

'Heard a ruckus. Saw the trailer had been moved and figured something bad was up. But I never thought . . .' She gazed at the bloodied man writhing before them, his left shoulder and arm lying half-severed from his torso.

His thin screams rose around them. 'My arm! My arm! You've killed me.'

'No, she hasn't,' Forever pointed out. 'Just listen to yourself.'

Blood rushed from the gash in a steady stream. Nora turned away, gagging, but Forever called her attention to it.

'Somehow you missed an artery. Amazing. If you'd clipped one, it'd be spurting halfway across the campsite and he'd be dead in a few more minutes.'

Nora leaned hard on the ax, afraid she'd fall if she let it go. Blood, black in the moonlight, slid from the blade, darkening the earth around it. 'That's good, right?'

Forever shrugged. 'Depends on whether you want him to live to testify against you. Might have been better for all concerned if he'd bled out. Want me to finish the job?' She drew the knife from her belt. It glinted in the moonlight, deadly, seductive.

'Jesus, no!'

'You sure? You honestly think you're going to get a fair shake from that sheriff?'

The mutter of an engine interrupted their conversation. Headlights swept the campsite, spotlighting Nora clutching the dripping ax, newly upraised, Forever with the knife held low and loose, ready for the upward slash that would cut through to viscera as it burrowed beneath the ribs to the heart.

Caleb cut the engine and stepped from the cab with hands held high.

'It's me. It's just me. What the hell happened here? Nora, are you all right? Please tell me you're all right.'

Forever sheathed the knife.

Nora dropped the ax.

Caleb stopped a few feet away and lowered his arms. Her move. Her choice.

She nodded.

He closed the distance and wrapped her in a hug, whispering soft words against her ear, lifting his head only to speak briefly to Forever.

'Call 9-1-1. Get the sheriff up here. And tell them to send an ambo. Tell him I don't know who the hell he found in the woods, but it wasn't Brad. Tell him Brad's very much alive, although maybe not for much longer. That'll get his ass up here. And you,' he said to Nora, shuddering in his arms, 'you're alive, too. You didn't need Forever, you didn't need me. You saved your own life.'

Miranda, that wily survivor, had hauled ass with the camper as soon as Brad ran into the night after Nora.

A deputy found the camper at the truck stop on the outskirts of Blackbird, sans Miranda, who presumably was already hundreds of miles away, perched high in the cab of some semi beside a very satisfied – for the moment – trucker.

'Wait until he wakes up with his throat cut. A shame for him that Brad took the gun. I'd rather be shot.' Caleb had pulled a chair close to the sofa in the cabin, where Nora lay beneath two patchwork quilts, soft and faded with age. 'My grandmother made these,' he said as he folded them around her. She propped herself up on the pillows and took the mug he offered her. Steam curled from it, sinuously wrapping her face in fragrance. Familiar, but . . .?

'What kind of tea is this?' She bent her head to it, but it was still too hot to drink.

'Lipton. I may have dosed it with bourbon. Old family remedy.'

'Quilts and bourbon. You must have quite a family.'

'I do.' His face softened, and Nora thought of how, despite his love for the forest, he kept a place in town for the days he had custody of Abby and drove there on the others to eat at the café where she worked. She'd managed a single text to her own mother – 'I'm fine. And I'm so sorry. I'm just not ready to talk yet. But soon.' – and thought that if there were a special place in hell for bad daughters, a reservation awaited her.

'Warm enough?' He stepped away to tend the fire snapping briskly in the grate framed with river stones.

'Finally.' It was July, but she was freezing; hadn't been able to get warm enough since he'd plucked her from the forest floor and driven her to the clinic himself, daring the sheriff with a few choice words to interfere.

He resumed his place beside her and took her hand, probing gently at the wrist. 'Hurt?'

'Some. I thought I'd wreck it again, swinging that ax, but I guess the other wrist took the brunt of it. It's sore, but not sprained.' She held up her other hand, turning it this way and that, staring at it in amazement, both awed and horrified at what it had done.

'You really whacked the hell out of him. He's lucky he's not dead. I guess you hit him right on the joint between the clavicle and arm bone and carved his arm away just like a turkey leg. Missed the artery by about a millimeter. Good thing I'd sharpened up that ax. I hear he's quite the curiosity down at that hospital in Denver. They're waiting to see if everything works after they sewed his arm and torso back together. He'll be a real attraction in prison.'

Maybe Brad had been half-mad from the pain. Or maybe deputies had talked with him later, when the painkillers had kicked him into drowsy delirium. Or maybe he hoped to get off easy by putting all the blame on Miranda.

Whatever the reason, he'd babbled away about the whole scheme. He and Miranda were indeed unemployed, at least in the traditional sense that neither had held down a straight-world job in more or less forever, each of them trading on their looks, turning tricks, either for cash outright or, in Brad's case, skillfully fleecing moneyed older women – or men.

At this, Nora winced, recalling his familiarity the night

they'd met. He must have taken in the cowboy Cadillac and the Airstream and picked her as his next mark.

'Why'd she kill them? The truckers, I mean? Those guys must get robbed by hookers all the time without getting killed.'

'Brad said she only shot the guys who got rough. You know, taking that whole she-asked-for-it business and turning it on its head.'

'I thought she cut their throats.' She imagined Miranda like Forever with her knife, except sawing through a tracheal tube rather than a tree branch.

'I guess some were shot, too. Cops are still working it all out. Anyway, despite leaving a trail of bodies, she seems to have been the brains of the operation,' Caleb said. 'It was her idea to stay in the area after she killed the trucker in Blackbird. She figured, rightly, cops would look at the pattern and start patrolling truck stops up in Montana. And Brad got caught on a surveillance tape robbing a convenience store outside Albuquerque when the cops were tied up with the murder at the truck stop there. They needed to lie low for a while. Somewhere along the line, they'd bought one of those fly-by-night life insurance policies. If they could pass Brad off as eaten by a bear, they could cash in on that. But then you came along in your trailer and Miranda got greedy. She wanted to pin it all on you. He says they drugged your whiskey that first night to make sure you wouldn't see him leaving the campsite. And then the deal got even sweeter when you gave her a golden opportunity to offer to "buy" the trailer.'

Nora let go of his hand to pull the quilts to her chin. They'd wanted to keep her overnight at the clinic in Blackbird, but she refused, having had enough of bright lights, sterile surroundings, and endless questions. The sheriff, perhaps fearing exactly the sort of fury she'd expressed over her earlier treatment, had sat stoic through her recitation.

'All of this could have been avoided if you'd just taken me seriously,' she'd told him as the nurse peeled away the tape holding the IV line to her skin, withdrew the needle, swabbed the spot yet again and pasted a Band-Aid across it. The back of her hand was starting to resemble a pincushion, what with the repeated IV insertions.

Nora watched the sheriff trying to impose an expression of contrition over the resentment that hardened his features as he reassured her that the previous charges against her would be dropped and that he couldn't imagine, under the circumstances, any being filed for nearly chopping a man in two.

'Lucky for you, he had a gun. He raised it, right? Pointed it at you?'

Surely they could tell that the ax had fallen across the back of his shoulder?

'It was dark,' she ventured.

He gave the smallest shake of his head. A long look passed between them, an unspoken bargain on the table. You save my ass, I'll save yours.

'But luckily there was a full moon. It let me see everything.' She spoke slowly, as if recalling the moment, giving herself time to think. Falling back on all those years on the job uttering phrases calculated to mean nothing at all. '"I've got you now," he said. I figured I was dead.' Quid pro . . .

He nodded and closed his notebook. 'That's what I thought. It's was self-defense. You had no choice.'

Quo.

THIRTY-FIVE

Caleb offered her the bed but Nora preferred the couch, an unspoken way of emphasizing her time in his cabin was temporary.

She slept and slept and slept. The clinic had supplied her with the sort of medications she figured that, had she been anything like Miranda, she could have sold on the street and funded a few weeks on the road. But she hadn't needed them. She'd wake, creep to the bathroom and back to the couch, and lie in a half-sleep, sometimes hearing Caleb moving about the cabin, a shadowy comforting presence. She'd close her eyes when he entered the room to tend the fire, or place things on the coffee table he'd pulled close to the couch. An insulated mug of coffee. Another of a strong, fragrant beef broth that sent strength into her extremities despite herself. Once, a silky banana pudding, so reminiscent of childhood that she nearly wept.

Sometimes he simply sat beside her, either in silence or talking so softly she barely heard him, whether to her or to himself she was never sure. He'd speak of his day in the woods, the things he'd seen, an otter twisting sinuously down the creek, riding the wavelets like the pro it was. Lichens of startling hues and patterns. A lynx that leapt to the top of a tall boulder at his approach, then crouched, flattening tufted ears against its head and hissing at him like a housecat.

Or he talked of the case, how law enforcement was slowly fitting the pieces together. He predicted a plea agreement for Brad 'if he's smart, although I'm not convinced of that'. As for Miranda – whenever he spoke of her, his voice would drop so low, with such an edge of ferocity, that she tried to tune him out. Easier to let herself be pulled back down into the blackness than contemplate what that woman had almost done to her.

Her phone, plugged into a charger, also sat on the coffee
table and at night when the house was silent but for the crackle
of the low fire and Caleb's soft deep breathing audible through
the open bedroom door, she'd steel herself for whatever
indignity it might deliver next.

Because the long email from Artie had been a real
treat.

'I know you,' it read. 'And I know that despite yourself,
you'll feel bad about what happened to Joe. Don't. I didn't
want to tell you this earlier, but it's out on the internet now.
Before you two came up with this cockamamie plan to roam
the country, Joe was about to lose his job.'

She nearly dropped the phone at that. She fumbled with it,
holding it close to her face.

'It was either that or face a lawsuit. One of the paralegals
accused him of harassment. More than one. I guess it had
been happening for a while. But with this whole #MeToo
thing, they got together and compared notes. They formed a
secret Facebook Group: Joe and His Johnson. I guess there
are photos. Your husband was quite the texter.'

Nora no longer saw the words on the screen. She heard
Joe's voice as he pulled her close, whispering, 'Come on,
babe, let's hit the road. Just you and me. Leave all these
committees and meetings and obligations and crazy fifty-hour
weeks behind. We never have time for each other anymore.
You can write one of your books. It'll be romantic.' *And I can
get out from under a lawsuit.* Funny how he'd left that part
out.

She'd thought the image of Joe moaning against Charlotte
was bad. Now others arose: Joe with Jenny-April-Keisha – she
couldn't remember all the paralegals she'd waved hello to on
her visits to Joe's office. Joe's Johnson in all sorts of places
it didn't belong.

She pressed her fingers to her temples. Blood throbbed
hot beneath her skin. Apparently, it was impossible to die of
shame.

She couldn't help herself. Typed 'Joe's Johnson' into her
phone. The secret Facebook group was secret no more. The
public had latched onto the site with glee. 'Shame she didn't

chop off his Johnson with her ax before she went after that other guy.' Hilarious.

Did it mitigate the news the sheriff had delivered the morning after she'd nearly chopped Brad in two?

He'd driven all the way up to the cabin and bent beside the sofa, Caleb hovering close beside him.

'Nora. Nora. Ms Best.'

She slitted her eyes.

'We regret to inform you . . .'

No, he didn't say that. But something like it, coughing up some hackneyed phrases, a rush of words from which even her fogged brain extracted the fact that despite the obvious evidence that carnivores had feasted upon the body, none had swallowed the bullet that had taken Joe's life.

'Mrs Gardner, when we find her, will be facing a homicide charge. Or at least an accessory to homicide, if it turns out Mr Gardner shot your husband. We'll charge him with your kidnapping, of course. As for her, there'll be more than one homicide charge, if we can link those truckers' deaths to her. They're a little more problematic. Lots of different agencies involved, and we're having trouble placing the Gardners at all the locations. It'll take us awhile, but we'll get to the bottom of this. Don't you worry.' That last sounded almost sincere.

But she wasn't worried. She just wanted him to go away, so that she could fall back asleep. She rolled over and turned her back to him, burrowing her face against the couch cushions.

A hand fell upon her shoulder, gentle, warm. Caleb, then.

'Nora. There's one more thing.'

She turned over.

'We need an identification.'

She'd have to rise. Shower. Dress. Endure a ride to town. Gaze upon the unspeakable remains. She forced the words in a raspy, stranger's voice. 'No. I can't.' She closed her eyes.

'You don't need to go anywhere.' The sheriff again. 'Just . . . is this your husband's? We found it with the, ah, at the site. Your initials are on it. And his. But we have to be sure.'

She cracked her eyelids again. The object in his hand caught the knife-edge of sunlight slicing through a gap in the curtained windows on either side of the fireplace, the infinity sign engraved into the ring glowing a false promise.

'Yes.' The voice again, words nearly inaudible. 'That's Joe's wedding ring.'

THIRTY-SIX

She couldn't stay on the sofa forever.

Caleb walked in one morning, not his usual tiptoe, but a vigorous stride. He shoved the curtains aside, yanked the quilts away, and held a mug of coffee just out of reach.

'Hey!'

He waved the mug, filling her nostrils with the scent, then pulled it back so fast he nearly spilled it. 'Up. It's time.'

'But I don't want to.' She did, however, want that coffee. She wanted it very badly. She held out a hand.

'Nice try. Halfsies doesn't count.'

She sat all the way up and placed her feet on the floor. Her head spun. 'Give it to me. I really need it.'

'And you'll get it. All you have to do is stand.'

'Are you kidding me?'

He held the cup out, the aroma so strong she could almost taste it. Almost.

She stood, advancing upon him step by step as he backed away, not handing the mug over until they stood before the bathroom door.

'Nora. There's no way to say this nicely. You stink. As in, you really reek. I've come across skunks that smell better than you do right now. There's a shower in there. Soap. Towels.'

Nora swallowed the coffee in a few gulps and handed the mug back.

'Shut up. I get the picture. Just bring me more of this.'

Something almost as good as coffee awaited.

She stood beneath the shower until the water ran cold and her skin glowed red from scrubbing, then toweled herself half-dry and hurried into clean clothes – he must have persuaded the sheriff to let him retrieve them from Electra – drawn as relentlessly as a ravenous grizzly toward the scent of bacon.

The cooked kind, sizzling toward crispness in a pan, not cold and slimy, rubbed over her naked body.

Caleb didn't comment on her improved appearance, nor her newly fragrant self, and let her eat in silence, slathering sourdough toast with butter and thick huckleberry jam and replenishing each slice on her plate as soon as she'd finished the one before.

'Leave the dishes,' he said when she was done. 'There's somewhere we need to be.'

Another trip to the sheriff, she figured. No wonder he'd lavished such a breakfast upon her. His attempt at casual conversation once they were in the truck furthered the impression.

'They haven't found Miranda. They keep getting sightings, but she's managed to stay one step ahead of them. On the plus side, she hasn't killed anybody else yet. Can't believe she tried to pin the whole thing on Forever. Like she's capable of killing anyone.'

Nora squirmed in her seat, studying the pine trees flashing past, stripes of light, dark, light, dark. She'd been the one who'd floated the idea of Forever as a suspect. She remembered how eagerly Miranda had latched onto the idea – but she also remembered the way Forever had stood over Brad's bloodied body, the knife balanced easily in her hand, offering to finish the job as casually as she might have suggested dispatching a lobster before dropping it into the pot, placing the tip of her knife beneath its eyes. The abrupt shove, the lobster going motionless before the splash.

'Where is she now, anyway? Forever, not Miranda.'

She'd thought maybe Forever would drop by the cabin while she was ensconced upon the sofa, lower herself cross-legged onto the coffee table, pull some magical healing potion out of her backpack that would make her forget everything that had happened since she'd clumsily steered the truck and trailer into the campground.

The campground into which Caleb was now turning his own truck. She turned to him in surprise.

'They'll open it again in few more days,' he said as he swerved around the chain and took the far loop. 'The contractor will want to find new campground hosts, maybe more than one couple. This place is bound to be overrun once we open it again. I thought maybe I'd ask Forever, although it didn't seem her style. But she's been gone for days now. Probably moved on.'

He slid a glance her way. 'Be good to have someone who could walk right into the job already familiar with the campground. Free campsite, of course, and a monthly stipend. Not much, but enough for groceries and an occasional dinner at the Buckhorn. Oh, and the cool uniform.' He laughed, trying to lighten the import of an offer that, if she accepted, would define the next several months of her life.

She sat in stunned silence, wanting to acknowledge the generosity of his suggestion, blurting practicality instead. 'That'd be fine if I still had Electra. But the sheriff hasn't released her. I guess she's evidence. And I suppose I've still got enough money in my bank account for a tent, but I can't imagine spending an entire summer in one.'

His knuckles whitened on the wheel. 'About that.'

The broken stump stood by the roadside, heralding the turnoff into her old site. He stopped the truck a few yards away and cut the engine.

'How do you feel about going back to where it happened?'

How did she feel?

About being in the same place where the footsteps had pounded loud behind her? Where an exultant chuckle, the words 'Got you now' were meant to be the last she ever heard before Brad put a bullet in her brain? Where the arc of the swinging ax pulled her arms forward and down? The slight hitch as the ax found its mark, then sank in?

She stared at the stump. That night, it had loomed inky and ominous. Now, in the sun's noonday glare, it looked like . . . a stump. A hunk of dead wood. Beyond it, out of site, lay the clearing. The big pine. The creek.

She drew a quivering breath. 'We can go in.'

He started the truck but didn't put it in gear.

'I checked with the sheriff this morning. They've removed any evidence they need from the trailer. What do you call it?'

Her throat tightened. She wanted to tell him to turn around, drive to town, to whatever impoundment lot where Electra sat, surrounded by lesser vehicles; wrecks, no doubt, or flashy SUVs seized in drug raids. Rescue her.

'Electra,' she managed to get out.

He touched his foot to the gas. The truck rolled forward.

The clearing came into view, the trailer gleaming within.

'Electra is all yours again.'

He was good enough to leave her alone with Electra.

She hovered on the steps until he drove away with the silent hand-to-ear signal to call him when she was ready.

She opened the door.

The smell hit her first, cigarettes and weed and the yeasty reek of spilled beer.

She recalled the night she'd seen Miranda and Brad – still thinking it was Joe – whooping it up in Electra, music thumping, Electra rocking from the force of their stomping dance steps in the few feet of space between the dinette and the bedroom.

'Poor baby,' she murmured as she stepped into the chaos of emptied drawers and cupboards, overturned cushions, clothing tossed carelessly everywhere. Maybe by Brad and Miranda in their revelry, maybe by the sheriff and his deputies, looking for evidence, whatever it might be.

She permitted herself a moment's fury. Then located the rubber gloves, the sponges and rags and paper towels, the cleaning products, the trash bags. She set her phone on the counter, and clicked to a music app – not the blasting crap that had so entertained Brad and Miranda, but something slow and bluesy, music that both acknowledged rage and shrugged it away because what else could you do but keep moving forward?

For the first time since the sheriff had confirmed what she'd suspected about Joe's fate, she let herself think about him. She wondered if Brad had subjected him to the same treatment, marching him through the woods at gunpoint, setting up his death as easily explainable by the savage environment of the forest, where creatures ate one another every day and humans most definitely were not at the top of the food chain.

But this time, Brad hadn't left anything to chance, relying on a maybe-conditioned bear. Because that was Caleb's theory. 'I remember, the first time I stopped by your campsite and you made me that kickass coffee, you said something about the grease spot on the picnic table,' he mused one night in the chair beside the sofa. 'No way to prove this, but I think Brad was leaving food around the campground, training that bear to come by. That way, Miranda's story about him getting dragged off by a bad bear would make sense. Same goes for you. I get why the sheriff didn't believe you when you said he'd smeared you with bacon – it sounds insane even now – but when you look at it that way, it makes perfect sense. If you didn't freeze to death, the bear was sure to find you before you found your way back to the campground.

'But with Joe, he couldn't afford to take any chances. Probably thought the bear would eat whatever part of him had the bullet. Good thing for all concerned he shot Joe in the head.'

Good thing for everyone but Joe. For his sake, she was glad it was a bullet rather than a bear. He'd inflicted so much pain upon her, but at least hers was of the mental variety, the kind you could recover from – she hoped. There was no recovering from a bullet to the frontal lobe. She'd raged at Joe, contemplated taking him back, and hated him – and herself – even more because of it. She'd wished him dead, or thought she had. And now?

'You're going to feel guilty about this,' Caleb had whispered one night as she lay motionless on the sofa. 'Don't.'

But she did, guilt settling on her shoulders like the quilts he'd folded around her with such care. She suspected, as she attacked the mess in the trailer, it would be her companion for a good long time. Even though it had belatedly occurred to her that it was never Joe she wanted back. It was her marriage, the reliable security implied by the ring on her finger. As though that had been a guarantee. As though anything in life were guaranteed.

BB King's voice cut through to her consciousness, a nudge as pointed as any of the midnight messages Caleb had tried to impart, the bluesman uncharacteristically upbeat in a jaunty swinging tune about moving on.

She almost laughed, swiping the cloth across surfaces in rhythm to the music, hips swaying, occasionally singing a snatch of remembered lyrics. She swept and mopped the floor, bagged foodstuffs that had broken open and put the rest back in the cupboard. Clothes went into a separate trash bag, to be taken to the laundromat in town and washed. The idea of the sheriff's plump, sweating hands pawing through her underwear made her think maybe she'd run everything through the washer twice.

She turned to the bathroom, and nearly backed right out again. The mirror was covered with smeary red lip prints. She imagined Miranda kissing her own image, pumped up with pride for having gotten the trailer to herself. God! A thought occurred to her. What if Miranda and Brad had celebrated by . . .

She straightened and rushed to the bedroom, tearing the sheets from the mattress in violent disgust. These, she'd wash three times. Just in case. Clean sheets sat miraculously undisturbed in a shallow drawer beneath the bed. Just in case, she flipped the mattress, then fitted the new sheets around it.

Back in the bathroom, she rubbed hard at the bespoiled mirror, erasing even the faintest outlines of Miranda's pouty little mouth. Her own face came into focus. Her hand dropped to her side, the paper towel fluttering to the floor. Unavoidably gray streaks glinted in her hair, which fell straight to her shoulders, with none of the product- and blowdried-poof she worked into it each morning. She gathered it up in one hand twisting it away from her face, wondering how it would look short. For certain, it would save her a lot of time in the morning. And if she cut away the blonde-tinted length, the gray – a good, silvery gray, she noted with some relief, not the dull kind that just made people look tired – would seem purposeful, even edgy. A defiant, take-me-as-I-am style. But her face. The bruising had finally subsided to shadows mimicking exhaustion rather than a violent attack. But at their worst they'd drawn attention away from the crow's feet fanning ever deeper, the triplicate lines scoring her forehead more emphatically, and there was no way to pass off the creases at either side of her mouth as dimples. She sighed and popped open the vanity drawer, extracting moisturizer, concealer, foundation, blush, eyeliner, eyeshadow, eyebrow pencil, dropping them with a clatter on the edge of the little sink, nearly obliterating its surface.

So much for take me as I am, she thought. Then thought again. Retrieved the trash bag. Swept the whole lot into it. After a moment she reached in, rescued the moisturizer, then knotted the bag against further temptation, gathered it up with all the others and jogged down the road toward the heavy steel trash cans that claimed to be bearproof, and tossed them in. No changing her mind now.

Electra was clean, but woefully empty of food. The truck sat waiting. Caleb had even unhitched it from Electra so it would be easy for her to hop in, drive to town. Maybe she'd run into him at the Buckhorn again. Or, maybe . . . a slow smile crossed her face.

She found her phone, tapped his number.

'Any chance you want to come by for dinner?' She opened a cupboard and considered the lone box of pasta that had survived. 'And, uh, could you please bring some of that sauce with you?'

THIRTY-SEVEN

Whatever other substances they'd consumed during their short time in Electra, at least Miranda and Brad had rejected the wine.

Nora had a bottle of Barolo open and breathing by the time Caleb arrived, a bit of overkill for the casual meal they'd planned, but she had a new appreciation for that eat-drink-and-be-merry saying.

'We're drinking the good stuff tonight,' she said as he handed her a Tupperware container of the sauce, still warm. She poured him a glass of wine and another for herself. They clinked.

'What are we drinking to?'

BB King's lyrics hummed in her head. 'To movin' on.'

The anticipatory smile faded from his face. 'You're leaving?'

'No. I mean, yes. At some point, sure. I guess.'

She realized she hadn't thought about it; that the need to foresee all the possibilities and to plan and prepare accordingly that had driven so much of her life had vanished, fallen away like a burden whose weight she'd taken for granted until it was gone, leaving her lighter, freer. Because who could have foreseen all the things that had happened since she'd nearly walked into that bathroom in the Denver house? And how could she possibly have planned for it? Yet she'd come out on the other side, thinking only as far ahead as cleaning Electra, inviting Caleb in, enjoying a meal together and . . . She raised her glass again.

'I meant movin' on – as in, to whatever comes next.'

They took their meal outdoors and ate under the stars. Caleb built a fire while the pasta cooked and afterward they sat by it as they had before, chairs pulled close together so that he could take her hand.

'How long does it take?' she asked without elaborating, counting on him to understand.

His hand tightened around hers.

'A minute. Forever.'

He lifted the bottle. She nodded, and the wine gurgled into their glasses. 'I don't want to liken my situation to yours. Diane and I have had years to get past all the pain and work out the way to a place of . . . let's say, cordiality. Of course, Abby is a powerful incentive. With Joe dead, you're never going to get that chance. On the other hand, under the circumstances, you might never have gotten to that place anyway. Might never have needed to.'

He turned to her, half his face in firelight, half in shadow. 'When Diane and I split, there was this huge sense of relief. Took me months, years, to figure out I was grieving, too. If I can offer any advice, it's this: let yourself feel it. But don't get stuck in it.'

She lifted his hand to her lips. 'I don't intend to.'

She dropped his hand, rose, and walked into the trailer. She left the door open.

She'd been right about him.

He took things slow, from undressing her and then himself, to spending long moments looking at her while his fingers traced the length of her body with the barest butterfly touch. She'd left on the tabletop light with its red shade and in its warm glow she saw his eyes were open, looking hard into hers when their bodies joined and she looked back and held his gaze until the last unbearable moment.

Later he laughed and she raised up on one elbow and demanded to know what was so funny.

'I was just thinking how whenever I see one of these fancy trailers, I wonder why anyone would go through the trouble and expense when a tent is just as good. But you know what? This is so much better than getting tangled up in a couple of sleeping bags. I could get used to this.'

His words hung there, full of possibility that she could either accept or reject.

Neither of which she was inclined to do.

So she chose deflection, burying her hands in his hair, even more disheveled than usual after their tumble, pulling him to

her, murmuring, 'You mean like this? Would this have been
hard to do in a sleeping bag?'

A refrain she repeated at intervals throughout the night as
they slept and woke and loved and slept again until she nudged
him saying, 'What about this? Do you think we could manage
this in a tent?'

Until Electra's interior gleamed rosy with the light of dawn
and he fell back onto the mattress, hands raised in surrender.

'You win! Everything is better in here. But –' his smile was
sly – 'we should try the tent, too. You know, just to be sure.'

'Mmmm,' she murmured, noncommittal and, in the next
second, sound asleep.

She awoke to the smell of coffee and opened her eyes to
the sight of the Thermos on the wall-mounted nightstand across
an empty expanse of bed.

Regret and relief did brief battle. Relief won out. Sometimes
the morning after was better savored alone, languidly stretching
muscles newly relaxed, mind wandering through a highlights
reel of the previous hours.

She took her sweet time getting out of bed, showering and
dressing, making breakfast of the coffee and an apple that had
survived, glancing occasionally at the note Caleb had left
propped on the dinette. Simply: 'See you at the Buckhorn
tonight?'

He'd played it perfectly, letting her know he wanted to see
her, the question mark leaving it up to her, freeing her from
expectation. Would she go? She answered herself aloud.

'Maybe.'

The word echoed around the trailer. Other than the tousled
bed, Electra was shipshape and ready to go – if that's what
she decided. She could hitch her to the truck, tow her to the
hosts' campsite and settle in, delaying decisions for an entire
summer. Because so many awaited. There were arrangements
to be made regarding Joe's body. Finances – whatever was
left of them – to be untangled. Her agent, at long last, to be
dealt with. And, dear God, her mother.

Caleb had made the morning coffee with the cone she used
in emergencies. It sat drying in the dish rack that fit atop the

sink. She put it away and retrieved the stovetop espresso pot and topped off the Thermos with a jolt of the strength she'd need for the too-long-delayed tasks ahead.

Thermos in one hand, tablet in the other, phone in her pocket, she headed for the flat creekside rock that somehow managed to be – barely – within cell range and gave herself a final moment's peace before tackling the unfinished business of her previous life.

'Forever?' she called out.

Just in case, not expecting an answer, but still hoping the woman would appear, as she was wont to do at moments when Nora needed help most. The creek chortled a mocking reply as it sped past. A squirrel scurried higher in a tree above, tail twitching in agitation at the disturbance. 'Forget it,' the wind sighed.

Once again, she was on her own. But this time, her life wasn't at stake.

'No big deal,' she said to the squirrel. 'Just financial ruin.' If she took the campground host job, she might be able to postpone things until summer was over, but sooner rather than later she'd have to sell the truck. And Electra.

Stupid to cry over things, she told herself some moments later, when her tears subsided. She was alive. That was supposed to cancel everything else out. But to have gotten Electra back, and then face the possibility – no, the necessity – of losing her again, this time the tears came harder and lasted longer.

It was better, really, that Forever was nowhere around. Nora wasn't sure she'd ever heard Forever laugh, but she could just imagine the reaction from a woman who carried all of her possessions in a pack on her back. Nora, who only twenty-four hours earlier had assured Caleb she couldn't stomach a few weeks in a tent, tried to imagine spending every single night in one, no matter the weather.

'Not an option,' she told the squirrel, swiping the back of her hand across her face.

She'd have to figure out a way to manage, beyond just selling the truck and trailer. The ring, she thought. Her engagement ring. Maybe she could sell it, combine the money with whatever she got for the truck and trailer, and use it to pay back her book advance with maybe a little left over to live on. Maybe she could finagle a deal from Lilith, something involving paying back part of the advance and then following up with monthly installments, almost certainly more than a campground host's stipend. She'd have to find a new job, somewhere where her newfound notoriety as suspected (though absolved) husband kidnapper wouldn't get in the way. Which left out her old field of public relations. You never wanted the messenger to garner more attention than the client.

As for her nascent writing career – best to get that over with, too.

She took a breath, scrolled through the numbers on her phone, tapped Lilith's and held the phone far from her head in anticipation.

Lilith delivered as expected.

'Nora? What the ever-loving fuck?'

That was for starters, delivered at a volume that shut up even the squirrel. Nora lay the phone on the rock and backed away until Lilith ran down. She approached cautiously, palming the phone.

'I'm so sorry,' she whispered into it.

'Are you freaking kidding me?'

Back onto the rock went the phone, Nora nearly toppling into the creek in her haste to escape continued condemnation. She teetered, grabbing at the whippy willow branches for support, as Lilith's next words screeched from the phone.

'How soon can you deliver a manuscript?'

'*What?*' she called from across the rock. She crawled back to the phone and picked it up. 'What did you just say?'

Lilith, as she put it 'didn't give two farts in a headwind' about her initial book proposal. 'But woman scorned! Suspected of murder!'

'Just kidnapping,' Nora tried to interject.

But Lilith was on a roll. 'Naked in the woods! And nearly chopping a man in two!' Dollar signs underlay every word.

'Just his arm. And they reattached it . . .'

'I don't suppose,' Lilith mused, 'there's a sexy detective somewhere in this. Maybe a little dalliance to liven things up?'

Heat crept up Nora's face. 'Because suspected of murder, naked in the woods, arm-chopping isn't lively enough?' But it was impossible to get the best of Lilith.

'If you haven't gotten yourself laid already, go out and get some,' Lilith ordered. 'Take notes. Oh, and forget about wandering around the country. Save that shit for later. Find a place where you can settle in for the next couple of months and write the damn book. We'll want to get this puppy out there before people forget all about you.'

There was more, a one-sided negotiation involving rebranding and deadlines and other dotted i's and crossed t's, with Nora acquiescing to all of it because if she'd learned one thing in her whole life, it was that there was no arguing with Lilith.

She hung up in a daze and sat speechless beneath a sun that shone brighter, caressed by a wind that blew more gently. Electra was saved! She tossed the phone high in the air and caught it. Rose to her feet and did a little dance atop the rock, bowing to the squirrel, who'd crept partway down the tree and watched in chattering puzzlement at antics stranger than its own.

She straightened and turned to the phone again, channeling all of the elation from her conversation with Lilith into the strength she'd need for the next call.

The phone buzzed once, twice.

A woman's voice.

'Nora?'

'Mom. Oh, Mom. Don't cry. I'm fine. Just like I told you. I'm really all right.'

THIRTY-EIGHT

She'd cried, if possible, even harder during the conversation with her mother than she had at the thought of losing Electra.

Especially after Penelope Best assured her she forgave her daughter the unforgiveable.

'All those texts,' she said. She promised Nora they'd kept her from succumbing to despair as story after story about her daughter's supposed escapades filled her computer screen, competing in number only with notes from friends and neighbors who'd known Nora since she was a little girl and she couldn't possibly have done those awful things, could she, Penelope?

'Oh, Nora, you should have heard them. All the biddies came around. I was the most popular person in town. And, oh, such dreadful food they brought. As if bribing me. "Here, I've brought you a coffee cake. Now tell me about your wayward daughter." That cake was like a brick. And someone showed up with beaten biscuits. Remember them?'

Nora did, golfball-size chunks of near-flavorless dough, almost hard enough to chip a tooth on, taking their name from Revolutionary War-era recipes that called for flour, lard, water, a bit of soda and salt and then commanded: 'Beat for twenty minutes with an iron mallet.'

As a child she'd unaccountably loved them, on their own or better still, split and slathered with butter, topped with a bit of ham.

'I threw them away. If only you'd been here. Or were here now. I don't suppose . . .'

The same plea she'd offered at intervals for years. 'I don't suppose you might be coming home.' At Thanksgiving. At Christmas. To see the azaleas in spring, feast on Silver Queen sweetcorn in the summer, marvel at the migration of geese by the tens of thousands in the fall. Even though the Eastern Shore hadn't been home for decades.

There were, of course, occasional trips back. Fleeting visits, her job and Joe's so demanding. 'Of course, dear. I understand completely.'

'I've got a job, Mom. Campground host. It'll keep me here through the summer. After that . . .' She let her voice trail off, hope extended, short of a promise. Some things just don't change.

The emotional whiplash of the pair of calls left her limp, exhausted. The rest of it – the paperwork for Joe, decisions about a cremation or a burial that would demand far more difficult discussions with his parents than she'd just had with her own mother; the necessary conversation with a financial adviser – could wait.

She gathered up her things and returned to Electra. Caleb had mentioned dinner at the Buckhorn, but that was hours away. Lunch beckoned. A cheeseburger, maybe fries and a milkshake. She could start running again tomorrow. In the meantime, there was one more thing.

She dumped her things on the dinette table and felt about among the cushions. Too many were the same size, and no doubt had been shuffled when the sheriff and his deputies had searched the trailer. And who knew what Brad and Miranda may have done with them?

She unzipped one after another, feeling within, fingers probing the corners with increasing desperation. No ring.

Miranda. Goddammit.

Was she sashaying through a truck stop, the ring winking on her finger, on her way to an assignation with her next victim?

Or was she even now standing before a jeweler, making goo-goo eyes at him, flashing just enough cleavage to keep him from driving the hard bargain demanded?

'Bitch,' Nora muttered. 'Bitch, bitch, bitch,' she chanted as she drew the final cushion toward her and tugged the zipper open. She wriggled her hand in. Gasped when her fingers encountered something hard. But it wasn't the ring. This was much, much larger. And flat.

She withdrew it by degrees, knowing what it was even before Forever's knife in its leather scabbard came fully into view.

* * *

A bit of paper seesawed from the sheath when Nora withdrew the knife.

'Sorry about the ring,' Forever had written. 'But I really needed it. And I need to get rid of this, and disappear for awhile. Take good care of it. It's been a good friend to me. Rest assured there's no innocent blood on it. I only used it when I had to.'

Nora turned the knife over and over in her hand. Heard Forever beside the stream, recounting using bear spray on a guy who'd tried to rape her on the trail. 'Then I got this.' Patting the knife.

The way she'd stood over Brad, knife drawn, casually offering to dispatch him.

Her talk of hitching rides. Her travels near Big Bend. A dead trucker in El Paso. Other dead truckers – some shot, others with throats slit. Had Miranda killed them all? Or . . .?

She hastily sheathed the knife. Lay it on the table. Considered it awhile. Then nodded, unfastened her belt, pulled one end through a few loops and threaded it through the slits in the scabbard, and refastened her belt. The knife lay flush against her hip, not heavy, slowly warming. It felt good.

She stood in the doorway and swept the campground with her gaze. In addition to returning the truck and trailer, the sheriff had even brought back the ax, propping it against the pine tree. She retrieved it and slid it into one of the storage compartments beneath Electra.

She circled the campsite, running her hands over the picnic table, the discolored spot that Brad had smeared with grease to 'train' a grizzly. Leaned in close to the big Ponderosa for an indrawn breath, inhaling the vanilla scent of its bark. Lifted her face to the sun, the air-kiss of wind. Parted the willows, made her way through them toward the creek, perching on the stone, kneeling over the waters as though asking a blessing.

Across the creek, a heavy rustling.

She started to her feet.

'Forever? Forever!' She hadn't left after all. Nora took a step toward the edge of the rock, face alight with welcome.

A massive head thrust its way through the underbrush, dwarfed by the roll of furred shoulders, the distinctive hump.

The black snout quivered, testing the air, finding her scent. The head swung her way, golden eyes fixed upon hers.

Nora froze in a crouch, the only thing in motion her brain, frantically calculating the distance to the trailer – and the bear spray – at the speed of one terrified woman, versus the distance from one side of the creek to another at the speed of a thousand-pound and presumably voracious carnivore. The answer was not on her side.

The bear dipped its head to the creek. Drank deep. Raised its head and stared once more at her. Water ran from the sides of its mouth and dripped back into the creek. It tilted its head, flashing its incisors in an extravagant yawn, a sight that turned her guts to water.

It stood, raising itself to a terrifying height, and hitched its back up and down against a tree, groaning in pleasure as it scratched. It fell back down upon its forepaws and shook itself like a large – very large – dog. Then, after a final slurping drink, it turned its massive haunches to her and ambled away.

The bushes closed behind it. The forest fell silent. It was as though he had never been there.

Nora stayed unmoving a very long time. She finally rose and made her way back to Electra on shaking legs. She didn't look to see whether the bear was following her. Somehow she knew it wasn't.

She bent and removed the chocks from Electra's tires. Got into the truck and backed it up to the hitch the way Caleb had showed her, taking only a half-dozen tries to align them correctly.

Attached the hitch, the safety chains.

Only one thing left now. She found pen and paper.

'Thanks for helping me find my way.'

Even though she hadn't found it yet. But it was time to start.

The forest was home to the bear; the creek, his territory. Just as it was Caleb's, and Forever's, too. But it wasn't hers.

The bear. She added a postscript: 'You should keep the campground closed.' She knew he'd catch her meaning.

She clipped the note to the post denoting the campsite.

She found her phone and texted her mother. 'Hang onto the next batch of beaten biscuits that comes through your door.'

She put the phone aside and restarted the truck, steering confidently out of the campground and onto the main road, picking up speed. She glanced in the rearview mirror at Electra sailing behind.

She was going to find her way.

ACKNOWLEDGMENTS

Thanks to Kathy Best for letting me borrow her most excellent surname for my protagonist. I'll try to make sure Nora lives up to it. Profound gratitude to agent Richard Curtis, who lets no manuscript go before its time. Deep appreciation to the team at Severn House – Kate Lyall Grant, Carl Smith, Natasha Bell, Anna Telfer, Jem Butcher, Michelle Duff and Kathryn Blair. The Creel crew – Alex Sakariassen, Matthew LaPlante, Camilla Mortensen, Bill Oram, Stephen Paul Dark and Jessica Ravitz – helped kick-start this project in the magical surroundings of the Rocky Mountain Front. Impressed and somewhat frightened thanks to my daughter-in-law Jessica Breslin for detailed information (with illustrations!) regarding anatomy and an ax. Another nod to my mom, who continues to shake the sand from her shoes into her late eighties as the rest of us scramble to keep up. And all love to Scott, a fierce defender of my writing time, even when my lighthearted fantasies of owning an Airstream took a very dark turn in the service of fiction.